The Ticklemore Tattler

LIZ DAVIES

Copyright © 2021 Liz Davies
Published by Lilac Tree Books

This book is licensed for your personal enjoyment only. This book may not be re-sold or given away to other people. If you would like to share this book with another person, please purchase an additional copy for each recipient. If you're reading this book and did not purchase it, or it was not purchased for your use only, then please purchase your own copy. Thank you for respecting the hard work of this author.

This story is a work of fiction. All names, characters, places and incidents are invented by the author or have been used fictitiously and are not to be construed as real. Any similarity to actual persons or events is purely coincidental

The author asserts the moral rights under the Copyright, Design and Patents Act 1988 to be identified as the author of this work.

All rights reserved. No part of this publication may be reproduced, stored in a retrieval system or transmitted, in any form or by any means without the prior consent of the author, nor be otherwise circulated in any form of binding or cover other than that which it is published and without a similar condition being imposed on the subsequent purchaser.

CHAPTER 1

JULIETTE

Juliette Seymour eyed the man sitting on the other side of her desk with undisguised dislike. He was leaning back in the chair, one leg cocked across the other, his trousers riding up so she could see his socks (fawn stripey ones) and had a smug expression on his face, which she was dearly tempted to remove with a slap. That she'd never slapped anyone in her life before and she certainly didn't condone violence made no difference; she still itched to smack him.

How dare he come into the office and tell her he intended to close the newspaper down!

She'd poured her heart and soul into the business for the last seventeen years. Didn't that count for something?

Obviously not, she realised, as the obnoxious little man kept talking.

'My father, as you know, hasn't been well for some time, and has signed all his business interests over to me. This little rag doesn't make a profit, not many of the local newspapers do – although you can hardly call this a newspaper, can you? I mean, it only goes out once a week and the readership consists of three old-age pensioners and the vicar.'

Ralph Trudge-Smythe guffawed, and Juliette shoved her hands under her thighs and sat on them. Just in case.

'The Tattler has been publishing a newspaper since 1907,' she replied mildly.

'And it probably hasn't made a profit since.'

Another guffaw. The insensitive b— The phone rang, making her jump.

Juliette was about to answer it, hoping it might be an advertiser, and she got as far as dragging her hands out from underneath her legs before she decided not to bother. There was hardly any point anymore, was there?

'You have three months,' Mr Trudge-Smythe said once the phone had stopped ringing as the answering service kicked in. 'That should be enough time to find another job.' He looked her up and down. 'Or not, as the case may be.'

Juliette's blood began to boil and she clenched her teeth.

He got to his feet. 'I'm sorry but business is business. Surely you can understand that? The Tattler isn't making a profit and hasn't done in years. It's time to knock it on the head.'

That was exactly what she would love to do to Ralph Trudge-Smythe...

Despondent, she was unable to settle to do any work after he'd gone. She pottered ineffectually, rearranging some perfectly good copy on a page then moving it back to where it had been originally, before she listened to the message on the answering machine from some guy who wanted details about how much it would cost for a quarter-page spread.

Eventually she threw in the towel, shut up shop, and went to share her woes with Nell.

The Treasure Trove hadn't closed for lunch yet, and Juliette amused herself whilst Nell was serving a customer, by picking assorted items up, scrutinising them, and putting them down again. Nell had some gorgeous things, and Juliette instantly fell in love with an old manual typewriter and thought how good it would look on her desk in the office; until she remembered she would have neither a desk nor an office in three months' time.

'It's lovely, isn't it?' Nell said, appearing at her side. She was several years younger than Juliette and an incredibly astute businesswoman. Looking at what

Nell had achieved in the two-and-a-half years since she and her husband divorced, made Juliette feel incredibly old and ineffectual.

Nell continued, 'I got it from an old lady who used to write racy novels in her time. When she showed it to me, it still had a typed sheet from one of them in the roller. It made me blush, I can tell you. She'd stopped writing years ago but kept the typewriter for sentimental reasons. I wish I could get my hands on a book or two of hers and sell them all together. I'll lock up, shall I? I wasn't expecting you today.'

Nell was a chatterer. Juliette was more recalcitrant. But then, they do say opposites attract and the pair of them had established a firm friendship over the years.

Juliette watched her lock the drawer to the old-fashioned till and slip the key in her pocket before setting the much more up-to-date alarm on the premises, and the two of them slipped outside and into the street and the warm spring sunshine.

'Bookylicious?' Nell suggested.

'How about the Tavern? I could do with something stronger than blackcurrant tea.'

Nell gave her a concerned glance and Juliette tried to put a smile on her face, aiming to cover the distress she was feeling.

It must not have worked because once they'd ordered their drinks at the bar, collected a menu and had taken their seats, Nell asked, 'How bad is it?'

'Bad, bad. Not life or death bad, but life-changing bad.' Juliette took a deep breath. 'I've just had a visit from the Tattler's new owner. Lord Trudge-Smythe's son, Ralph, owns the paper now and he's going to close it in three months.' She took a gulp of her gin and tonic.

'Oh, sweetie, that's awful. What will you do?' Nell stretched across the table to give her a hug.

'That's the problem – I don't know. I've done this for so long I'm not sure I could do anything else.'

'Could you get a job with another newspaper?'

'I doubt it; certainly not around here. And not at my age, either.'

'Fifty-one isn't old. Not like it was years ago. There are loads of women who get a second wind in their fifties and beyond. And I don't see why you couldn't get a job with another paper – look at Kate Adie. She was still reporting from war zones in her fifties.'

'Bless you; Kate was a BBC reporter, not a political journalist, but thank you for trying to lift my spirits. I've been away from the scene for too long and I don't have any contacts anymore. It would be impossible to get back in. No, the only thing I'm good at is writing about cats stuck up trees.'

'Don't be daft!' Nell shot her a cross look. 'You're

putting yourself down and that's most unlike you. Your reporting is much better than that.'

'It may well be,' Juliette replied dryly, 'but even if you're right I don't want to live in London, or put in the awful hours, or do all the smooching that needs to be done. I like my life just the way it is.' Neither did she think she had the stomach for it anymore.

'Then you'll have to fight to keep it.'

'I can't fight Ralph Trudge-Smythe.'

Nell leant forwards. 'I'm not talking about fighting the closure – you'll never win. I'm talking about buying him out and owning the newspaper yourself.'

Juliette blinked in surprise; the idea hadn't occurred to her. Could she do it? 'What if he doesn't want to sell?' Juliette said the first thought that came into her head.

'He's a rich git, isn't he?' Nell scoffed. 'Of course he'll want to sell. Probably for far more than you can afford.'

That was true. He wasn't going to simply give the business away. 'It's pointless then, isn't it?' she said with a resigned sigh. Typical, no sooner had the idea been planted in her head, than it was uprooted and thrown on the compost heap.

'Not if you convince him it doesn't mean that much to you, and you just fancy keeping it on for posterity,' Nell argued. 'He might just think the sum you offer him is better than no sum at all.'

'But he's right, the paper is barely breaking even. It probably costs more to keep it going than he's making, what with tax and so on. If *he* can't make a profit, what makes you think *I* can?'

'Because I know you. You need to think outside the box. Take the paper in a different direction.'

'I don't know where to start.'

'Then speak to someone who does,' Nell replied reasonably. 'If nothing else, it'll give you the tools to make an informed decision rather than floundering around in the dark.'

As usual, Nell's advice was sound. If she didn't look into it properly, Juliette knew she might be making a big mistake – one way or the other. She didn't want to set her sights on trying to buy the newspaper only for it to be a massive white elephant, but neither did she want to let the opportunity pass her by when there was a chance she could run the publication at a profit.

It was most likely a pointless exercise, but Juliette thought she might as well give it a go. What did she have to lose – she was going to lose it anyway.

She thought for a moment, wondering where she should start. To make the Tattler profitable there would have to be some significant changes, and she recognised she needed some advice.

And she hoped she knew just the person who could point her in the right direction.

CHAPTER 2

JULIETTE

Oliver Pascoe was exactly the way Juliette remembered him, only more so. More distinguished, more attractive, more confident, more *everything*. She hadn't seen him for years, not since she'd quietly resigned from the publication where they'd both been working at the time, to give birth to the baby she was carrying.

'There were rumours, you know,' he was saying, as they slipped into a booth in a trendy wine bar in the centre of Birmingham. 'About why you left. Wild ones.'

'Did you fan them?'

'Not me. I guessed, of course, but it wasn't my story to tell.'

'And you call yourself an investigative journalist?' she quipped.

'Not anymore, I don't.'

Juliette waited for him to expand and when it seemed he didn't intend to say anything further, she asked, 'Are you going to tell me what you do?' Darn it, she'd been hoping he was still in the business.

'Only if you tell me why you disappeared so suddenly. One minute you were tracking down some story in the House of Lords, the next, poof.' He snapped his fingers. 'You were gone. Tarian Waytor – remember him? Sleazy fella, worked on the sports desk? – anyway, he put it about that you'd got too close to someone high up and they'd had you done away with.'

Juliette raised her eyebrows. 'Crikey, that's a bit far-fetched. I didn't exactly hunt down those kinds of stories. Reporting on a bill going through Parliament is hardly dangerous stuff.'

'We all know you did rather more than that.'

Juliette looked at Oliver. She had done more than that and she had uncovered more than she should have done on occasion, but it was all water under the bridge and oh so long ago. It was another lifetime.

'You want to know the real reason I quit?' she asked him.

Oliver nodded, the silver streaks at his temples catching the sunlight streaming in through the wine bar's windows. Birmingham's Little Venice had been an unexpected venue to meet. She hadn't thought she would manage to speak to Oliver, never mind meet him in person. With vain hope, she had dug out her ancient and dusty Filofax, found Oliver's number and dialled it, never expecting it to still be operational, or if it was, for him to answer. It had been so long ago and people today changed phone numbers like they did their socks, so she thought it might have been allocated to someone else. To her surprise he had answered. She'd assumed he was still living in London and had been fully prepared to travel there to meet him, but he'd surprised her once again.

Juliette took her mobile out of her shoulder bag and scrolled through it, then held it out to him. 'This is the reason I left.'

Oliver stared at the photograph. 'She's beautiful. How old?'

'Brooke is eighteen and is in her first year at Bath Uni.' Juliette lifted her chin proudly. 'She's doing a degree in journalism and publishing.'

'Should I have to look out for her in the future?'

'Undoubtedly. She's incredibly bright. That girl is going somewhere.' She'd also cut her teeth on the Tattler, so to speak, which was another reason Juliette hated to let the newspaper go. It might be sentimental of her, but her days of being hard-edged and hard-nosed were well and truly over. Brooke and

Ticklemore had seen to that.

'Just like her mother,' Oliver said.

'Hmm.' Juliette didn't call getting pregnant by a married man as being terribly bright.

'Anyway,' Oliver added, 'it's nice to see you're alive and well and haven't been "done away" with.'

'How *is* Tarian?' she asked, suddenly eager to delve into the world of tabloid publishing again, and for a while Oliver filled her in on what he knew.

'I've been out of it for quite some time myself,' he added, when he had exhausted all his news regarding their shared acquaintances.

She polished off the last of the wine in her glass and decided she wanted another. It was remarkably pleasant sitting in a bar on a Saturday afternoon and talking about something other than what was happening in Ticklemore, or trying to get Brooke to share anything more than an airy "it's great, Mum" about her life in university. Juliette felt more alive than she'd done in weeks. Maybe it *was* time for a change?

After fresh drinks had been brought to the table (a far cry from the Ticklemore Tavern where you had to go to the bar yourself) Oliver told her what he did for a living.

'I've gone down the typical ex-journalist route and become an author.'

'What of?'

'Biographies.'

'Have I read any of yours?'

He raised one eyebrow. It had been a kind of party trick of his, and she remembered he used to use it sparingly and to great effect. She also remembered she'd had an almighty crush on him, and a faint echo of those long-ago feelings pricked at her mind.

'Silly me, how would you know if I've read any of yours, and if I had, then I wouldn't be asking.' She took a sip of wine to cover her embarrassment.

'Much as I love seeing you again, what is it you wanted to pick my brains about?' he asked, leaning back and stretching out his long legs.

He'd not put on an ounce of weight, unlike her, and he didn't look his age, either. She knew for a fact he was fifty-five, but one could easily knock ten years off that.

'I – this is going to sound ridiculous – I want to buy a newspaper. A local one obviously, not a national. And as far as local rags go, it's rather on the small side.'

'Why?'

'Because I run it and the owner wants to close it down.'

'Again, I ask why?'

'Isn't that a good enough reason?' she demanded

crossly.

'Just because you *can* do something doesn't mean to say you *should*. Why do they want to wind it up?'

'Because it's not making any money.'

He did the eyebrow raise again. Why had she thought it was sexy once, when it was actually quite annoying.

'There you go,' he said. 'So, what's the real reason you want to buy a failing newspaper when newspapers are yesterday's news – excuse the pun – and it's making a loss?'

'Because it's all I know,' she blurted, infuriated with him for cutting straight to the heart of the matter.

'Explain.' He tilted his head to the side, his gaze intense as his grey eyes zeroed in on her. He'd been damned good at his job once. She suspected he still could be, if he wanted.

Juliette sighed. 'I was born and bred in a village called Ticklemore. When I discovered I was pregnant, I went back there to live. After Brooke was born, I batted about doing odd bits of work here and there, until my mother, who was friends with the Trudge-Smythes – who own the newspaper – got me a job running it.'

'How large is the readership?'

'Around two thousand.' She shrugged. It probably

wasn't even that.

'How many staff?'

'Just me. But it keeps me busy, you know?'

'And it's a connection, albeit a small one, to the life you once had?' he guessed.

She swallowed, recalling how grateful she'd been to be given the opportunity to run the Tattler, and how resentful and faintly contemptuous she'd felt at the time, too. It was a far cry from the job she'd once held.

Now though, she loved it. Outside of her family it was her whole world.

'I suppose. It provides a service, too,' Juliette said. 'The nationals are all well and good, but they don't let the locals know that Jo Bloggs is planning on building a whopping great big barn next to the library, or there's a new apprenticeship scheme for toymakers in the village.' She paused. 'I made that first one up, as an example.'

'I'm sure people can find out things like that elsewhere.'

Oliver was playing Devil's Advocate she knew, but he was still being annoying (annoyingly accurate, if she was honest). 'Of course they can, but they have to specifically go looking for it. I gather all the news into one handy weekly publication. It's called a newspaper,' she added, archly.

'You really want to do this, don't you?'

A lump lodged in her throat and she coughed to clear it. 'I do.'

'You've been running it for how long?'

'Seventeen years.'

'And it's not making any money?'

She knew what he was inferring and once again he was right. It was a question she'd asked herself more than once since Ralph Trudge-Smythe had dropped his bombshell earlier in the week – if she hadn't made it viable in all the years she'd been running it, what made her think she'd be able to turn a profit if she owned it?

Which was why she was sitting in a bar opposite the far-too-attractive and still very perceptive Oliver Pascoe, and hoping he'd be able to give her some pointers. Unfortunately not, since he'd swapped journalism for writing.

'I was hoping you could put me in touch with someone who could give me some advice,' she said. 'I know traditional newspapers are dying, and that most people get their news from the TV or online, but I still think small, local newspapers continue to have their place in small, local communities. I just need some ideas on how to go forward with it. I'm aware the Tattler can't carry on the way it is. Relying on advertising to make ends meet is no longer viable.'

Speech over with, Juliette slumped back in her seat and took a hefty gulp of her drink. If Oliver couldn't suggest anyone, then she was stumped. She was too close to the newspaper to look at it objectively, and she'd been doing the same thing for so long when it came to generating revenue, that she didn't know where to start in order to do things differently.

'I can't think of anyone off the top of my head, but leave it with me and I'll see what I can do,' he said, and Juliette had to be content with that.

It was nice catching up, and it was even nicer seeing Oliver (had she mentioned how attractive he was and how she'd once had an immense crush on him?) but she was under no illusion that she'd hear from him again.

She was in this on her own, and it would be up to her to sort it out.

All she hoped was that she didn't make the wrong decision.

CHAPTER 3

OLIVER

That was a blast from the past Oliver thought, as he made his way back to his flat on the outskirts of the city. When he'd answered the phone to an unknown number on Thursday, he'd expected it to be a sales call or one of those people who wanted to know if he'd been involved in an accident that wasn't his fault. What he hadn't been expecting was to hear Juliette Seymour's rounded, well-modulated voice.

Even more unexpected had been his reaction to her. When she'd said she wanted to pick his brains she'd undoubtedly meant a quick chat over the phone, but he'd suggested they should meet. He'd been prepared to go to London for the day, assuming that she was still living in the capital, but when she'd said she'd have to check the train times as she'd probably have to change at least once, he realised that wasn't the case.

In a little village not far from Hereford, she'd said when he asked her where she lived, and she seemed more than happy to meet him in Birmingham. He should have suggested meeting somewhere vaguely in the middle, such as Worcester, but he didn't want to appear too keen. Besides, whatever it was she wanted from him, as soon as she got it he'd probably never set eyes on her again. It had been what... nearly twenty years?

He wondered what she'd been doing all that time. She'd been a shrewd and intelligent political correspondent when he knew her, but she'd suddenly disappeared from the newspaper they'd both been working for. At the time, he'd suspected she'd had a better offer elsewhere, but when he failed to see her name attributed to any features in rival publications, he'd begun to wonder if the rumours about her and Otis Coles were true. The politician had been incredibly ambitious even then, and Oliver suspected Juliette might have discovered some secret, and Otis had used his wealth to shut Juliette up. Not in the manner that daft Tarian Waytor at hinted at, but more of the "I'll-make-it-worthwhile-if-you-go-away" kind of thing. The longer Juliette was away from the reporting scene, the greater the likelihood that Otis Coles had paid her off, he'd thought.

It was nice to know the real reason. Being a political reporter with the long hours such a career involved, wasn't conducive to single parenthood. Or to dual parenting either, as he knew from all-too-personal experience. His own marriage had dissolved (more of a fizzle than a bang) due to the weight of his work commitments. It was one of the major regrets in his life.

Another was not checking up on Juliette Seymour after she'd left so abruptly.

She may have been a woman in her thirties and more than capable of steering her own ship, but he was certain there had been a connection between them.

Neither of them had acted upon it, of course – he'd been in the throes of a divorce and she, well… she'd been spending more time than was wise with Otis Coles.

As Oliver unlocked his car, he froze as something occurred to him. Was *Otis* the father of Juliette's baby? He didn't have any proof this was the case, but it would certainly explain a lot. He wondered whether Otis was aware. And if he was, how would the man feel about Oliver knowing he had an illegitimate child?

Somehow, Oliver guessed not many people were privy to the information.

Interesting...

What was also interesting was what Juliette was doing now. He would never in a million years have guessed she'd be running a tiny, local fish-wrap. Not that fish and chips were wrapped in newspaper any longer, more's the pity, because that was all some publications were good for.

He wondered what the Tattler was good for, and he made a note to look it up as soon as he got home. He'd look up Ticklemore too, just out of curiosity. He wanted to know where Juliette had come from, and where she'd run back to.

Her appearance hadn't changed much. A few more lines around her eyes, a softer set to her mouth, her curves slightly more rounded. She was still slim and elegant, but her hair was longer than he remembered, falling in soft waves to below her shoulders, and her skin was more luminous. It must be all that country air and healthy living, he concluded. Back then, there had been too many late nights, too many parties you simply had to be at (outside usually, waiting for the important people to appear), too many deadlines.

He'd enjoyed working there but had also been happy to move on. Now he was his own boss (although he did still have deadlines to meet, and one was looming in the not-too-distant future) but he had no one to answer to apart from his editor, and his days were very much his own.

Which was why he decided to help Juliette as much as he could.

He had the time, he had some ideas, and the thought of a new project excited him.

It had nothing whatsoever to do with Juliette herself. Nothing at all. He'd do the same for anyone.

CHAPTER 4

JULIETTE

'Is that you, Juliette?' her mother called, from the depths of the kitchen.

'Yes, Mum.' Juliette threw her keys in a bowl on a little table in the hall and walked through to join her mother.

'Did you have a nice time?' Audrey asked.

'Not really; it was more of a business meeting,' Juliette replied, opening the fridge and having a nose inside, which was exactly what Brooke did when she came home, and it made Juliette feel like a naughty teenager as her mum tutted at her.

'Who was it you went to see?' her mother asked, shooing her away. 'Dinner won't be long, so don't you dare fill up on snacks.' Her mum had invited her to eat with her this evening and Juliette was more than happy to oblige – she hardly ever bothered cooking for herself now Brooke wasn't around.

'His name is Oliver Pascoe. I used to know him when I worked in London.' Juliette moved away from the fridge and lounged against one of the cupboards instead.

Audrey's eyebrows lifted a fraction. 'Was he a journalist too?'

'Yes.' Juliette wondered if it was too early to crack open the bottle of wine she'd seen in the fridge door.

Her mother gave her a sideways look out of the corner of her eye, and Juliette knew what was going through Audrey's mind, without being told. Juliette never talked about the past, so she supposed it was only natural her mother would wonder whether the man she'd met with today was Brooke's father. She'd never told Audrey who he was, and she never would. It might not be fair to Brooke, but it was a secret she intended to take with her to the grave. It wouldn't do anyone any good to know, least of all Brooke.

It would probably cause more damage, if it came out. Otis was gaining power and influence, and was aiming for the top job in the UK. He would undoubtedly be Prime Minister one day.

'What was your meeting about?' her mother asked curiously.

Juliette's answer of 'This and that,' was met with another shrewd look.

She recognised it for what it was – her mother knew there was more to the story than Juliette was letting on. Should she come clean and tell her that Ralph Trudge-Smythe was planning on closing the newspaper? Or should she keep it to herself until she had decided what to do?

Although Juliette was good at keeping a secret (the biggest secret of them all was the identity of Brooke's father), this wasn't quite in the same league and, as her mother would find out sooner or later, she thought she might as well prepare her. Besides, two brains were better than one, and her mum might have some ideas that wouldn't occur to Juliette. Not about the newspaper business, but she might have more insight into what Juliette could do if she failed to buy the Tattler, or if she came to the conclusion she wouldn't be able to make it profitable.

'Mum, I've got something to tell you.' Juliette said, then paused.

Audrey tilted her head to one side and stopped what she was doing. She placed the tea towel on the counter and turned to give her daughter her full attention. Juliette took a deep breath.

'Ralph Trudge-Smythe told me he's planning on closing the newspaper,' she said.

Her mother's reaction was just as she expected; Audrey's mouth dropped open and her eyes widened.

'He can't do that!' she declared.

'I think he can, Mum, and he will. The newspaper is barely breaking even. It makes perfect business sense to close it down.'

'What about all your hard work? Doesn't that count for something?'

'Not when it comes to business.'

'Do you want me to have a word?' her mother offered.

'Thanks, Mum, but I don't think it would do any good. Besides, you shouldn't be getting involved.' Audrey was friends with Ralph's mother, Bunny, and Juliette didn't want her to do anything to jeopardise that.

'No, I suppose you're right. I've heard Lord Trudge-Smythe isn't too well, the poor man; Bunny was only telling me the other day that he was going to see a cardiologist.'

'I knew he was getting on a bit. If he's got health issues no wonder he's handed the reins over to his son. Can you keep this to yourself for a while, though?'

Her mother picked up the tea towel again and resumed wiping the pans she'd used to prepare the tray bake which was currently in the oven. It smelt delicious and through the oven door Juliette could see it bubbling away.

'Of course I will.' Audrey stopped wiping for a moment. 'Ralph has been waiting for so long to get his hands on the business, he probably can't believe his luck. New broom and all that; I expect he's throwing his weight around and stamping his authority. I wouldn't be surprised if some things do need altering, but I hope he's not changing things for the sake of it. What will you do?'

That was the problem, wasn't it? Juliette didn't know.

How long should she leave it for Oliver to get back to her? One week. Two? What if he never did? She could be two weeks, or a month, down the line with no plan in place. She had to start thinking seriously about it now, and one of the first things she needed to consider were her finances.

It was time to open another spreadsheet – Juliette loved spreadsheets – so after dinner and with the dishes washed, she returned to her own house and sat at her desk. As she started her laptop, she realised there was something she wanted to do before she began work properly, and that was to look up Oliver on the internet.

The most logical place to start with was Amazon, so she typed in his name, but the results were disappointing. A couple of people called Oliver Pascoe had written books, but they were all fiction and when she clicked on the author links, she realised none of them was him. Wondering if he was using his initial she typed in O. Pascoe and the results were even more disappointing. He might have a middle initial, but if he did she didn't know it, and the only option open to her was to start at A and work her way through to Z. Which she did.

It didn't help; she still couldn't find him.

Had he been lying to her when he'd told her he was an author? Or maybe he hadn't had anything published yet? That was a possibility, she conceded. Next, she Googled him, and it wasn't a surprise to see there were quite a few hits. Some of them were images, most were about features he'd written, and there was also a Wikipedia page which didn't tell her a great deal more than she already knew.

Without meaning to, she clicked on an image of him and his face filled the screen. The photo must have been taken several years ago, because there were a few less lines around his eyes and his hair was darker. But apart from that, he hadn't changed much at all. It was deeply unfair, she thought, how some men managed to get better with age. Oliver certainly had. He'd been terribly good looking when she knew him in London, but this afternoon he seemed to have grown into himself, had become more mature maybe, and certainly more relaxed. He'd always been confident and sure of himself, but back then he'd had to be.

Juliette got the impression when she met him today that he was happier in his own skin now, than he had been when she knew him previously, and she assumed the slower pace of life away from the rough and tumble of journalism suited him better, the way it suited her.

She just hoped he'd come up with some new ideas, but she couldn't depend on that, so it was time to bite the bullet and do some planning. With that in mind, she stopped stalking him, opened a new spreadsheet and got to work. Until she knew exactly how much she'd be able to offer Ralph Trudge-Smythe, and for how long she could go without paying herself a salary, she wouldn't be able to move forward.

***

Juliette rose from her office chair, placed her hands on the small of her back and eased the kinks out of it. That hadn't been much fun, had it, she thought after examining her finances. The future wasn't exactly looking rosy. When she'd confirmed she was pregnant, Otis had paid maintenance for Brooke and would continue to do so right up until her nineteenth birthday. But that was only a few months away and then it would stop. The thought was sobering.

Juliette's outgoings weren't excessive; when she'd sold her place in London she'd had enough left over once she'd settled the outstanding mortgage, to buy a little cottage in Ticklemore for her and Brooke. The household bills were manageable, and she made sure Brooke didn't go without. She also owned a little car, but apart from that, the only other things she spent her money on was the occasional meal out with friends or drinks with Nell. She liked clothes, and one of her weaknesses was getting her hair cut every couple of months, but that was it; which meant she had some savings behind her. Just as well, really, considering she might have to live on them for some considerable time.

She now faced a dilemma – should she use some of those savings to buy the newspaper and then try to live off the rest until the Tattler became more viable (how that was going to happen she had no idea at present). Or should she cut her losses and start looking for another job. If she took this particular route, she might well need those savings to live on until she found something else. However, she couldn't make a decision until she knew how much Ralph was going to demand for the business, and whether she managed to come up with any innovative ideas to turn it around.

Juliette realised she only had herself to blame for the situation the Tattler was in. She was the sole person employed to run the newspaper, no one else; everything was on her shoulders, from the copy, the layout, the advertising, the photographs used, *everything*.

Knowing deep down that it wasn't doing well, should have stimulated her to do something about it before now. Other independents had failed over the years as more and more people took to their phones and their tablets for their daily news, and local newspapers were quickly becoming a thing of the past. She'd been aware of this, but she hadn't done anything about it. She'd buried her head in the sand, hoping it would go away, because she enjoyed her life just the way it was. But if she had made a few small tweaks earlier on, she might not be facing the situation she was in now. It had gone so far though, that it needed more than a few little tweaks. It needed a complete overhaul and a total rethink, and she simply didn't know where to start.

It was sad that her only hope if she wanted the Ticklemore Tattler to continue, might rest on a man she hadn't seen for nearly two decades. She was a woman in her prime and she should be in charge of her own destiny. The future was up to her, and no one else.

She needed to do some serious research and she vowed to start on Monday. Tomorrow, Sunday, she was driving to Bath and taking her daughter out for lunch. Juliette understood that she should start thinking about the issue with the Tattler sooner rather than later, but Brooke was everything, her family was everything. No matter what happened in her own life, Brooke would always come first, whether her daughter appreciated it or not. Juliette hadn't seen Brooke since Christmas and she was so excited at the thought of giving her a hug, she couldn't think of anything else.

Wondering whether she should share her predicament with her daughter, she powered off her computer; she'd done enough for today, and she was finding it hard to concentrate as her thoughts kept going around in circles. Brooke might be able to cast a fresh pair of eyes over the situation, and Juliette hadn't been lying when she'd told Oliver her daughter was very bright and had a shining future ahead of her. She was going into journalism just like her mum; all Juliette hoped was that she'd do a better job of it, and not make the same mistakes she had – although she would never in a million years call Brooke a mistake. Her daughter was the best thing to have happened to her, and even if she had her time all over again Juliette wouldn't change a thing.

Pushing the worries about herself, her future, and the Tattler aside, she headed towards the kitchen and was just about to grab a bottle of wine (out of her own fridge this time), when there was a knock on the front door. Before she could answer it, she heard footsteps in the hall and Audrey poked her head around the kitchen door. She was dressed up to the nines.

'I'm just off out,' her mother announced.

'So I see. Going somewhere nice?'

'Only to the Tavern – it's quiz night. You can come with me if you like.' Audrey got a compact mirror out of her bag and checked her appearance, smacking her lips together.

Juliette seriously thought about the offer for a moment, before dismissing it. Was this what her life had become? Having to rely on her mum for company on a Saturday night? Audrey had a better social life than she did. To be fair, her mum was only sixty-eight (she'd had Juliette rather young), and she was still a very fit and vibrant woman, and there were occasions when Juliette felt the older of the two. It wasn't a pleasant feeling.

Audrey departed after giving Juliette a quick peck on the cheek, leaving her alone with her thoughts, the bottle of wine, and whatever she could find to watch on TV.

It shouldn't have been such a surprise – Juliette had been doing roughly the same thing every Saturday for years, apart from the occasional date (normally disastrous, or at the very least uninspiring) and the odd drink or meal out with friends.

The highlight of her life recently had been a few meetings with the Toy Shop Team last Christmas. A group of villagers had joined forces to help an old man open a toy shop in which to sell his handmade and totally beautiful toys to generate money for charity.

Apart from this afternoon, that is. Seeing Oliver had been a highlight indeed, and also a bit of an eye-opener. The couple of drinks she'd had with him had been lovely; which was incredibly sad. How had she come to the point where she thought meeting an old colleague to garner some business advice was lovely?

Going out for dinner with a handsome man was lovely. Enjoying a play or a ballet with friends was lovely. A business meeting should be as far from lovely as it was possible to get. Interesting, informative, beneficial? Not lovely.

But it had been. And she didn't know whether that was because of the man who'd been sitting across the table from her, or because it had been so long since she'd done anything other than have a quick gin in the Tavern, that the novelty had knocked her off kilter slightly.

Whatever the reason, she couldn't seem to get Oliver Pascoe out of her head. The bottle of wine and the weepy romantic comedy didn't help, either.

CHAPTER 5

OLIVER

Before meeting with Juliette earlier, Oliver hadn't intended sitting in front of his computer this evening, but there was nothing he wanted to watch on TV, he didn't fancy reading, and he wasn't in the mood to go to the pub. His local was nice enough and he had a few mates who might be there, but he couldn't be bothered. After seeing Juliette, too many long-forgotten memories of his years in London had found their way to the surface and were now darting about in his head, and he didn't seem able to rid himself of them.

It might have been a mistake to suggest meeting her, but his curiosity had proved irresistible.

That was what was riding him this evening – curiosity. Oliver wanted to know much more about Juliette Seymour than he'd discovered tonight; like whether she had a notable other on the scene. He wasn't sure why he wanted to know that, he just did. It must be the reporter in him… he was never happy until he knew the full story.

He wondered what hers was. She didn't appear to be married; she'd used her maiden name when she'd told him who it was on the phone, and he'd checked out the third finger of her left hand and hadn't seen a ring. Had she been married in the past and now no longer was? Did she have a significant other? He knew she had a daughter, but did she have any other children?

He was surprised how badly he wanted to know more about her.

Grabbing a cold beer out of the fridge, he popped the cap and took a swig from the stubby brown bottle, the flavour of fermented hops exploding on his tongue as he took a deep swallow. Wiping his mouth with the back of his hand, he wandered into the little spare room that he used as an office, sat down at his desk and logged onto his computer. It came on instantly and a rush of satisfaction went through him. His computer was one of the tools of his trade, and he'd treated himself to a top of the range model, super fast and super efficient.

The first thing he did was type in Ticklemore, and he was soon learning all about the village. It seemed charming and quintessentially English but not in a thatched roof kind of way. The photos showed old red-bricked buildings with slate roofs, and plenty of hanging baskets filled with bright flowers. There was a green, a small river with a narrow stone bridge spanning it which didn't look wide enough for anything larger than a single person to cross, and a pretty high street filled with independent artisan shops.

As Oliver stared at the images of the village, he realised there was something missing – he couldn't seem to get a feel for it – so he went into Google Maps, grabbed the little orange figure from the bottom right of the screen and plonked him in the middle of the main street. Instantly he was transported into the village. Using the mouse, he slowly turned and looked around; it was almost as if he was there in person.

He wondered where the offices of the Ticklemore Tattler were, and he "travelled" up and down the high street a couple of times, trying to see it, but he couldn't.

Now that he had some idea of what the village was like, it was time to have a look at the newspaper itself. Coming out of street view, he went back to the search page and typed in "Ticklemore Tattler".

To his surprise, there were far fewer hits than he

expected. There was a small amount of information on a sidebar to the right of the screen and there were a few other sites with mentions of the newspaper, but he couldn't see an actual website. He scrolled up and down, but there was nothing. He checked the spelling, wondering if he'd typed it incorrectly, so he tried another variation, but the spelling he'd originally used was correct as far as he could tell.

Grabbing a sheet of paper and a pen, he made a quick note – *where is the website* – and added several question marks. Then he underlined it. A website should be easy to find and should ideally appear somewhere on the first page, preferably in the top three items. This one didn't, and he scrolled five pages in and still couldn't find it; which led him to believe that the Ticklemore Tattler didn't have one.

Oliver sank back in his seat and blew out his cheeks. That was the first thing Juliette needed to rectify. Every business worth its salt had to have a website these days.

Before he could take his quest to help her any further, he needed to see this newspaper for himself. He needed to get his hands on a physical copy, to read what the features were, to check the layout, to see what was being advertised and by whom. He didn't profess to be an expert in publishing – he was a journalist, nothing more, and not even that now – but he did have some kind of an idea how a paper should be run.

And, more importantly as far as he was concerned, Juliette had asked him for help.

That was quite telling itself, that she had reached out to *him* after all these years. Wasn't there someone else she could have asked? Someone who knew more about producing a newspaper than he did? Possibly not, he mused – it depended who she'd kept in contact with.

In a way he was flattered that she'd thought of him, and he was also intrigued. Never in a million years would he have imagined that Juliette Seymour would have ended up in a small village out in the sticks, running a provincial newspaper. The woman he had remembered had been a bit of a party animal, but then she'd had to be; they all had. You had to be seen, you had to move in the right circles, even if it was on the outside looking in. There were more late nights than you could shake a stick at, more deadlines, more hunches, more stories than could ever be told. She'd been in the thick of it. Ostensibly she'd been a political reporter, but she had been rather more than that. Politics had its secrets too, and she'd uncovered her fair share of them. She had been a damn good journalist, and when she'd abruptly disappeared off the scene it had been a surprise to all of them, himself included.

When he'd answered his phone, Juliette Seymour's voice was the last he'd expected to hear. And when he'd realised who it was, a shiver of *something* went through him. Excitement maybe? He'd been very attracted to her once. She had been funny, beautiful, lively, highly intelligent and good at her job, but he'd kept his distance, emotionally and physically, despite his marriage being so far on the rocks his wife had told him to leave. He had still been married and had two children, and that had been the end of it. Which was why he'd been so surprised when Juliette had contacted him. Yes, they'd worked well together, and they had probably been friends as well as colleagues, but he had been married at the time and there had been rumours about her and a politician.

Now she'd come back into his life, and he wasn't sure how he should feel about it.

But he'd said he'd help and he would, to the best of his ability, but the first thing he needed to do was to visit Ticklemore and see the Tattler for himself.

Without allowing more time to think, he shot off a text to her asking if he could call in to see her. He suggested Tuesday – his time was his and he had no appointments looming – but after he'd sent it he wondered if he was appearing too keen.

Then he laughed at himself; *she'd* been the one to

contact *him*, not the other way around. He was just doing what he'd said he would do.

Second-guessing himself yet again, he debated whether he should have just sent a quick email to advise her about getting a website and left it at that.

But then again, there was that little thing called curiosity, and he was mighty curious about her.

Oliver finished his beer and debated fetching another from the fridge before deciding not to. With nothing else to occupy him this evening he thought he might as well get some work done, and he needed a clear head for that. Whoever it was it who had said "write drunk, edit sober" had never written a biography. Oliver always had to have his wits about him when writing his books. Things could, and did, get picked up at the editing stage, but he didn't want to risk introducing errors into his manuscript in the first place. His current work in progress would be vetted by the man in question and possibly his legal representatives, but Oliver didn't want to make a rookie error, and another beer might see him do exactly that.

As he turned his attention back to the computer, he hesitated.

It was decidedly odd that Juliette Seymour had resurfaced at this precise moment, and not only that, she had contacted *him*. Of all the people she could have got in touch with, it had to be him.

Was it a coincidence? Or was there something more to it? Something he had yet to work out?

Because, if it was nothing but a pure coincidence then it was a darned great big one, he thought, as he narrowed his eyes and clicked on a folder. It was the biography of the man he was currently working on… and the man whom Oliver believed to be the father of Juliette's daughter – Otis Coles.

CHAPTER 6

JULIETTE

'You want to do what?' Ralph sounded as though he had a bag of marbles in his mouth, his accent reminding Juliette of the way TV presenters used to speak in the 1950s. He also sounded incredulous and rather scoffing.

'Buy the newspaper.' She nervously twisted the cord of the office phone around her fingers and winced. She had a feeling this wasn't going to go well.

'My dear girl, whatever for?'

The scoffing worsened and not only that, Ralph had put her back up. "Dear girl" indeed! She was hardly a girl and the way he'd said it was incredibly patronising. She was tempted to tell him exactly what she thought of him, but common sense won out and she decided a charm offensive would better serve her needs.

'I've worked here for so long,' she said, allowing a slight wheedle to creep into her tone. 'I don't think I'd be able to do anything else.' It was partly true, although she hated to admit it.

'I'm sure you could find another job. There's always temping or bar work.' He snorted down the phone. 'Anyway, why am I dispensing career advice? I've got a lot of other things to be getting on with, so—'

'I'm serious,' Juliette interrupted. 'I want to take the Tattler off your hands.'

'A second ago you said you wanted to buy it. Now it sounds as though you're doing me a favour.'

'I will be, in a way. How much will it cost to dissolve the business?'

'About as much as it would cost to sell it,' Ralph Trudge-Smythe shot back.

'Exactly! If I bought the newspaper off you, your books would balance as it were. The amount you'd receive from the sale would cover the cost of any associated fees. If you dissolved it, you'd be losing out – it would cost you money.'

There was silence on the other end and Juliette could almost hear the cogs whirring in Ralph's brain. He might talk as though he was chewing on cut glass, he might have a double-barrelled name and live in one of the oldest and grandest manor houses in the county, his father might have a seat in the House of Lords, and he might come across as a rich bumbling buffoon, but she was well aware Ralph was a successful businessman, and was much more hard-nosed than his father.

'Let me have a think about it,' Ralph said, and Juliette knew she wouldn't get any further with him until he'd had a chance to mull it over, crunch some numbers, and probably find a way of shafting her.

She knew he'd want to get as much as he could from the newspaper and she didn't blame him; in his shoes she'd probably do the same, but she didn't want to be taken for a ride. What the paper was worth in monetary terms, what the paper was worth to the community, and what it was worth to her, were three totally separate things. In financial terms it wasn't worth much at all, otherwise why would Ralph be closing it down? To the community, it served a purpose but was it sustainable in the long term? Probably not in the format it was currently in. She'd resisted going digital with it, loving the feel of a traditional newspaper and the smell of one.

Most of the people who bought the paper were from the older generation, she knew, and some of the more community-minded also bought it, but youngsters today (when she said "youngsters" she was talking about thirty-year-olds and under – which made her feel incredibly ancient) obtained most of their information from Facebook, Twitter, or other sites on the net. They had no reason to buy a newspaper. Which meant if she was to take the Tattler forward and make it a viable and sustainable venture, she had to find a way of engaging them.

She hadn't picked Brooke's brains when she'd visited her yesterday because she'd wanted to get her head around it first before she told her daughter the news, who would no doubt have very strong opinions of her own. Besides, she wanted to hear about Brooke's escapades about her life in university, and not talk shop during their precious time together.

Juliette concluded that her dilemma was a bit like the question of what came first, the chicken or the egg – she needed to put the work in to get some idea whether she could carry on running the newspaper if she bought it. But she didn't want to spend all that time and effort if Ralph wasn't prepared to sell it to her.

It might be a better use of her time if she was to begin looking for another job. She had a CV to brush up on, and some supporting letters to prepare.

Ralph had said he was going to think about it, and she had to be content with that.

Not feeling in the mood to do any actual work, she stared out of the window at the street below. It was a typical Monday, with delivery vans parked half on the pavements, mums pushing prams, pensioners with shopping bags on their arms or dragging those trolley things behind them. A woman was being pulled along by a large dog, and children (those who were too young for school) trotted by their mothers' sides. It was a busy, vibrant street and the window was open, allowing the sounds of people, cars, and birds to drift into her office.

If she did leave, she wouldn't miss the offices themselves; although, when she said *offices* what she was referring to was the small room she was currently sitting in, the loo, and a tiny kitchen area.

If she did happen to buy the newspaper, the office would be the first thing about the business that she'd change. At present, it might be a nice separation of her personal and professional life to live in one place and work in another, but if she was honest she could do her job quite easily from home and save herself some money.

That was a thought – she needed to know how much the rent on this place was. She needed to have full access to the newspaper's financial accounts before she signed anything. She had no idea about accounting, so she needed to hire someone who did, which meant an expense she didn't want but had to have. There was so much to think about, that she felt quite daunted.

She'd also have to have a solicitor, one who specialised in the buying and selling of businesses, especially since it was a concept she was buying and not bricks and mortar, or stock or physical things as such, but the name and the rights to publish under that name. At least that was what she assumed she was buying. She wasn't sure about any of this at all.

She wasn't entirely sure about anything anymore.

Her eyes drifted towards her phone. She didn't know who she was expecting to call, but Oliver had already been in touch on Saturday asking if he could come to Ticklemore tomorrow and meet up. She'd texted back immediately to say she was looking forward to seeing him and had sent him the address of the office.

Juliette didn't have any idea why she'd asked him for help in the first place, and he might prove to not have the expertise she needed, but she remembered the way he used to think outside the box, and that ability of his to come up with ideas no one else had, and she hoped he'd be able to do the same now.

She also wondered if she would ask him what pen-name he was writing under or if he had yet to publish anything. She wanted to know, but she didn't want him to think she'd been stalking him. Idly, she wondered if he had looked her up on the internet and guessed he probably had, so he had some idea what he was letting himself in for. She guessed he hadn't found much, and she was surprised he'd decided to carry on nevertheless.

Juliette smiled softly to herself; from what she remembered, Oliver had always liked a challenge, and the Tattler was certainly going to be that.

Despite knowing she should be thinking about saving every penny, Juliette decided to pop into Bookylicious for a spot of lunch. She didn't fancy eating a sandwich at her desk, and she certainly didn't fancy eating it alone with just her thoughts for company. Hattie Jenkins would be certain to take her mind off her troubles.

Hattie was a lively, opinionated, and slightly eccentric octogenarian, and she always brightened up Juliette's visits to the café-cum-bookshop. The old lady made her laugh, and Juliette guessed it was because Hattie reminded her of her grandmother, Gloria, who had been a few years older than Hattie when she had died.

Juliette wondered how Alfred was doing. Alfred was Hattie's partner. He was around the same age as Hattie and it was rather sweet when they'd got together last Christmas as a result of trying to get the Toy Shop off the ground. It was also uplifting to think that such an elderly couple could find love.

Maybe there was hope for her yet?

Not that she'd been looking – she hadn't. She'd been quite content with her life up until now. But during these past few months a lot had changed. To begin with there was Brooke going to university, and Juliette hadn't realised she was going to feel so empty, so bereft. It wasn't as though she and her daughter had lived in each other's pockets; hell, the child had hardly ever been at home. But now that she wasn't there at all, Juliette felt as though her right arm had been cut off. Brooke still had some of her clothes in the wardrobe (the ones she never wore) and her bedroom was just as she'd left it, apart from a bit of tidying up and vacuuming that Juliette had done, but the essence of her had gone. It had left, along with the girl herself, in the overloaded car when Juliette had taken her to the halls of residence and deposited her there, quietly weeping. Juliette had been weeping that is, not Brooke. Brooke had been full of giddy excitement, looking forward not back.

Perhaps that was what Juliette should do. Until last September, she had been content with her life in the village. Before her daughter started her own life and Ralph had dropped his bombshell on her, Juliette had been coasting in a kind of suspended animation. Not now though, not any longer. Whether she liked it or not, whether she wanted it to or not, her life was about to change.

Maybe *content* was the wrong word to use, but she had been so focused on caring for Brooke and on her job, she hadn't had time for anything else. Could she consider moving on?

Juliette spotted Hattie as she opened the door, the delicious smell of coffee wafting over her as she made her way inside. Hattie's eyes lit up and she gave her a wave, pointing her towards an empty table. Juliette took a seat and picked up the menu even though she knew what she was going to have – whatever Hattie recommended.

'The velvet cake is on today, but if you want to have some proper food first, I can recommend the roasted red pepper & tomato soup with ricotta, and a slice of sourdough bread,' Hattie told her.

'I'll have that, please, and a black coffee.' Hattie's choices were always perfect and the soup sounded delicious.

'I'll bring it right over.' Hattie turned to walk away, and hesitated. She turned back. 'What are you going to do now?' she asked.

Juliette blinked. 'What do you mean?'

'About your job.'

Juliette blinked again, then frowned. She tilted her head to the side. 'How do you know about it?' She'd told her mother, but no one else.

Hattie tapped the side of her nose and gave her a little wink. 'I know lots of things.'

She certainly did, Juliette thought. Hattie knew far too much for her own good, sometimes before the people concerned knew them.

That wasn't strictly true, Juliette amended; Hattie was inquisitive and loved nothing more than to get involved in other people's business. Take Alfred for instance – Hattie had most definitely got involved in his business and, as it happened, things had turned out wonderfully.

Juliette asked, 'Does the whole village know?'

'I don't think so.'

'Good. Do you mind if we keep it that way? At least until I decide what I'm going to do.'

'I'd like to think you'll stay there,' Hattie said. 'Do you know who's taking it over?'

Juliette gave a small smile. Hattie wasn't privy to the full story, was she? 'He isn't going to sell it – he's closing it completely.'

'*What!* He can't do that! The Tattler is part of Ticklemore. It's been around longer than I have, and that's saying something. It would be like closing the church or diverting the river – it's part of Ticklemore. He can't just shut it down.'

'I thought you knew this,' Juliette said, 'otherwise, why did you ask me what I was going to do?'

Hattie looked sheepish. 'I didn't know anything. Your mum was in here yesterday with a face like a wet weekend, so I guessed there was something going on. I pretended I knew about it, so don't go blaming her because she spilt the beans. She didn't tell me the whole story, though.' Hattie looked disappointed. 'She just said you might be out of a job and did I know of anything going? Naturally, I assumed the Tattler was changing hands.'

'You sneaky thing!'

'You'd be surprised how often that ploy works on people,' Hattie grinned.

'And there was I thinking you've got some kind of psychic ability.' Juliette laughed, despite her vague irritation. Hattie was incorrigible.

The old lady pulled out a chair and sat down. 'Here's what I think,' she offered. 'You've got to stop him from closing it down.'

'I know that,' was Juliette's none-too-patient reply. 'Unfortunately, it's easier said than done.'

'Is it?' Hattie gave her a shrewd look. 'Some things are impossible,' she continued, 'some things are very difficult, and some things are doable if you put enough effort into it or if you want it badly enough. I might be wrong, but I don't believe taking on the Tattler yourself is impossible. It probably wouldn't even be very difficult. It's not as if you don't know what you're doing. So in that case, it falls into the other category, doesn't it?'

'It's not that easy,' Juliette protested again. 'Ralph Trudge-Smythe has got to want to sell it to me.'

'I am sure he will, if you offer him enough.'

'That's the problem, isn't it? I might not be able to offer him as much as he wants. I tried to convince him that the money he'd make from the sale would cover the cost of all the legal fees and everything else. Because even closing a business these days costs money, so if he shuts it down he would lose out.'

'I'm sure things didn't used to be as complicated in my day,' Hattie grizzled. She shook her head, got to her feet, and patted Juliette on the arm. 'If there is anything I can do…' She trailed off. 'If there's anything *any of us* can do…'

'Thank you, I appreciate it, but the ball is in his court now. I'll just have to wait and see.'

And even if he threw the ball back to her and the outcome was positive, she might not be able to purchase the newspaper anyway. Without a sound business plan and a firm idea of where she was going from here, there would be little point in her taking it on. If the steady downward trend in sales of the newspaper continued, she wouldn't be able to pay herself a wage, and without a wage she wouldn't be able to live.

As soon as she'd finished her lunch, she vowed to return to the office and try to brainstorm a few ideas. The problem was, she didn't know where to start.

CHAPTER 7

OLIVER

The village of Ticklemore was even prettier than Oliver thought it would be. It helped that it was a beautiful spring day; it mightn't be quite so nice in winter, perhaps. As he drove from one end of the main street to the other, his eyes scanned the buildings on either side looking for the butcher's shop, above which, Juliette had informed him, the Tattler's offices were located.

He parked with ease at the far end of the village, locked his car, and sauntered up the street checking out the shops. Briefly he wondered whether to pop into a little cafe with a book shop attached, quirkily called Bookylicious, to have a quick coffee before he met with Juliette, but on checking the time he realised he might be late if he did.

Ah, there was the butcher shop, he saw, noting the

window had a wonderful display, the meat looking far more attractive than the shrink-wrapped goods in the supermarket he usually frequented. He was tempted to buy a few bits to take back with him, before he realised he probably wouldn't be bothered to cook them because he rarely cooked these days.

Then he snorted; he'd never been bothered to cook, preferring to grab something on the way home, or eat out. Apart from when he was married of course, because back then his wife used to like him to be at home for the evening meal. Unfortunately that had happened extremely rarely, and he usually arrived home to find something dried up left for him in the oven, which he subsequently threw in the bin, and he'd usually ended up making himself some toast. No wonder his marriage hadn't lasted.

A door and a narrow flight of stairs next to the butcher's led him to the first floor. The door at the top was closed but there was a shiny plaque on it saying "Ticklemore Tattler" and underneath was a handwritten note stuck on with Blu Tack which stated, "please knock".

Oliver knocked.

A voice shouted, 'come in' and he pushed the door open. Inside wasn't what he'd been expecting at all; it was smaller for a start. He didn't know why, but he'd assumed it would be much larger, much busier, and far less feminine. The newspaper offices where he had worked in the past tended to be strictly functional, rather masculine places to work now he came to think about it, but this little office looked more like someone's cosy living room.

For one thing, it had billowing white curtains at the window, which was open and the sounds of the street below drifted up. A desk sat at right angles to it with a vase of flowers on top, and a pretty floral cushion was propped on the guest chair, which wasn't the usual office variety, but more of a winged-back armchair. A woven rug lay on the polished hardwood floor, and the walls were painted white. The room was light and airy, with accent colours of pink and green. The office was a pleasant place to be, but from what he could tell this was a one-man band. There were no other workstations he could see, and no people apart from Juliette.

She had been sitting behind her desk, but as soon as he stepped into the room she rose to her feet and came around it, holding out a hand. He took it, but instead of shaking it, he drew her to him into a brief hug. He had no idea what made him do that, but it seemed natural. They were old friends, and it didn't feel right to simply shake hands.

She smelt delectable, her perfume slightly floral with an undertone of vanilla. And she felt as good as she smelt, he noticed. It was extremely pleasant and he released her quickly, more than a little surprised at his reaction to her. He hadn't felt such an intense attraction to a woman in a long time, and it put him on the back foot somewhat. Disconcerted, he sank into the chair she gestured towards, and cleared his throat.

'So, this is where it all happens, is it?' he asked.

Juliette seemed a little embarrassed and she gave a small laugh. 'Yes, this is it. It's not much, but it's home. Well, not home, I don't live here, but you know what I mean.'

She seemed flustered, and it was quite endearing. He'd never known her to be flustered before. She'd always been supremely in control, almost an ice maiden, although he'd guessed powerful emotions had simmered below the surface because, more than once, he'd seen them lurking in the depths of her eyes. This new Juliette was even more of an enigma than the one he had known previously, and he was intrigued to know more.

There it was again – curiosity. Once a journalist, always a journalist, he thought to himself mockingly.

The pair of them gazed at each other in silence for a few moments, Juliette nibbling at her bottom lip. She seemed nervous and he wondered at the reason. Was she regretting asking him for help, and if so, why? For a second he also wondered whether she knew whose biography he was writing, but he dismissed the thought as soon as it had crossed his mind. She couldn't possibly know; no one did, apart from his agent and his editor, and the man in question, of course.

'It's lovely,' he said looking around, ostensibly meaning the little office but including her in the compliment.

'I do my best,' she said, with a small laugh. 'Thank you for coming. I'm not sure what you can do, but I'm hoping you can do something, even if it's just someone to bounce ideas off. I've approached Ralph Trudge-Smythe with a view to purchasing the Tattler, but so far he hasn't come back to me with either a figure or a decision.'

Oliver tapped his fingers on the arm of the chair, thinking. 'If he does, it will be a ball-park figure, an amount pitched to see what your reaction is. Whatever he offers, I suggest you laugh and ask him to try again. It won't be a serious amount; he'll just be trying his luck. Can I ask you a question?'

She nodded, shifting slightly in her chair, her attention firmly on him. Her gaze was intense, and he hadn't realised her eyes were quite so blue.

'How much are you willing to pay for it?' he asked.

She shrugged. 'I don't honestly know. I know how

much I *could* pay, but that doesn't mean to say I *would* pay it. If I did, I'd have nothing left to live on, and I don't think I'd be able to draw a wage from the business for several months.'

'Many start-up businesses don't pay their owners a wage in the beginning,' Oliver pointed out. 'It's not unusual; but you are right, you don't want to leave yourself trying to live off fresh air. OK, then.' He rubbed his hands together. 'Let's get down to brass tacks. The first thing I need to do is to have a look at this newspaper of yours. Do you have any copies handy?' He'd be shocked if she didn't, but unlike the offices he was used to, there were no piles of rival publications, or stacks of newspapers lying haphazardly around the place.

Juliette continued to stare at him for a second before nodding, then she got up, went to a tall, white filing cabinet behind her, opened it and pulled out a newspaper. She sat back down and handed it to him across the desk.

He took it. It was the size of a tabloid (he hadn't been expecting anything larger) and the publication's name was emblazoned in old fashioned script across the top. It was quite distinctive and he guessed it hadn't changed since the very first edition had rolled off the presses. He liked that; it suggested continuity and would be familiar to readers. Aside from that, the front page followed the usual format, with the headline, a photograph, and a lead story. The rest of the page contained a smaller story, and two adverts at the bottom.

He scanned the inside of the paper. There weren't many pages – the Tattler had far fewer than the national tabloids, but that was to be expected. It did, however, have everything he expected to see – more stories, more adverts, a classified ads section (which wasn't very big) and towards the back were a couple of pages dedicated to sporting activities. Although he wasn't sure whether a tug-of-war actually was a sport, since it was mentioned as a throwback to what had gone on in last year's summer fete.

The newspaper was perfectly fine, but nothing to make him sit up and take notice. And that might be one of the reasons it wasn't making any money. The layout was old hat, and so was its content. If it was to survive and to flourish it needed a drastic change, but at the moment he wasn't sure what.

'How often is it printed?' he asked.

'Weekly,' Juliette said.

'Who does your printing?'

'A small press in Hereford. I put it to bed two days before they print and they deliver on the day it's published.'

'Who do they deliver it to?' he asked.

'Why, me, of course,' Juliette said.

'Do you mean they deliver to this office?'

'Yes, that's right.'

'What happens to the newspaper after that?'

'I take it to the newsagents on the corner, our local Co-op, and a few other places.'

Oliver was astounded. 'You really are doing everything yourself! You don't deliver to peoples' houses as well, do you?' he joked.

'Er, yes, actually I do. When Brooke was younger, she used to help. I paid her out of my own pocket. But she grew out of that quite some time ago, and there aren't enough funds to pay a paperboy or girl.'

'How many do you deliver?'

'Not as many as I would like,' was her dry reply. 'About a hundred. The rest are sold through the local shops and I deliver to a couple of nearby villages too, because they don't have a publication of their own, which is why I include their news alongside ours.'

'So it's not just the *Ticklemore* Tattler?' Oliver said. 'It caters to a wider locale. Who's your demographic?'

'Older people mostly, and those people who are heavily involved in the community, such as the Women's Institute – although they tend to be on the older side, too. Youngsters aren't that interested.'

'What, you mean they don't like reading about cats stuck up trees?' he joked.

Juliette shot him a sharp look. 'As you can see,' she said frostily, 'the Tattler is about far more than cats being stuck up trees. Although, I *would* report on it if the fire brigade turned out – my readers love a bit of drama.' Her expression softened.

'How many copies do you sell?'

'Roughly about a thousand.'

Oliver sucked in a slow breath. No wonder the paper wasn't making any money. Not only was digital news taking over from printed news, but anything that happened in the community very often tended to spread very quickly via social media, making physical newspapers redundant. Advertising was still viable for bigger businesses, but if you wanted to sell your car, for instance, you're more likely to go to sites like Auto Trader. And how was she meant to compete with Facebook Marketplace, Gumtree, or eBay? The answer was quite clear – she couldn't. Therefore her newspaper had to have a complete overhaul and a new focus, but at the moment he couldn't for the life of him think what that could be.

'I'm so sorry, would you like a coffee?' she offered suddenly, and a faint blush spread across her cheeks and he guessed it was from embarrassment at forgetting her manners.

'I'd love one,' he enthused. 'White, no sugar, please.'

He became aware of the faint aroma of coffee, and when she walked past him and disappeared through a small door behind him, he realised there must be a kitchen back there.

A few minutes later she returned with two cups of proper coffee, not the instant variety, and he sipped his with appreciation, before putting it down on the table. The mug was decorated with the Tattler's name running round it.

Juliette noticed him looking at it. 'I've got a couple of T-shirts, too,' she said. 'I wear one of them when I'm out doing public things, like the summer fete. Everybody knows who I am in the village, but sometimes it helps for them to see me as Juliette from the Tattler and not Juliette from down the road.'

'And sometimes it doesn't?' he guessed.

'That doesn't happen much around here,' she said. 'It's too small, too gossipy. And I have to live here.'

He was pleased she'd picked up on his meaning. 'If you found out something shocking, something that people should know about, would you report on it?'

'That would depend. If it was in the public interest, then yes, I would. If it was just Joe Blogs sleeping with Jane Doe, whilst being married to… oh I don't know… Maisie Martin, then no, I wouldn't.'

'Maisie Martin?' Oliver chuckled. 'Do you know anyone by that name?'

Juliette peered at him over the rim of her mug. 'No, I don't. And if I did, I probably wouldn't tell you,' she joked.

'Just in case her husband might really be having an affair?' he smiled back.

'Exactly.'

'I'm not that man anymore,' Oliver said. 'I haven't been that man for a long time.'

Juliette continued to gaze at him and he wondered what she was thinking.

'How many years is it since you've not been a journalist?' she asked.

'Quite a few.'

'What made you give it up? I never thought you would stop chasing stories.'

'I never thought *you* would, either,' he countered.

'I don't care what some people say, it's not easy doing that job and being a single parent. Women like to think they can have it all, but that's not necessarily true.'

He could tell she was pricklier than a hedgehog about it. 'Now your daughter is in university, have you thought about moving back to London?'

'Not a chance! I like living here. I like my life just the way it is – which is why I don't want it to change.' She barked out a slightly bitter laugh.

'But it *is* going to change, isn't it? Nothing stays

the same forever,' he pointed out. 'Think how boring that would be. You could look at this as a new opportunity.'

'I'm trying to…' Her eyes clouded with worry and she swiftly dropped her gaze, but not before he saw.

'It will be all right, you know,' he tried to reassure her, but he wasn't sure whether he believed it himself. The prognosis for the Tattler wasn't good. Not unless she, or both of them, could come up with something new and innovative, because things couldn't go on the way they were.

When she looked back at him, there was a new emotion in her eyes. Was it hope? He had hope, too – he hoped she wasn't setting all his sights on him, because at the moment he didn't have any answers.

He wished he did; because he really, really wanted to help Juliette. And he wasn't sure it was purely for altruistic reasons, either. Selfishly, he wanted to see more of her, and if he couldn't come up with a couple of ideas to help her turn her business around, he guessed he might never see her again.

CHAPTER 8

JULIETTE

'Juliette?' The voice belonged to Sara who managed the Ticklemore Toy Shop. 'Can you pop in when you've got five minutes? I've got something I'd like to share with you and I hope you can write a piece on it.'

'Of course. How about this afternoon? I've got someone with me at the moment.' Juliette's gaze drifted to Oliver, who was lounging in her armchair and looking very much as though he belonged there.

'Great, I'll see you then,' Sara said.

Juliette hung the receiver back on the cradle. It was one of those old-fashioned phones looking as if it came from the 1930s or 40s, and she loved it. She'd bought it from Nell at the Treasure Trove, and it had been a bit of a bugger to get it to work, but the phone company had done wonders and she could now use it as a proper phone. It had its limitations though; if somebody wanted her to press one for this, or two for that, then she was in a bit of a quandary, but she usually just hung on and eventually she nearly always got to speak to a real person without the hassle of going through all those options. It probably wasn't the best business decision she'd ever made, but she hadn't been able to resist the purchase.

'Sorry,' she said to Oliver. 'I don't like leaving the phone unanswered. I do have an answering service, but I try to pick up calls when I can. That was the lady who manages the Ticklemore Toy Shop, although it's not just a toy shop any more. Back last November, Hattie, an old lady who works down the road, met Alfred, who had a shedful of handmade wooden toys. To cut a long story short, they got together, and along with quite a few other people in the community, the Ticklemore Christmas Toy Shop was born. Except it's no longer a Christmas shop, it's now an all-year-round shop and it sells more than toys. It's become a kind of cooperative for local craftspeople to showcase and sell their work. It's very successful.' She frowned. 'I wonder what she wants?'

'Why don't we go and find out?'

'Now?'

'Why not? I'd like to see a little more of the village to get a better idea about things.'

'I told her I'd be there this afternoon,' she said, her

frown deepening. She didn't like being unreliable, and being early could sometimes be as bad as being late.

'Do you think she'd mind if you turned up earlier?' Oliver asked.

'Probably not, but how about if we have lunch first?'

'Sounds good to me,' he said. 'Where do you suggest?'

'We can go to the Ticklemore Tavern. I usually frequent Bookylicious, but Hattie works there.'

'And that's a problem because...?'

'Never mind. You'd have to meet her to understand.' She pushed her chair back and got to her feet. 'We'll go to the pub. They always do a decent pie and chips.'

'Great, that'll save me having to think about food later.'

'Thinking about food is one of my favourite activities,' Juliette said, as she locked the door to the Tattler's office and trotted down the stairs behind him. He looked just as good from the back as he did from the front, she thought. Then, annoyed with herself, she shook her head. Why was she thinking about him like that? She didn't know anything about him anymore. Although her internet search had told her he was divorced, he might have a girlfriend or a partner at home, and Juliette would bet her last pound that the woman wouldn't be at all happy to know Oliver was being ogled by someone.

Her flirting days were long gone, of course. But it didn't stop her appreciating a fine figure of a man when she saw one. Oliver might be in his mid-50s, but he was still darned attractive. He had a presence, a certain charisma, and she was just as susceptible to it as the next woman.

In her London days, she'd known him to use it to his advantage, to get people to open up to him, and she didn't blame him for that. She used to do the same thing. It was what you did. Anything to get ahead of the game, to get your hands on a story before anyone else. She hoped she hadn't abused it.

She did have some integrity and some morals, although those morals had deserted her when she'd met Brooke's father. She'd been defenceless and helpless in the face of him and she'd been unable to resist, much to her shame. It hadn't been one of her better moments, but it had resulted in Brooke and in some ways she'd always be grateful to him for that.

Why on earth was she thinking about that right now? Then she realised Oliver had brought long-buried memories, thoughts, and feelings to the forefront of her mind, and she should have expected that when she'd phoned him. He was part of her old life, not her new one. But she'd reached into the past and had dragged him into the present, so she only had herself to blame if those memories resurfaced.

On reaching the pavement she turned to him and smiled brightly, trying to dispel any negativity.

'It's this way,' she said, leading him in the opposite direction to the toy shop, and towards the quaint little pub.

She was conscious of the curious gazes of the regulars as she walked inside, Oliver behind her, and she smiled at a few of them but she didn't introduce him. She guessed the rumours might very well be flying around by the end of the day, regarding her relationship with a strange and rather attractive man, but she knew that if she introduced him they'd want to know where he was from, what he did for a living, why he was here, and so on.

She had no intention of adding fuel to that particular fire. It would be bad enough as it was and, in a way, she almost looked forward to the speculation – it was sometimes quite amusing. It had been one of the things she'd found difficult in the beginning when she'd returned to live in the village after being in London for so many years; the way everyone knew everyone else's business, especially Hattie. She wondered how long before Hattie found out about Oliver – if she hadn't already heard, Juliette thought to herself with a smile.

'The food here is quite good,' she told Oliver as she handed him a menu. 'So are the ales. They do some speciality ones; not that they interest me – I'm more of a gin girl. What are you having?' They were standing by the bar, and Juliette had got her purse out.

'No, let me, I insist,' Oliver said.

'Don't be ridiculous,' she protested. She'd asked him to help and he had driven all this way, so it was only fair she picked up the tab. Once upon a time she used to have a budget for this kind of thing, but not anymore. The closest she came to entertaining anyone these days, was treating them to a scone and a cup of tea in the café. She didn't exactly have business meetings, although she often met with the people she was writing stories about. Usually it was on their turf, so they were the ones who provided the tea or coffee.

'Would it do any good if I insisted?' Oliver asked.

'No, it wouldn't. Just tell me what you want then go and find a table for us.'

'I'll have a lemonade, please, as I'm driving, otherwise I might have indulged myself in one of those ales you mentioned.'

Juliette ordered the drinks and then joined him at the table. He was nose-deep in his menu, scanning it quickly, and she wondered whether he would order one of the more fanciful dishes on the menu. That was another thing she'd found difficult in coming back to Ticklemore – she had become very used to the extraordinary range of restaurants and bars in London, and the diversity of the food on offer. Bookylicious served up gorgeous light meals and snacks, but they weren't a patch on some of the things that could be found in swanky London restaurants. Not that she used to go to swanky London restaurants that often, but she'd revelled in it when she had. Even the little takeaways on the corners sold dishes that weren't to be found in Ticklemore.

Logan, who owned the Ticklemore Tavern, strolled over to take their orders. As he was scribbling on his pad, Juliette was conscious of his curious looks at Oliver. She grinned inside, then sobered; if Oliver was here just for fun, that would be one thing, but he was here for business, and hopefully to help her get herself out of a hole, so it was quite serious. Which made her wonder why this almost felt like being on a date?

She gave herself a mental shake for being so silly. It was clearly such a long time since she had gone out with a man, any man, that sitting in a pub on her own with a handsome guy felt like a date. She needed to get a life, or so her daughter kept telling her.

Maybe Brooke had a point, although Juliette

wasn't quite sure Brooke meant for her mother to start dating. How would she feel if Juliette brought another man into their little twosome? Would Brooke be accepting, pleased that her mum had found love again? Or would she be horrified her middle-aged mother had taken a man to her bed?

Juliette almost gasped in horror at the direction her thoughts were taking her. Was she seriously thinking about allowing another man into her life? And not just any man. Her imaginary lover was no faceless date she had yet to meet, because the image that had popped into her mind was Oliver's head resting on her pillow.

She needed to stop this at once. Meeting him on Saturday had been bad enough, but having him here in Ticklemore was doing absolutely nothing for her equilibrium.

Desperately hunting around for something to talk about, she blurted, 'Tell me, what books have you written? You didn't say.'

'No, I didn't, did I. I've written a handful of biographies, nothing fantastic…'

'Who have they been about?'

'Figures in public life mostly.'

'Anyone I'd know? '

He hesitated, as if unwilling to tell her. Which was silly, because his books must be out there somewhere, even if she couldn't find them on Amazon.

'Er, possibly. Reginald Carson, Philly Cresswell, to name a couple.'

Julie was impressed. Both of those men could often be found treading the halls of the Houses of Parliament. One had been a chief whip, the other was high up in the civil service. She made a mental note to look up their biographies later, once Oliver had gone.

'Did you find it strange, going from journalism into that kind of writing?' she asked.

'Some things were different, other things quite similar. I had to do a lot of research and homework, because although I interviewed the people in question, often for hours on end, I had to speak to those people around them, sometimes their parents, sometimes their spouses and their children, to verify the facts. I was putting my name to the book, so I wanted to make sure that firstly the information was accurate, and secondly I wasn't going to land myself in a heap of trouble.'

'When you say putting your name to it,' Juliette asked, 'what name were you putting?'

He gave her the kind of look she interpreted as he knew that she'd checked him out on the internet. She blushed, feeling slightly wrong-footed.

'I write under the name O.M. Martin. Martin is my mother's maiden name,' he explained.

'Oh, I see,' Juliette said, not seeing at all. 'Why don't you write under your own name?'

'Because of its previous associations. I didn't want people to be biased. As you well know, journalism can often be sensationalised, and some of my stories certainly were. I didn't want readers to associate what I wrote then with what I write now. I want it to be a serious piece of work. Of course, my editor knows, so does my agent and now, so do you.'

Juliette was pleased to be included in the very short list, and rather flattered too, to think that he trusted her with such information. 'How do you know I'm not going to spread this about?' she asked him.

'It wouldn't matter if you did, but I know you, Juliette, and you're not the type of person to break a confidence.'

He was right; she wasn't. Which had occasionally caused her problems in the past. It sometimes did now, to be honest, but not quite to the same degree – the stories she wrote now, the features she produced, were rather run of the mill, and very little in them would be embarrassing or incriminating to anyone.

Now and again someone trusted her with a snippet of information they wouldn't like to get out (she must have that type of face), but she never published it.

That said, as she had mentioned to Oliver earlier

this morning, if there was something that needed to be exposed because it was in the public interest to do so, then so be it; that's what she'd have to do.

After that, the conversation drifted away from the slightly awkward to the more mundane. She discovered he was currently single, and living in a flat on the outskirts of Birmingham. She told him she was also currently single, and living in a cottage in Ticklemore. They swapped news about their parents – both of his were still alive, and so was her mum but she had no idea about her dad because he had left them the second he'd found out Audrey was pregnant. Audrey hadn't bothered much with men since.

It was ironic, Juliette thought, that although her and her mother's circumstances weren't identical, they were similar enough to comment on. Both of them were single mums, neither of them had a partner on the scene when the babies were born, and neither of them had had a serious relationship since.

Her mum seemed perfectly content with her life. It was full, and she was hardly ever in. And when she was in, she was busy doing things, usually for the WI, or sometimes for the church, or the community centre, or anything else she could think of. Her mum had all ten fingers in more than ten pies (if that was possible) and she seemed to love it. In fact, Juliette thought she'd just caught a glimpse of her mother on the high street, rattling a collection tin for one of the charities the WI supported. She must remember to walk on the other side of the road when she took Oliver to the Toy Shop. She didn't want her mum asking awkward questions. To be honest, she didn't want her mum asking any questions at all.

After coffee Juliette paid the bill, ignoring another of Logan's questioning looks, and led Oliver back out into the street. Thankfully Audrey was nowhere in sight, so Juliette ushered him quickly along the road, only slowing her pace when they reached the door to the toy shop.

Unable to resist, Juliette paused for a second to look at the window display. It was changed every week by Zoe, who was an apprentice to Alfred and learning from him how to make old fashioned wooden toys. But she was so good at window displays that Sara, who managed the shop and who also happened to be Alfred's daughter, insisted she came in every week to change it.

It always looked beautiful and today was no exception. There were currently eight individual craft people renting space in the shop, including Alfred, and each one of them was represented in the window. But not as separate entities; the display incorporated all of them into one glorious eye-catching whole.

Oliver said, 'Oh this is pretty. I like the rabbit.'

It was a spring woodland theme, and Oliver was referring to a pull-along rabbit sitting next to a jar of sculpted glass bluebells. There were also brightly painted pots filled with daffodils and crocuses, pretty flowery scarves, a willow basket filled with speckled eggs, a stuffed squirrel, and the backdrop was a wonderful silk screen depicting a meadow with trees in the background. There was plenty more to look at, but Juliette wanted to find out what the shop's manager wanted her to write about.

'Come on,' Juliette said. 'Let's see what Sara wants.'

She pushed open the door, and Sara came forward to greet her with a smile. They did a double-cheeked kiss, then Juliette moved to the side. This time she would introduce Oliver. It would be rude not to.

'Sara, this is Oliver Pascoe, an old friend of mine from London. He's just popped to Ticklemore for a visit. Oliver, this is Sara. As you can see, she runs the Ticklemore Toy Shop brilliantly. What have you got for me, Sara?' Juliette asked.

Sara gestured towards the counter. On it was a cardboard box and inside, nestling in a bed of tissue paper were a selection of items which were similar to those sold in the shop. Sara bent down and picked another box up off the floor. This one had a different selection, and Juliette ran her fingers over the most exquisite bead necklace which was draped over a small velvet box.

Sara stood back. 'What do you think? I'm just about to take some photos of them.'

Juliette wasn't quite sure what she was supposed to be looking at. The contents of the boxes were beautiful and the items in them complemented each other perfectly, but why was she being shown them? Was it for an Instagram post?

'They're lovely, but...' She trailed off.

Sara rolled her eyes. 'Silly me, I forgot to tell you what they were. These are subscription boxes.' She looked at Juliette as though she was supposed to know what that meant.

'I don't quite follow?' Juliette gave her a confused look.

'Haven't you heard of them? They're all the rage right now. Loads of companies are doing them, from cosmetics, to books, to… oh, I don't know, all kinds. People pay a monthly subscription to the sorts of companies they like to get things from. For example, if we're talking about cosmetics, then every month they would get a box filled with all kinds of goodies through the post. With books, it might be around a particular theme, for example, crime, and then you could get say, two or three of the recently released best sellers together with maybe a signed copy of something, and a bookmark, and perhaps a magnifying glass and, I don't know – there are all kinds of things. So we thought we'd do one ourselves. We have a theme, of course, as you can see with these.' Sara stopped to draw breath and indicated the two boxes on the counter, before continuing. 'This is just the start. We can do one that might be just scarves, or just toys, or a mixture of things for a particular age group.'

Juliette glanced around the shop, wondering if the people who would like scarves or jewellery, would also appreciate receiving a wooden toy abacus. She suspected not.

'Not all the crafters in the shop would contribute to all the boxes every single month,' Sara continued. 'And that's probably going to be a bit of a nightmare on the admin side, sorting out who has contributed what for that month and who is eligible for part of that payment. But that's where I come in; I'll do all the organising – it'll keep me busy,' she laughed.

Juliette shook her head in admiration. She was well aware just how busy Sara was. The former headmistress was supposed to be retired, but retirement hadn't been up her alley at all, Juliette knew. Sara had been bored, which was why Hattie had suggested she run the toy shop.

Alfred had been trying to do it himself, but it had proved to be too much for him. He was in his eighties and he didn't particularly like the selling side of the business. He much preferred toy making, so that's what he now did, and he was also busy passing his knowledge and his expertise onto a much younger generation, of which Zoe was part.

'I see,' said Juliette. It was a wonderful idea, and anything which brought in revenue and raised the profile of the shop was well worth doing. 'Do you want to put together something for the feature or would you prefer me to do it from scratch? Either way, I'm going to need some prices and I'm going to need to come in and take some photos of the crafters with the boxes, and with you, of course. Shall we say tomorrow after the shop closes? I want to catch the light, but I don't want there to be a shop full of customers while I'm trying to do it.'

Oliver, who had been silent up until now, broke in, 'Do you take the photos for the paper yourself as well?' He was looking at her strangely.

'Yes, I do. Why? Is that a problem?' Juliette asked, feeling worried.

'Not at all. It's just that you seem to do everything.'

'I have to, don't I? The newspaper can't afford to

pay anyone else. So I do it all.'

'I'm not criticising or anything,' Oliver said. 'I'm just trying to get to know the business better, before I make any suggestions.'

Juliette opened her eyes wide at him, wishing he'd stop talking. It wasn't as if she wanted to keep everything secret, because people would know soon enough whether the Tattler was closing or whether she was taking over the reins. And she didn't mean simply running it, although there was nothing simple about the Tattler; it was quite a complex process. She just wanted to keep it under her hat for now until things were more definite.

Too late, Sara had already cottoned on that something was up. 'Why does this gentleman—?' she gave Oliver a professional smile. '—need to get to know the business? Do you mean *this* business?'

'Definitely not.' Juliette sighed. 'He's talking about the Tattler. Look, I don't want it bandied about, but Ralph Trudge-Smythe told me he's closing it down.'

'*What?* He can't do that! I know I haven't lived in Ticklemore for long, but I do know the paper is part of the community. Where would people find out when the church was having a jumble sale? Where would people go to check that their neighbour hasn't asked for planning permission for a five-storey hotel in the back garden?' Sara grimaced. 'That last was a bit of an exaggeration, but you know what I mean.'

'I think you'll find he can do so, and he quite possibly will,' Juliette informed her. 'I'm trying to buy it off him, but so far he hasn't come back to me with a figure, or to let me know whether he'll sell it to me in the first place. Which he might not.'

'What will you do if he doesn't?' Sara asked.

'I've no idea at the moment. I don't want to think about it, to be honest, not until I know for sure what is going to happen with the Tattler.'

'If there's anything I can do...' Sara offered.

'Don't worry about the article, it will get written,' Juliette hastened to reassure her. 'I've got three months yet before he plans on closing it, so I'll try to get you as much publicity as I can for your subscription boxes.'

'That's very kind, but I'm more concerned about you. We'll get plenty of publicity in other ways. We've got Twitter, and Facebook, and Instagram, so I'm sure we'll be fine.'

They said their goodbyes but once Juliette and Oliver were outside again, Juliette turned to him and said, 'That's the problem, isn't it? Twitter, Facebook, the internet… how can I compete with that?'

'You can't,' Oliver said. 'Not directly at least; in the same way you can't compete with the nationals, or with Sky News, or the BBC for that matter. All you can focus on is the local stuff, news that can't easily be obtained elsewhere or what would take too long to find out, because people are lazy and they like things handed to them on a plate. I take it you haven't told many people the Tattler might close?'

'No, just my mum and now Sara. Hattie in Bookylicious also knows. She knows everything. Nothing gets past that old lady.'

'What was their reaction?' Oliver asked.

'They were all shocked and quite upset. The Tattler has been going for over a hundred years. It's part of Ticklemore's history and they can't imagine being without it. But if you asked for the reaction of one of those teenagers,' Juliette pointed to a group of kids just getting off a bus, 'I'm pretty sure they wouldn't care, and that's if they had any idea what the Tattler was in the first place. If the newspaper is to survive, it needs to appeal to a wider demographic and I simply don't know how I'm going to do that.'

'It's the same as a lot of things, isn't it?' Oliver said. 'People don't want it to go, but they don't use it themselves. It's like when shops close down in small towns and villages; people are upset to see them boarded up or lying empty, but they didn't make the effort to buy from them in the first place. They can't have it both ways. If, *when*, this Ralph Trudge-Smythe person decides to sell it to you, you're going to need to make sure everyone is aware if they don't use the Tattler, it will fold. You need the community behind you for this, because without it, you'll fail.'

Juliette knew what he was saying was right, but it didn't make it any easier to hear. It was also easier said than done.

'I can't do anything further until I know what Ralph Trudge-Smythe is going to do,' she said, feeling more despondent than she could ever remember feeling. Even when she'd discovered she was pregnant, she hadn't felt quite this low. Mind you, she said to herself, she'd been a lot younger and far more resilient back then.

'Yes, you can,' Oliver insisted. 'You need to start making plans. And even if the owner doesn't let you buy the Tattler, there isn't anything stopping you from setting up on your own. You just call the paper by a different name, that's all. And it might be a good thing – a fresh start and all that.'

'But I want to keep the Tattler's name,' she objected. She knew she sounded petulant, like a toddler denied a toy, but she couldn't help it. It had so much history, so many connotations, and its good name was irreplaceable and invaluable.

'Ideally, that would be best, but the world isn't ideal, is it?' he pointed out.

Juliette wished Oliver would stop being so logical.

She wished he would stop talking altogether if all he was going to suggest was that she should carry on regardless. Carrying on wasn't an option under the present circumstances, was it?

Everything still boiled down to finances – and no matter whether it was called the Tattler or something else, the newspaper wasn't making enough money for her to live on.

Oliver was staring into the distance and he had such a faraway look on his face she wondered what he was thinking.

Suddenly he stopped walking. 'Do you know what?' he said. 'The woman in the Toy Shop has given me an idea. How about subscriptions?'

'You want me to get a subscription box together?' Juliette had no idea what he was talking about, but she was willing to hear him out. 'I think you're going to have to expand on that.'

'Many magazines have a subscription, don't they? I think you should do the same. Maybe offer a discount. For example, each edition costs fifty pence to buy, so per year that would cost a reader twenty-six pounds. What if you offered a yearly subscription for twenty pounds?' He looked pleased with himself, but Juliette had yet to be convinced.

'I'll be losing six pounds,' she pointed out.

'Only if that reader religiously bought every single

copy in the year. How many of them do that? Even the most dedicated reader tends to miss one or two copies. And twenty pounds doesn't sound much, even if it does have to be paid all at once; whereas physically going out and buying a newspaper might be more of an effort.' He paused and his eyes lit up. 'Have you thought about an app?'

Juliette didn't know what to say. What app? What was he talking about? Goodness gracious, she knew she'd asked for ideas, but now she had the feeling she was getting far more than she'd bargained for.

Suddenly overwhelmed, she desperately longed to return to the serenity of her office and to trundle along in the same manner she always had. Everything was moving far too fast. She needed time to process it.

But what she really needed, was time to process Oliver himself, because she was in danger of getting swept away by him. And she wasn't referring solely to his enthusiasm, either. Seeing the passion on his face and watching his excitement grow, she recalled how she used to feel before Brooke came along, when her own passion and excitement for her job had run high – and it terrified the life out of her.

As did the niggling notion she was starting to feel more for this man than was good for her.

CHAPTER 9

OLIVER

Oliver wasn't entirely sure what he had done to make Juliette mutter a couple of excuses about how busy she was and then scuttle back up the street towards her office. She'd been pleasant enough, polite and friendly, but he was certain he'd seen a mild panic in her eyes and he wasn't sure what had caused it. Perhaps he'd come on a bit strong; he did tend to get carried away when an idea occurred to him, but *she'd* asked *him*, and he was only trying to deliver.

Maybe she wasn't ready for this. When she said she wanted his help, perhaps she didn't mean it in the way he'd assumed she'd meant. Maybe she wanted help to keep the newspaper just the way it was. But if that was the case, it wasn't going to happen.

The Tattler couldn't carry on as it was. It was well known that the writing was on the wall for newspapers all over Britain, as the industry was in decline. There was no denying that the younger generation rarely bought a paper, and it was going to be damned hard to give them a reason to do so.

Although, he acknowledged, it did tend to get easier to persuade people to buy local papers when they were part of the community and they wanted to know what was going on in their patch, so to speak. Announcements were always popular in local newspapers, he knew. But on the other hand, there was social media for that. Juliette was going to have her work cut out if she wanted to compete.

He knew his suggestion of making the newspaper available on subscription was a valid one. He also knew that moving the newspaper from physical copies to an app, might appeal to people under forty. It certainly appealed to him. He rarely bought a newspaper himself these days, preferring to obtain all his news from the internet because he had a greater selection at his fingertips, and it was also more environmentally friendly. Which was rather ironic, considering he had spent a big part of his life working for a publication that depended on cutting down trees to make a profit.

When he'd got back from Ticklemore yesterday, he'd decided to set up a meeting with Otis Coles. He didn't need to and there wasn't anything scheduled, but he felt an urge to meet with the man face to face again.

To his surprise Otis's secretary had given him an appointment for this afternoon. Oliver had been anticipating a wait of at least a couple of weeks, if not longer. Politicians were rarely so accommodating as this, and when they were it usually meant they wanted something. Oliver wondered what it could be.

The man made no secret regarding his ambition. He wanted the UK's top job and there was nothing wrong with that. Knowing that the biography would take at least eighteen months between Oliver finishing writing it and the book hitting the shelves (and that was assuming he could finish the first draught today – which wasn't about to happen) it was a decent chunk of time and a lot could happen between now and then, especially in politics.

Whatever the reason, Otis had agreed to meet with him and Oliver had a sinking feeling it would affect the book in some significant way.

These were the things going through his mind as he travelled to London today.

It would have been easier if he could have met Otis Coles in his constituency offices, but there was a vote in the House of Commons and Otis needed to be in London for it, so his secretary had informed Oliver. Otis had time between meetings for a half-hour chat, as long as Oliver was flexible about the time and didn't mind a bit of a wait.

Hanging from a strap when he boarded the Tube, his body swaying to the rhythm of the train, an old excitement coursed through him at being in the capital again. He used to live for being in the thick of things; journalism was in his blood and right now his very veins were thrumming with the remembered thrill of the chase.

But that wasn't why he was here today. There was no chase. There was no story, as such. In all his research and digging around, Oliver had uncovered nothing unsavoury regarding Otis. There had been many high points in the politician's life, and some low ones (the tragic death of his brother, Finley, from cancer, for instance) but nothing scandalous.

There would be no revelation, no surprise, and no twist at the end. The story he was commissioned to write was the tale Otis wanted him to tell, consisting of an account of Otis Coles's rise from obscurity to power (not the ultimate power, not yet, but Oliver knew it was imminent) and would be factually correct in as much as it could without it being libellous. Although Oliver was under no illusion many things would be omitted, things that it wouldn't be in Otis's interest to tell. Take Brooke, for instance…

Oliver's biography of the man was already starting

to garner interest. His editor was responsible for that, as was his agent, and the publishing house which would be producing the book. It was in everyone's best interest to make this a popular book. It probably wouldn't be found on the shelves of the local supermarket, but it would be talked about in the broadsheets, and on the more highbrow TV programmes. In it, there would be one or two surprises – carefully orchestrated surprises – but nothing shocking, and certainly nothing which would be detrimental to Otis or to his career.

When Oliver had been approached to write Otis's biography, he'd been under no illusion this would be Otis's version. He had been more than happy to do it, but a little part of him, a part which he was finding increasingly difficult to subdue, wanted to know the whole story and not just the one Otis was prepared to share with the world.

Oliver blamed Juliette for his curiosity. If he hadn't met up with her again, and if he hadn't discovered her secret (and Otis's), maybe he wouldn't be feeling so restless today. His nose was twitching, figuratively speaking, and it was the same twitch he used to have when he was onto something. The question was, should he ignore it, or should he go with his gut feeling?

Scratching the curiosity itch would be far more fun

and far more satisfying, but no matter what the journalist in him wanted, the man in him couldn't entertain the idea. Let sleeping dogs lie, was the best thing to do.

On reaching his destination, Oliver had to go through the necessary rigmarole of security and checking and double-checking, before he was finally allowed into the hallowed halls of the Houses of Parliament, and he wondered whether Otis's insistence on meeting here was a deliberate ploy on the politician's part.

All their previous meetings, four of them to be exact, had taken place outside of London; the first had been in a neutral restaurant with Oliver's agent and a couple of other people in attendance, one of them being Oliver's editor, where both parties had sounded each other out and had laid down the ground rules. Another two had taken place in Otis's constituency offices in Surrey, and the last one had been at Otis's home.

The inference from this, Oliver guessed he was meant to take, was that he and Otis were becoming closer, and that Otis was opening up to him and showing him the person behind the politician by inviting him into his home.

Now Otis had shown him the private man, maybe Otis thought it was time to remind Oliver of the public one?

Oliver had a hunch regarding the reason, and if he was right he knew that timing was crucial. The current political party had been in power for more than four years and a general election was looming in the autumn. It was common knowledge the Prime Minister was standing down and retiring from public life. He was getting on in years and his wife was unwell. Otis, on the other hand, was considerably younger, and Otis's wife, if the magazines were to be believed, was brimming with health and vitality.

They made a formidable pair. Oliver guessed she was being groomed to become the wife of the next Prime Minister. Once again, this wasn't a surprise. There was no news here. The news would be if Otis *failed* to become the leader of the party. If someone pipped him to the post, for instance. But he was the front runner by miles, and he was practically guaranteed to be voted in. He was a popular choice by both the backbenchers and the general public.

When Oliver was shown into his office, Otis Coles rose from behind his walnut desk, with his hand stretched out and a wide smile on his face.

Otis stepped forwards, grabbed Oliver's hand and pumped it, patting him on his arm with the other – a classic show of power – and said, 'My dear Oliver, what a pleasure. I was going to suggest you popped by, so you asking for a meeting is fortuitous. Is there a problem with the book?'

Oliver wore a smile as genuine as the one Otis bore. 'Everything is fine. I just thought we could have a bit of a catch-up. Did you want to see me about anything in particular?' He thought it best to let the politician go first, because Oliver didn't have a set agenda.

Otis gestured for Oliver to take a seat. 'Can I get you a coffee? Tea? Or something stronger?'

'Coffee would be great, thanks.'

Oliver studied the man as Otis pressed a button on his phone and spoke. He was as charismatic as Oliver remembered from his last meeting. Tall and slim, he obviously looked after himself. He wore handmade suits, his hair was expertly styled, and his nails were manicured. Oliver had no idea where he bought his ties from or his shirts, but they looked expensive.

Everything was understated, nothing was obvious or flashy – the average man in the street probably wouldn't be able to tell that the politician spent more on a suit than they earned in three months. The people who *would* know were his peers, and it was those who Otis aimed to impress.

The general public saw a well-put-together, well-turned-out man, good-looking in an unthreatening sort of way, who had a non-existent accent. Although

Oliver had heard him speak with a cut-glass accent when he needed to, but he'd also heard him talk with a faint hint of Yorkshire in his voice. Otis Coles was a man for all seasons, a man for all people, and he worked bloody hard to maintain the impression.

It was obvious what Juliette had seen in him all those years ago, and Oliver wondered how many other women had seen (still saw?) the same thing. Did Otis still indulge in a little extra-marital activity? Oliver hoped not; anyone can fall by the wayside once, anyone can make a mistake and he hoped Otis had made his with Juliette. Just Juliette. But he thought not. He suspected there were others, because, for this type of man, weren't there always?

Oliver didn't want to see Otis fall, but if you were in public life you had to expect the scrutiny which came with it. The higher you rose, and the higher the demands made upon you, the further you were likely to fall. Oliver quite liked the guy. He was a breath of fresh air in politics, even though he'd been around the block more than once.

He played the game, he knew the rules, he also bent them slightly as he had pointed out once or twice, and some of these instances were in the book. Not many, just enough to show his human side, and just enough to show the public that he wasn't too rigid, that he could bend and sway if the circumstances warranted. Otis had been keen to show he was compassionate, thoughtful and measured, yet firm and decisive – all the things people want from the leader of their country.

Oh yes, Oliver had a fairly good idea why he was here, and it wasn't because he'd asked for a meeting.

'Should I go first?' Otis asked, and Oliver had a feeling he wouldn't be expected to contribute to the conversation at all.

'Please do.' Oliver leant back slightly, resting his hands on the arm of the chair, his legs stretched out in front of him. Appearances were everything, and he didn't want Otis to think he was in awe of him (Oliver was, but he didn't like to admit it, not even to himself). The man was a legend in his own lifetime, but the problem with legends was they tended to have feet of clay. Oliver prayed he hadn't found Otis's.

'Grantham is standing down before the next election,' Otis began. 'I expect you are aware of this?'

Oliver nodded. It was common knowledge. Grantham Bridges made no secret that he'd had enough of politics. When he'd said he wanted to spend more time with his family, which was usually a euphemism for "I've been forced to resign to avoid a scandal", in the Prime Minister's case it was perfectly true.

'I'm going to be next leader of the party,' Otis

announced.

Oliver nodded again; once more this was no secret. Everyone knew he was in with the best chance, everyone knew he was the odds-on favourite. If you put a bet on whether Otis would become leader of the party, you would undoubtedly win.

Otis leant forward, placed his elbows on his desk and steepled his hands together. It was a calculated, earnest, sincere gesture. He probably paid as much attention to his mannerisms, as he did to his appearance, Oliver suspected. When you were in the public eye, every nuance was scrutinised, therefore it was sensible, necessary in fact, for the man to calculate every move he made and every word he uttered.

Politicians were in a way more like actors than actors themselves. They had to be these days and Oliver admired him for it. There was no point in disliking him because of what the job entailed. They all did it – they had to. It was just that Otis was rather better at it than most.

'I'm going to be the next Prime Minister,' Otis said. There was no fanfare, no bravado, it was a simple statement of fact.

Once again, Oliver nodded. He was beginning to feel like a wobble-headed doll. He felt like saying "tell me something I don't know" but he kept quiet.

'I want the book to come out shortly after I win the election, and I want to change the title,' Otis continued.

Oliver shrugged. The title didn't make a great deal of difference when it came to biographies. It was who the book was about which was important. It would have Otis Coles's name emblazoned across the top, with the title as more of a subtitle underneath. 'What do you want to call it?'

'The Journey. I want it to reflect how I became Prime Minister. My next one will be called The Destination.'

Otis gave a small smile. 'You're planning your next biography already?'

'Why wouldn't I? The next one will be all about what I achieve in office. Of course, it won't be able to be written until afterwards. I anticipate that to be a good many years hence.'

'Not just five?'

'Oh, no. I'm planning a second term, and a third. After that, we shall see.'

The man was confident, Oliver gave him that. He shouldn't be impressed at his audacity and sheer bloody-mindedness, but Oliver couldn't help himself. Otis was supremely confident, fantastically self-assured, and he got Oliver's back up a little. This was the side of Otis Coles not many people outside of the

Houses of Parliament had the privilege of witnessing.

'It's going to be a bit of a rush considering I haven't finished the first draught yet, and I do have other commitments,' Oliver said, thinking of Juliette and the newspaper. Which also put an image in his head of her and Otis together, and he pushed it away crossly. He didn't want to imagine the pair of them, but even as he was trying not to think of it, he couldn't help himself, and jealousy jabbed at him. Which made him even crosser, because he had no reason to be jealous – Juliette wasn't his, and never had been.

'Whatever they are, put them on the back burner,' Otis instructed. 'I'd like this book out by Christmas.'

'This year?'

'Most certainly. Everyone buys books for Christmas, and I want this one to be a best seller. Don't you?' The question was a calculated one. Of course Oliver would like it to be a best seller. What author wouldn't?

'You do realise Christmas is only seven months away? The manuscript has got to go through a whole process before the book will be anywhere near ready to be printed.'

'I'm sure you can rush it through if you have to.' Otis was almost dismissive, and Oliver could practically see him waving a hand in the air as if to waft away an annoying fly.

'I've got to finish it, that's the first thing,' Oliver said. 'Then it's got to go through at least one round of edits, then the copywriting, then the proofreading. All that takes time.'

'I've no doubt it can be expedited. Timing is crucial, as I'm sure you can appreciate. As will your editor, and your publisher. It's in their interests to do so. What better time to release a biography about a Prime Minister, than a few months after he *becomes* Prime Minister? I'm aware we'll have to have a few more meetings, especially around the time I become leader of the party, and during the election itself. I want you with me, to experience it alongside me. Readers will love the first-hand account and all that. I'll let you in on what I'm thinking every step along the way. What more can a biographer ask?'

What more indeed? 'I still don't think it will be completed on time,' Oliver said.

'Why ever not? You've had long enough.'

Oliver had had precisely five months. Most of those five months had involved a great deal of research, meetings and interviews, and the sorting out of notes. He had written quite a bit, but there was an awful lot yet to get down. It could be done, he acknowledged, but did he want this man to rush him?

'The final, edited manuscript also has to be

approved by you and your legal team. That will take time, too,' Oliver pointed out.

'Oh, I suppose I could probably read it in an evening if I put my mind to it,' Otis said. 'As for my legal team, they will do as they're told.'

'But what if things need amending or rewriting?' Oliver asked.

Otis dropped his hands, resting them on the table, one curled around the other, making a large fist. He looked Oliver straight in the eye. 'I'm sure they won't have to be.'

Oliver interpreted the man's words as he was meant to; it was a warning, a threat – he shouldn't put anything in the book that would embarrass him, or would incriminate him, or embarrass or incriminate anyone else, except for those things Otis had told him to put in.

'I'll see what I can do.' Oliver was going to have to pull his finger out if this book was to get written. And he'd have to speak to his agent and his editor.

But what was bugging him the most, was that he'd have to renege on his promise to help Juliette.

And even more upsetting was that the reason he'd be letting her down was because of the man whom he suspected was the father of her child.

CHAPTER 10

JULIETTE

To say Juliette was intimidated was a bit of an understatement. She'd never been to the Trudge-Smythe's house before. It wasn't open to the public, although maybe it should be, she thought, gazing around at the immaculately tended grounds. It wasn't a stately home as such, or a castle, but it was no less impressive.

She had been summoned there by Ralph, although why he couldn't have met her in the Tattler's office, she didn't know. But she could guess. It was a blatant display of his wealth and power, compared to hers. He wanted to intimidate her.

Trudge Manor mightn't be in the same league as somewhere such as Hatfield House, but it was certainly big, she saw, as she drove up the long drive. It swept around so the house wasn't face-on but at a slight angle. From the front it had a flat facade, but she could see how far back it went. You could fit several families in there, she thought, and they would never need to bump into each other.

She was well aware that was often the fate of some of the larger houses – they had been split into apartments. A cynical part of her wondered if Ralph Trudge-Smythe had considered that particular option. He seemed to be far more ruthless when it came to business than his father ever was. She also had the feeling he had no respect for history whatsoever and would trample roughshod over it if there was a pound to be made.

She switched off the engine and got out of the car, resisting the urge to crane her neck and gawp up at the building, just in case Ralph was watching. She didn't want to give him the satisfaction of knowing she was as impressed as he wanted her to be.

It wasn't a surprise to find the door was opened by someone other than the man himself, as Juliette was faced with a woman roughly her own age, who smiled a welcome and gestured for her to step inside.

'Mr Trudge-Smythe is in the drawing-room,' she said before Juliette could say who she was. As the woman closed the door, Juliette quickly scanned the enormous hall with its checkerboard marbled floor, the grand sweeping staircase, and the huge chandelier.

Paintings of dour-looking men and women lined the staircase and she guessed they were ancestors. Their watchful eyes made her shudder.

She was even more discombobulated when the woman knocked on a pair of grand doors, pushed them open and stepped back, gesturing for her to enter.

The drawing-room could have fitted her cottage into it twice over, she saw, and seated at the far end, their legs sprawling out in front of them, were three men. Juliette recognised one of them as being Ralph. The other two were strangers, but they wore suits and she guessed the reason they were there.

Ever since Ralph had phoned her, her heart had skipped a couple of beats. If it was bad news and he intended to wrap up the business, surely he wouldn't have asked to meet her? "Asked" was the wrong word – "commanded", might be a better choice.

She was here to be told how much Ralph wanted for the newspaper. Oh God, she wished she'd asked Oliver if he wouldn't mind accompanying her. Here, in this grand room, faced by three men in suits, she felt alone and out of her depth.

Then something Oliver said came back to her – even if the amount Ralph wanted for the Tattler was ridiculous or was beyond her means, it didn't necessarily indicate the end of a newspaper for

Ticklemore. She dearly wanted to keep the name (it made sense for business reasons as well as for historical ones) but it wasn't the be-all and end-all. She could start up again with a different name, although she still hadn't thought through how she was going to go about revamping the newspaper – she really must get started on that.

When she looked at it that way, she was coming to this meeting from a position of strength. She wanted to buy it, that was a given. But she didn't *have* to. It made financial sense for Ralph to sell it to her. But when she thought about it, did it make financial sense for her to buy it from him? How much was a name worth? What was the value of a reputation?

In some ways, Juliette was now synonymous with the Tattler. They were one and the same, and with her readership knowing who she was, she didn't think it would be too much of an uphill battle if she produced a Ticklemore newspaper which bore a different name. Especially once the villagers knew the reason for the change. Oliver was right though, she acknowledged – she needed the community behind her.

Reaching deep inside herself to find an echo of the woman she had once been, Juliette stalked into the room, her head high, a confident smile on her face, marched straight up to Ralph Trudge-Smythe and held out her hand.

Taken by surprise, (this was his show and not hers) he scrambled to his feet, took her hand and shook it. The other two men did the same, rather more slowly, giving each other glances as they greeted her.

Without waiting to be asked, Juliette took a seat, leaning back a little, and crossed her legs at the ankles. She was glad she'd worn her smartest suit, the sheer tights, and the nude-coloured high heels. She looked as though she could hold her own, even if she didn't feel like that inside.

Ralph cleared his throat and opened his mouth, but Juliette jumped in before he had a chance to speak.

She said, 'I hope you didn't bring me all this way just to tell me you aren't prepared to sell the newspaper to me, because that would be a waste of my time... and yours,' she added, as if it was an afterthought. She'd met this type of man before, although not for many years, admittedly, but handling them was a bit like getting back on a bike. You never forgot. They were like sharks, or perhaps she was doing sharks a disservice. They were more like playground bullies; as soon as they sensed weakness they pounced.

She shifted forwards and gave him an intense stare. 'Go on,' she said, 'Spit it out. How much would you like me to pay for it?'

When he told her, with a smirk playing around his lips, Juliette let out a bark of laughter. Then she got to her feet.

'Gentlemen, thank you for inviting me, but our meeting is over. There's no point in discussing things further. As you well know, the amount you're asking is ridiculous. Go ahead and close it down.' She began to walk towards the door, her heart pounding, wondering if they would call her bluff.

If they did, they did. Plan A was buying the Tattler. Plan B, she suddenly realised, was *not* buying it. She reached the door. Plan B it was.

'Miss Seymour? Wait a moment.'

She turned, one hand on the ornate brass handle. She put a mildly questioning look on her face, and hoped it fooled them.

It wasn't Ralph who had spoken, but one of his minions, and she realised neither of them had introduced themselves. How rude.

'You are...?' she asked.

'Merton Berrow. I was Lord Trudge-Smythe's financial advisor; I am now Ralph's.'

'When it comes to the Tattler, what have you advised him? I hope it wasn't to ask for such a ludicrous amount. I thought financial advisors were more intelligent than that.'

She saw an infusion of pink spread across his

cheeks. Good, she had insulted him. Now he was the one on the backfoot, and she was quite enjoying it.

Once again, Oliver had been right, although she hadn't realised it when he'd asked her whether she'd missed the cut and thrust, and the clash of wits. She had, although she wouldn't want to go back to doing anything like this full time. Once was probably enough. Playing with words was her business. But not in this way now, and not those kinds of words. These days, she preferred less highbrow stories (but equally as important, as far as she was concerned). But there was no real story here, was there? She was uncovering nothing, apart from Ralph's greed, and that was hardly anything new.

The figure they'd demanded had been a fishing expedition, to see if she'd bite. This whole negotiation was like a game of chess. Except, she held the winning hand. She almost smiled as she realised how mixed her metaphors were.

'Sit back down, Miss Seymour. I'm sure we can come to some arrangement.'

'I'm not sure we can,' Juliette replied. 'You're going to have to come down an awful lot to make my buying your newspaper a viable proposition. I'd like to buy it, obviously. But not that much. And unlike Mr Trudge-Smythe, my funds aren't unlimited. They're very limited indeed, so why don't I leave you gentlemen to have another little think, then come back to me with a more realistic proposition. I can see myself out.'

With that, she coolly opened the door. It was time to leave it there. She was walking out of Trudge Manor with the upper hand, although whether she'd keep it was another matter entirely. And next time (if there was a next time) she hoped to have backup with her in the form of Oliver.

Realising she hadn't heard from him in a week, she decided to give him a call. First though, she needed to get away from this place. She didn't want Ralph and the others to see her phone someone the second she was out of the door. She needed to continue to play it cool, at least until she was out of sight.

Calmly (on the outside at least – inside she was a bubbling mass of semi-hysteria) she started her car and drove down the gravelled drive, neither too slowly nor too fast, her pace measured. She didn't expect anyone to be watching, but just in case they were, she didn't want them to think she was running away.

As soon as she thought it was prudent to do so, she pulled into a layby, took out her phone and dialled Oliver's number. She was surprised to find her heart was hammering just as hard as it had been when she was in the drawing-room of Trudge Manor. The meeting must really have spooked her. She thought she'd handled it well, though.

'Juliette, lovely to hear from you. Sorry I haven't been in touch...' Oliver ground to a halt.

Juliette wondered if this was his way of backing out of saying he'd help her. She couldn't blame him, he owed her nothing. They'd been work colleagues, possibly friends even, but only as much as the job had entailed. That she had fancied him once had been neither here nor there. She still fancied him. But once again, it was of no consequence. He didn't feel the same way about her, she was sure of it.

'No worries,' she said brightly. 'I know how busy you are.' She wondered if she should make some excuse and ring off, but she might as well tell him her news, since she had him on the phone.

'Guess where I've been?' She carried on, before he could answer, 'I was summoned to a meeting with Ralph Trudge-Smythe and two men in suits. One of them said he was Lord Trudge-Smythe's financial advisor. I didn't get the other one's name or what he did, but my guess is that he was possibly a lawyer of some description. They made me an offer.' She paused, deliberately.

'How much?'

She told him, and his reaction was the same as hers. Oliver burst out laughing. 'I hope you didn't agree to it,' he spluttered.

'No, I did not! I can't afford a quarter of that,' she told him.

'What happened then?'

'Basically, I insulted them.'

She heard Oliver chuckling down the phone again, glad she was amusing him. It was quite funny when she came to think about it. Little old her against those three big men (none of them had been that big – unless you included their waistlines in the equation). They had meant to intimidate or impress her, but she wasn't quite sure of the reason. Did they think she had that kind of money? Or had they been simply making it impossible for her to buy? But if that was the case, it would have been far easier to simply inform her once and for all that the business was folding. There was no point in bothering with all the palaver.

There she was again, going round in circles and second-guessing herself. It was pretty clear, she concluded, that this was an opening gambit. All she had to do was hold her nerve and stop overthinking things.

'Where did you leave it?' Oliver wanted to know.

'With them. I told them to come back to me with something more sensible and then we could talk. I walked out of the meeting and left them to it.'

'That's brilliant – I wish I could have been there.'

'I wish you had been, too,' Juliette said before she had time to stop to think.

There was a brief uncomfortable silence between them, then all of a sudden he spoke. 'Why didn't you call me to let me know about the meeting? I would have come with you.'

'I didn't want to bother you,' she replied.

'It wouldn't have been a bother.' There was another short silence, then he said, 'If Ralph Trudge-Smythe comes back to you again and suggests another meeting, I'd like to go with you. Not because I don't think you can manage on your own,' he added hastily, 'but because it's not fair having three against one. At least I can even up the odds a bit.'

'I would be grateful,' she said. 'I did manage on my own, but I didn't like it. If it had just been me and Ralph, it wouldn't have been so bad. I didn't like him bringing reinforcements.'

'You could take it as a compliment. He clearly thought he needed backup.'

'I know *I* did.'

'From what you've told me, you most certainly did not. But I'm there if you need me.'

'I appreciate it, I really do.'

Another silence followed, this time not quite so strained, then Oliver said, 'Do you fancy meeting up?'

Juliette wondered if he had more ideas for her.

'Don't worry if you're busy,' he said, 'I perfectly understand.' There was a whole depth of meaning in that last sentence. What was it that he understood?

She did want to see him again, and not because of the newspaper. She wanted to see him because she enjoyed his company, although she wasn't so sure she enjoyed how he made her feel.

'I'm not busy,' she said. 'Or rather, I *am* busy, but not too busy to see *you*.'

'Good,' he said softly, 'because I'd like to see you, too. How about tomorrow? Do you have to work?'

'Probably, but I shan't.' She was lying; she would do some work, but she'd fit it in around him. Her hours were quite flexible, as was her workload. There were only four occasions during the month when her time was not her own, and that was when she had the publication deadline to meet, just before the paper went to the press. Tomorrow wasn't one of them.

'How about dinner?' he asked, and Juliette drew in a breath.

Dinner wasn't a business lunch. Dinner wasn't a quick meeting at her office. Dinner was a date. 'Do you mean what I think you mean?' she asked him – she didn't want to play games. She wanted to know where she stood.

'If that's what you'd like it to mean, then yes.' He

took a breath and she heard the hesitancy in his voice. 'I'd like to see more of you, Juliette.'

'Good,' she echoed, 'because I'd like to see more of you, too.'

Oh, lord, whatever she was doing, whatever *they* were doing, it felt good. It felt *right*. A tentative excitement glowed inside her – for the first time since before Brooke was born, she felt she might be falling for a man.

She just hoped she wasn't making a big mistake.

CHAPTER 11

OLIVER

What part of not having the time to help Juliette didn't he understand, Oliver asked the following day as he was getting ready to meet her.

He'd been deliberately keeping himself to himself, knowing he should ring her or text her at the very least, but he knew if he did, he'd get sucked in. He needed every minute he could spare to finish writing Otis's biography, and he'd been hoping she might take the hint, because he didn't want to tell her he was too busy. It was cowardly of him, he knew that.

But then she'd gone and rung him, and he'd been unable to resist picking up her call. And he *had* got sucked in, and another part of him was jolly pleased about it.

Which was why he'd found himself asking her to dinner.

It was obvious they both knew it wasn't simply a business meeting. Or even a meeting between two former colleagues. This was a date, and a surge of excitement shot through him. He couldn't remember the last time he'd felt this way about a woman.

Since the divorce he had dated sporadically, he'd even had the occasional girlfriend, but he hadn't been emotionally touched by any of them, and gradually things had fizzled out between him and whichever woman he'd happened to be seeing. Nothing had lasted.

A little voice in his head asked what was so different about this one? Why did he think this would last? He knew the answer – because this time it felt different. He couldn't put his finger on it, and for a man whose profession relied on how well he expressed himself, it was quite ironic.

He wanted to see her again, hopefully start a relationship with her, yet at the same time he wanted (*needed*) to finish Otis's biography. He was well aware he might have to take things slow and easy with her for the next few months – even without his deadline, that would be advisable – but he didn't want to, because he was also well aware this was a crucial time in Juliette's life. Even if he couldn't offer any practical help, she might welcome his support.

He wished he could have been there for her

yesterday, when she'd met with Trudge-Smythe and his cronies, but from what she'd told him, she'd coped admirably on her own. He would have been nothing more than window dressing. He still wished he could have been there though, just to see it.

Then he laughed at himself. There he was, thinking of Juliette as a slip of a girl confronting three greedy businessmen, when she had never been a slip of a girl; not when he'd known her twenty years ago and certainly not now. She might have been younger back then, but she'd known how to hold her own. She was nearly two decades older now, and just as capable.

They'd agreed to meet at seven p.m. in a restaurant on the outskirts of Hereford. He'd never dined there before, but he knew some people who had, and it had a good reputation. This was neutral territory, and would give them both some breathing space and an opportunity to get to know one another all over again without being on either his or her home turf, so to speak.

He dressed with more care than usual, picking out a dark pair of chinos, a crisp blue shirt, and a casual jacket. He didn't want to look too smart, although he did wonder whether he should have worn a suit. Although, if he had worn one, she might have had the impression this was a business meeting after all.

He arrived before her, as he'd intended, and waited in the bar area, nursing a tonic water, and feeling far more nervous than he thought he would be.

He saw her before she saw him, as she walked through the door. It was a fine spring evening, the chill of winter having been replaced by the promise of summer, and she was dressed in jeans and a blouse, with a jacket made of soft drapey material over the top. He was relieved to see he'd made the right choice regarding his own apparel.

His next thought was how lovely she looked. She was a striking woman, tall and slender, with cheekbones a model would die for, and those blue eyes sparkling out of a creamy complexion. He couldn't tell whether her dark-honey hair was coloured or not, as it fell softly to her shoulders and shone with glossy health.

He waved to attract her attention and got to his feet. As soon as she was close enough he held out both hands, and when she took them in hers, he drew her towards him and kissed her softly on the cheek. The same scent filled his nose, and he inhaled deeply. He didn't know what perfume it was, but he knew he would always associate it with her.

Pulling back a little and still holding her hands, he smiled into her eyes. 'You came,' he said. Part of him had been speculating whether she would now that it was clear he was offering more than just his help.

'So did you,' she replied, and he wondered if she was just as nervous.

To cover his anxiety, he indicated she should take a seat and asked, 'What do you want to drink?'

'What are you having?'

'Just tonic water.'

'I'll have the same, but could I have a twist of lime in mine, please?'

'Certainly.' He gave her order to the waiter, and then he had no idea what to say to her. He was tongue-tied, like a teenager on a first date, overwhelmed and excited by the possibilities, yet terrified of them, too.

'So,' she said, 'here we are.' She appeared to be as awkward as he felt, and he hoped she wasn't regretting accepting his invitation to dinner.

They could always talk shop as a way of breaking the ice, but he was reluctant, in case she had too many questions about what he was working on. It would be unfair not to answer her truthfully. He'd managed to avoid it so far, but he didn't want to tell her an outright lie. Neither did he want to share with her any details about the man whose biography he was writing.

He might, of course, be wrong about Brooke's parentage, but in his gut he knew he wasn't. He used to rely on his gut feelings quite heavily and they hadn't often let him down.

'How is your daughter enjoying her course?' he asked. 'Bath Uni, did you say?' He saw the relief flooding through her along with an eagerness to talk about her daughter.

That was safe ground, their children. He was more than happy to talk about his two boys. They were older than Brooke by a few years, and he and Juliette spent the time between being shown to their table and the arrival of their first course by talking about their respective offspring.

He deliberately avoided talking about his ex. He was still friends with Bertha, namely because they had the boys in common, but he wasn't close to her. He was just thankful that the agreement to separate had been mutual, although there had been some considerable bitterness on her part for a while afterwards. It wasn't her fault; he'd not been an easy man to live with.

He hoped he had changed. He was still a workaholic, but he wasn't as single-minded as he had once been. Separation and divorce had been a bit of a wakeup call, and he'd made considerably more effort after he'd moved out of the marital home to spend more time with his children. It was just a pity it had taken something so drastic for him to realise what he had been missing.

He didn't share any of this with Juliette. It was neither the time nor the place to discuss past relationships, and telling funny stories about his children was as far as he wanted to go at this point. If this tiny embryo of a relationship of theirs developed into something deeper and more substantial, there would be plenty of time to talk. He could hardly share his marital past, and for her not to share any information about Brooke's father. Not at the moment; and he was also aware that perhaps she never would. It depended on how much contact she had with Otis.

Partly because of how quickly and thoroughly she'd disappeared and also because there'd not been even a hint that Otis had fathered a child out of wedlock, Oliver had the feeling she didn't have much to do with the man. Which brought him back to the idea that Otis might not even be aware of Brooke's existence.

Blast, Oliver didn't want to think about Otis at all unless he had to, and certainly not when he was in Juliette's company, so he shoved the man out of his head and concentrated on enjoying the evening.

As dinner progressed to the main course, the conversation moved on. Over lunch the other Tuesday they'd caught up on past acquaintances so they didn't touch on the subject now, instead they tentatively got to know each other's tastes in things like music, films, books, and food.

'I haven't been to the theatre in years and years,' Juliette said. 'I think the last thing I saw was An Inspector Calls in a small theatre in the West End. I remember the performance vividly, though; it was interesting.' She said the word "interesting" as though it was in italics. 'When I say An Inspector Calls, the play I saw was only loosely based on it. I think they called it alternative theatre. It put me off going for a while.' She hesitated. 'And then I moved to Ticklemore, and Brooke put a stop to any further theatre visits. The closest I've got to seeing any kind of performance since, is watching her in the school play.'

'I don't go to the theatre often, either,' Oliver said. 'I tend to prefer going to the cinema.'

'Gosh, I haven't done that for ages, either! The last thing I saw was a Disney princess film. I haven't seen a grown-up film in…' She lifted her gaze to the ceiling as if she was trying to pin the memory down, before bringing her attention back to him. 'I honestly can't remember.'

'Is there anything you fancy seeing?' he asked.

'I don't know. I don't take much notice of what's on in the cinema. Our nearest is in Hereford, so I have to make a special effort to go there. I tend to just wait for films to come out on Sky or Netflix.'

'What sort of things do you like watching?'

'I like a good thriller, an intelligent one, not just a shoot-'em-up kind.' She gave a small laugh. 'I also like romantic comedies.'

'I like those, too. I thought Bridget Jones's diary was absolutely hilarious.'

'You did?'

He nodded. 'Admittedly it was a while ago. I don't think I've seen any since.' He hesitated, wondering if he should say it, then decided he was going to anyway. He added, 'How about if I take a look at what's on in Hereford, and if there is anything that takes your fancy, we could go together?'

Juliette's gaze was level, her expression unreadable. 'Are you asking me on a second date?'

'I suppose I am.'

'Just suppose?'

'No, I definitely am.'

'We haven't finished the first one yet,' she pointed out.

'I don't need to get to the end of this date to know I want another one with you.'

'Then yes, please, I'd like that very much.'

After that, things became decidedly easier between them. Until, that is, it came to the point where they were to part company.

They had lingered over coffee, sharing a cheese platter which had been surprisingly and pleasantly intimate, as their hands had brushed more than once as they reached for a grape or went for the same cracker. But Oliver (he hoped it wasn't his imagination) could sense the rising tension, and whenever his fingers touched hers, it ratcheted up a notch.

God, he wanted to lean across the table and kiss her, and when he imagined how she'd taste, his heart skipped a beat as desire coursed through him.

They kept catching each other's eye, too, and the looks between them were growing longer and more intense, neither of them willing to break contact.

There was a kind of electricity building, rather like the air when a storm was imminent. The slightest spark would ignite it, and the thought made him tingle.

After a friendly argument, Oliver paid the bill. 'I asked you to have dinner with me, therefore I should pay,' he argued. 'Besides, that was the argument you used when you insisted on paying for lunch the other day.'

'That was different, that was business,' she countered.

'If you're so bothered about it, you can pay for the

cinema tickets,' he suggested, with no intention in the slightest of letting her do so. She needed every penny she had in order to buy the Tattler, or to re-float it under a different name. The cinema was his suggestion, therefore he was determined to pay.

He held her jacket while she slipped her arms into the sleeves, then he followed her outside and walked with her to her car. Once there, he stopped, wondering if he should do what he wanted to do, or whether it was too soon. He didn't object to kissing a woman on a first date – it wasn't as though he'd not done it before – but this was different. He didn't want to rush things, or scare her off. He wanted to take his time to get to know her properly.

The decision was made for him as she leant back against the door of her car and made no attempt to get in. He hesitated, but before he could make any kind of move, she grasped his lapels and pulled him closer until he was standing with mere centimetres between them.

She was nearly as tall as him, but not quite. He bent his head slightly as she tilted hers up, and he stared into his eyes, losing himself in their depths. It had grown dark during the time they'd been in the restaurant, and the blue of her eyes had deepened to almost navy.

Her lips were slightly parted and he could feel her

soft breath on his face. Enveloped in her perfume, he breathed in the scent of her, and his pulse quickened.

She hadn't let go of his jacket, and when he continued to hesitate, she tugged at him again, her intentions glaringly obvious. She only let go of his lapels when he put his hands on the car door either side of her shoulders, caging her in his arms.

Then his lips gently met hers. For a few moments he kept his eyes open while he kissed her. Hers were firmly shut, and his drifted closed as he felt her arms wind around his neck. She came up off the car, and he wrapped his arms around her, crushing her to him, her chest against his. Not too hard, but enough for her to know he felt a very real and hungry desire for her.

He had no idea how much time passed as they stood there, kissing. But what he did know was when he finally came up for air, his heart was pounding so hard he thought it might be about to leap out of his chest. He was breathless and giddy, his emotions swirling, his mind deliciously devoid of anything except her.

His senses were full of her, and he didn't want the moment to end. But a restaurant car park wasn't the place to show her how much he wanted her. Although, he suspected that was exactly what he had done.

'You'd better go,' he said throatily, 'before I do something I'll regret.'

As the words left his lips, he couldn't understand why a sudden flare of hurt appeared in her eyes, then he realised and added, 'I don't regret kissing you. I just regret doing it here in a car park. Not terribly romantic, is it?'

Her soft laugh sent a shiver through him. 'How much more romantic do you want to get?' she asked.

'Oh, I'm sure I could think of something.'

She pulled him towards her again and he couldn't resist kissing her thoroughly; but the next time he let her go, he meant it. Although he would dearly have loved to take this further, he didn't think either of them were emotionally ready to jump into bed, despite his body saying otherwise. And from her reaction, he was fairly sure hers was saying the same thing.

But he didn't want to suggest anything. It was too soon, too new, and he didn't want to risk rejection. Besides, he liked to think he was too much of a gentleman to suggest going to bed on a first date, even though his body was crying out for her.

He kissed her again, this time a chaste and fleeting touch of the lips, then he released her and stepped back. 'Cinema?' he reminded her.

She didn't respond for several seconds and when

she did it was in a throaty voice which made his insides twist and tumble.

'Pick a day,' she suggested. 'I don't do much in the evenings.'

'Neither do I. Can I give you a ring tomorrow?'

'I'd like that.'

He took another step back, giving her room to open her car door, and watched her slip inside before he closed it gently. She started the engine and wound a window down.

'I enjoyed this evening,' she said, with a twinkle. 'Especially the last part.'

'Yes, so did I. They had a lovely selection of cheeses.'

She blinked at him for a moment then burst into laughter. 'So they did,' she agreed.

His voice soft, he said, 'Drive carefully.'

'Do you want me to text you when I get home safely?' she asked in a wry tone.

'I'd like it if you did.'

She nodded. 'In that case, I expect you to text me, too.'

He waited until her tail lights had disappeared from view, before he got into his own car and began the journey home. And all the time he was driving, she was the only thing he could think about, and an old Kylie Minogue song came to mind as he realised he couldn't get her out of his head.

How was it possible to fall for someone so quickly?

It hadn't exactly been love at first sight (he was thinking about when they were younger), but maybe love at second sight? He remembered opening the door of the Tattler's office and seeing her sitting there; maybe it had happened then? He hadn't felt it at the time, but it appeared to have crept up on him.

He still wasn't sure if it *was* love – it was far too early for that – but it was certainly something. And he was determined to find out what that something was and where it could lead, because the idea of seeing Juliette again made his heart sing.

CHAPTER 12

JULIETTE

'You look different,' Audrey said to Juliette the following morning. She had popped round to her mum's house because her mother had said she needed a hand with something, and Juliette was now wishing she hadn't answered the phone.

She felt different, but she didn't realise it was showing on her face.

'What do you want, Mum?' she asked, trying to deflect the conversation. She didn't want to discuss last night. She needed time to process it, to get her head straight, and having her mum firing questions at her was not what she needed right now. Because that's exactly what her mum would do if she knew.

'I've got to pop into the village and take some things to the church hall.' Audrey pointed to several black plastic bags and a couple of boxes sitting in her living room. 'They are for the jumble sale.'

'I didn't know the church was having a jumble sale,' Juliette said with a frown. 'When is it? I should put a notice in the paper. Father Todd normally calls me and lets me know.'

Her mother looked sheepish. 'Er, um, I think it might be my fault that he hasn't.'

'What do you mean?'

Audrey's sheepish expression morphed into downright guilt. 'I kind of... I didn't mean to, you understand... might have mentioned that the Tattler would be closing soon. I expect he probably thought there was no point in letting you know about the jumble sale, if that was the case.'

'Mum! How could you? I didn't want anyone to know just yet.' Juliette shook her head, cross with her mother but also cross with herself. She knew what her mum was like. Audrey wasn't a gossip and there wasn't a mean bone in her body, but she wasn't the best at keeping secrets. Which was why Juliette had never told her mum who Brooke's father was.

Juliette's expression softened. 'Don't worry,' she hastened to reassure her. 'Hattie told me she'd weaselled it out of you, and Sara also knows.'

Audrey looked shocked. 'The sneaky— I thought Hattie already knew!'

'That's what I called her when she told me how

she'd got it out of you.'

'At least it explains how she does it. I was starting to think she has the whole village bugged. How does Sara know?'

Juliette blinked slowly, cursing herself. Trust her mother to arrive at the very thing Juliette would have liked to have kept quiet, which was the part Oliver had played in Sara finding out. Should she tell a small fib and make something up? Or should she come clean and tell her mother Oliver had been to visit her in Ticklemore and had let the cat out of the bag?

Her mother beat her to it. 'Was it something to do with that man you were in the pub with the other day?'

Typical, Juliette thought; she ought to know by now how impossible it was to keep a secret in a little place like Ticklemore. She rolled her eyes, feeling like a kid – how did mothers have the uncanny ability to make their adult offspring feel like unruly children?

'Nothing much gets past you, does it?' she asked. 'If I didn't know better, I would think you were in cahoots with Hattie.'

'Marge Everson told me she'd seen you in the Ticklemore Tavern with a man last week. You were seen walking down the high street with him, too.' Audrey looked a little aggrieved. 'I was waiting for you to tell me about him.'

Juliette wasn't quite sure why she hadn't. She'd told her mother she'd met Oliver in Birmingham to discuss the paper, so why hadn't she told her he'd visited her in Ticklemore?

She wondered if it was the same reason she hadn't told her mum she was going on a date with him last night. And she had no intention whatsoever of telling Audrey they had shared a kiss. She didn't know whether they were in a relationship or not, and, if they were, whether it was going anywhere. Until it was on firmer footing, she didn't want to tell anyone. But she had to say something about it, so she decided to give her mother a pared-down version of the truth.

'That was Oliver Pascoe. Remember, I told you about him? He's a former colleague, and I've been picking his brains.'

'Why did *he* tell Sara that the Tattler was to close?' her mum asked. 'And why were you both in the Ticklemore Toy Shop?'

'Oh.' Juliette waved her hand in the air. 'That was because Sara has an idea for subscription boxes, and she wanted to have a chat about me writing a feature. Oliver just happened to be with me when I called in to talk to her about it.'

'Yes, that's a lovely idea, isn't it? It's all well and good having a shop you can walk into, but these days people want a bit more. You've got to be on the internet.' Her mother's face lit up. 'Why don't *you* do that? You could reach more people that way,' she said as if she was telling Juliette something new.

Maybe her mother was, at that, because Juliette hadn't bothered to go online with the Tattler, had she? Perhaps she should have done. But she'd been quite happy with the way things were, and it was definitely something the Trudge-Smythes could remonstrate with her about, if they were so inclined. She had been put in charge of managing the paper, but she had to admit she probably hadn't done so to the best of her ability. She'd been content to let things drift along in the same old fashion, and had made absolutely no effort whatsoever to drive the business forward. For the Tattler, the twenty-first century had yet to arrive. The newspaper was rooted firmly in the past, and so was Juliette.

With sudden insight, she realised that when she'd arrived in Ticklemore, pregnant with Brooke, to a certain extent she'd put her life on hold. She might have become a mother, she might be managing a newspaper, but she hadn't moved forward, had she?

Discomforted, Juliette walked over to the pile of jumble sale items and hefted a bag in each hand. 'Come on,' she said. Let's get this done, because I've got to go to work.'

She was conscious of the shrewd look Audrey sent

her and was aware the conversation was far from over as far as her mother was concerned. Audrey would pick it up again sometime in the future, probably quite soon, but for now, at least, she let it slide, so Juliette busied herself with loading the car.

She had to put the back seat of her mum's Ford down to be able to get everything in. 'Do you need me for the other end?' she asked.

'Yes, please, there's no guarantee the vicar will be there to help unload. And how about we pop into Bookylicious and have a sneaky fried breakfast? I bet you haven't bothered with anything more substantial than coffee this morning.' Her mother gave her a winning smile.

Juliette knew exactly what this was about. It was about her mother wanting to have a full English and using Juliette as an excuse to eat one.

'OK, I'll go to Bookylicious with you,' Juliette said, 'but I'll just have a Danish or something.'

Her mother's face fell. 'If you're not having a full English, I won't have one either.'

Was her mother really guilt-tripping her over a fried breakfast? 'You win, but if there's black pudding on there, I'm not eating it,' Juliette declared.

'You can tell them you want it without,' her mother pointed out, so that's what Juliette did. As she was giving her order to Hattie (trust the old lady to be on duty this morning) she told her she didn't want any black pudding, and not to bother with putting any mushrooms on her plate, either.

Her mother sighed dramatically. 'I'll have the lot,' she announced. 'And, I'll have her black pudding, too.'

'Black pudding is good for you,' Hattie said. 'It'll put hairs on your chest.'

'Thanks, but I can't stand the stuff, and I wouldn't eat it if you paid me.' Juliette expected Hattie to leave them to it as soon as she'd taken their order, but the woman continued to linger.

'How's that nice young man of yours?' Hattie asked her.

'I haven't got a nice young man,' Juliette replied, feeling a treacherous heat flood into her cheeks.

'Yes, you have, you went to the pub with him last week and you were seen together in the Toy Shop. You were looking at him like a lovesick calf.'

'I was not!' Juliette was pretty sure she hadn't been looking at him in any such way. 'This place takes the biscuit. Can't I have a simple conversation with someone without it being spread all over the village?'

'If that someone is a handsome fella, and a stranger to boot, of course you can't. People are going to speculate and most of them have got nothing better to do. Spill the beans.'

Juliette rolled her eyes, knowing Hattie was right. She may as well tell her what she wanted to know (some of it) – it might shut her up for a while. 'His name is Oliver Pascoe and he's an old acquaintance.' Juliette narrowed her eyes, daring Hattie to ask another question.

Hattie rose to the challenge. 'Is he your boyfriend?' Her eyes had taken on a knowing sparkle.

'No, he isn't.'

'But you like him, though,' Hattie observed.

Juliette was conscious of her mother's intense stare, so she shrugged casually. 'He's nice enough.'

Hattie let out a loud cackle. 'Nice enough?' she chortled, gazing around the room as if to share her incredulity with everyone.

Juliette could feel her blush deepening. 'That's what I said.'

'You think he's more than nice,' Hattie observed. She turned to Audrey 'Look at her. She's gone as red as a beetroot.'

'So she has,' Audrey agreed, gazing at Juliette assessingly.

'If he's not your boyfriend, then why were you having lunch with him?' Hattie demanded.

Juliette was starting to lose patience. 'Hattie, I don't want to be rude but it isn't any of your business,' she said, at exactly the same time as her mother announced in far too loud a voice, 'He's here about the Tattler.'

'What?' her mother said, when Juliette shushed her. 'Hattie already knows.'

'Not just me - the whole village knows the Tattler is about to close,' Hattie said. 'And before you say anything, it wasn't me who let the cat out of the bag. Was your Oliver here about that? Does he want to buy the newspaper?'

'No, he doesn't,' Juliette answered truthfully.

'So it really will close?' Hattie asked.

'Not if I can help it,' Juliette vowed. But it all depends on whether Ralph Trudge-Smythe wants to sell it, she thought. And even if he didn't, she wasn't certain she'd like to keep running a newspaper.

But even without those two obstacles, the question she had to ask herself was, would she be able to?

It was time she sat down and had a serious think about the newspaper's future – about *her* future – and the only way to do that was to do some major research.

And she knew precisely where she should start – subscriptions.

CHAPTER 13

JULIETTE

Juliette sighed, her huge breakfast sitting uncomfortably in her tummy. She should have stuck with coffee and a pastry. She should also be working, trying to think of new ways to promote the Tattler. She should be doing a lot of things, but what she was actually doing was daydreaming about Oliver.

If she closed her eyes, she could relive the whole glorious, wonderful moment when he'd kissed her. She could still feel his lips on hers, his arms around her waist, and his solid chest as he held her tightly against him.

It had been one of the most thrilling and exciting kisses she'd ever had. Her heart pounded just thinking about it, and the thought of seeing him again this evening made her tummy do somersaults. Maybe that was what was wrong with it, not the cooked breakfast.

It had taken her a long time to drop off to sleep last night because her mind had been too busy with the events of the evening. She simply couldn't stop thinking about him. She wasn't sure if it was a crush, infatuation, or whether she was falling for him. She suspected the latter, because no one ever heard of a fifty-one-year-old woman having a crush.

But falling in love bothered her and the reasons were many. For one, she hadn't been in love for a long time. Looking back, she wasn't entirely sure she ever had been. What she'd had with Brooke's father had been infatuation. But she hadn't been able to see it then. Which made her think that perhaps she wasn't able to trust herself.

If she had thought she was in love when she hadn't been, why should she believe her feelings now? Was she experiencing the same thing with Oliver, and she'd wake up a few weeks or months down the line and realise she'd been mistaken? That what she was feeling was infatuation, and she was calling it love?

She didn't think so, but she hadn't thought so back then, either. If anyone had dared to suggest her feelings had been anything less than pure love, she would have probably bitten their heads off. It had to have been love, hadn't it? Otherwise, how could she justify to herself what she had done? She'd slept with another woman's husband. She'd known he was married, although he'd told her the only reason he and his wife were staying together was because of his career and their children. She'd believed him, but she'd also accepted their relationship was destined to go no further.

She should have walked away the very first time she'd met him. She should have run as fast as she could and not looked back. But she'd been at a work thing, not a private event, so she'd been obliged to stay at the conference. She'd drank at the bar after the day's work was done and when the night's work was only just beginning. If you were at a conference, you didn't take time off, no matter how late it was or how many drinks you'd imbibed. It was work, pure and simple, but at some point along the way she'd forgotten that, and she'd found herself in his bed.

Maybe she could have forgiven herself if it had been just the one time. But it hadn't. She'd been unable to resist him, and look where it had got her.

Was this the same? Should she walk away now? If only she could be certain her feelings for Oliver were real.

She thought they were. She hoped they were, because although she was looking forward to seeing Oliver again, the terrible desperation to be with him wasn't there, not in the way it had been with Brooke's father. She had been physically, mentally, and emotionally unable to resist him. It had been an addiction, whereas what she felt for Oliver appeared more solid and substantial, rooted in friendship and not merely animal attraction.

Suddenly feeling slightly flat, she closed down her computer for the day and made her way home. But once there, the house felt cold, despite it being mid-May, and awfully empty. Even though Brooke had been out a great deal of the time during the months before she'd left home for university, her presence had still been very much in evidence. Juliette used to find signs of her daughter all over the house – empty cups, half-eaten plates of food, clothes left in unexpected and often inappropriate places, cans of half-drunk soda, makeup stains… Sometimes she could have sworn she still heard Brooke's music playing, and could smell her perfume in the air, as though she'd just left.

The house was incredibly quiet without her. Juliette's life was incredibly quiet without her.

She was glad to be going out this evening, and even more pleased it was with Oliver.

Oliver… those little butterflies were there again, and her excitement resurfaced, zinging along her veins, making her fingers and toes tingle.

She knew she was overthinking things. What she needed to do was just go with the flow and see where it led her. If nothing came of it then so be it, at least she'd had some nice times with a new (old) friend. And if something did come of it? Well then, she'd just have to live it one date at a time.

In some ways though, it couldn't have come at a worse time in her life. She should be concentrating on the newspaper and on her professional future. As today's pathetic attempts had shown, she was focussing more on her emotions than anything else.

But then again, if Oliver had come back into her life even as little as six months ago, would she have been ready for him? Or would she have been so stuck in a rut of her own making that she would have been happy to remain there?

She'd never know, would she? And thinking about it wasn't doing her any good whatsoever. She should learn to chill, as Brooke kept telling her.

It was jeans again this evening, Juliette decided, although this time she wore a knitted cable jumper on the top, and teamed her outfit with a pair of ankle boots and a chunky leather jacket. It was a far cry from her normal business attire of smart suits, high heels, and chiffon blouses.

When she thought about it, she acknowledged it was ridiculous to dress up in such a manner to go to work; it wasn't as though many people saw her when she was in the office. But she needed the demarcation between her home life and her work life, even when it was almost impossible to maintain. Take the Ticklemore summer fete for instance – she wouldn't dream of wearing a smart suit and high heels to that. Muddy fields and stilettos didn't work well, but no-one seemed to mind that she was dressed casually. Everyone knew she was Juliette from the Tattler, no matter what she wore.

Smiling to herself as she climbed into her car, she realised for the first time that she *was* the Tattler. She was part of the newspaper and it was part of her. She'd told herself she wanted to buy it mainly for the name, for the continuity and the history, but she really wanted to buy it because she felt it was hers. Ever since Lord Trudge-Smythe had handed her the keys to the office (not personally, he'd got someone else to do that) she felt at home. She'd been left to run it more or less single-handedly since that day, and she felt quite territorial and possessive over it.

She knew if Ralph Trudge-Smythe didn't sell it to her, she would start up again, with a different name and maybe a different format.

As she drove, her thoughts swirling, Juliette acknowledged she had to fight for it. Oliver was right – if she wanted the Tattler to carry on, she'd have to involve the whole community. She couldn't do this on her own. She needed Ticklemore's support and she hoped the village would give it, because the newspaper belonged as much to them as she believed it did to her.

With renewed determination, which she put to one side for this evening, she drove to Hereford and parked in the cinema car park. Getting out, she scanned the other vehicles, spotting Oliver's straight away, and a smile spread across her face. She hadn't seriously thought he might not turn up, but it was still a relief to see he was here ahead of her.

He was waiting in the foyer, waving tickets in his hand.

'I told you I was going to pay,' were the first words out of her mouth, and she prepared herself for some wrangling.

But Oliver didn't allow her to say anything else. His arms came around her and he pulled her towards him. His mouth met hers, stopping her protests over the tickets, and for a moment the cinema and all the people in it disappeared.

When she surfaced, she was conscious of some odd looks and a few sniggers, mainly from the younger contingent, and she blushed furiously, but Oliver didn't seem the least bit concerned. He was neither remorseful nor apologetic. In fact, he was grinning from ear to ear.

'What are we going to see?' she asked in case he

attempted to kiss her again.

He pointed to a huge poster behind her. It was for a ballet.

'I thought we would be watching a film?' she said, confused.

'So did I, but when I saw this I thought of you. I know it's not the real thing but it's the best I could manage at such short notice, and apparently it's almost as good as seeing the ballet for real.'

It was Swan Lake, and even though the love story didn't have a happy ending (it was similar to a tragedy like Romeo and Juliet) she was touched. It was rather a romantic thing to do. She just hoped her mascara wouldn't run when she cried, and she wondered whether she had any tissues in her bag.

It seemed sacrilegious to buy popcorn and soda for such a noble performance, so when Oliver returned from the food court holding two coffees and a bar of dark chocolate, she declared it perfect – grown-up refreshments for a grown-up performance.

Why didn't she feel grown up inside, though?

She quite liked this giddy feeling rushing through her. She felt young and alive, and the uncertainty of her future only added to that. When she was Brooke's age, with her whole life stretching ahead of her and the future had still to be written, she'd thought it was exciting and full of possibilities. But she recognised that as one grew older, an uncertain future wasn't something to be excited about, yet here she was, poised to start a whole new chapter of her life, and the words she'd use to write it were up to her. Not completely of course (one could never know exactly what direction one's life story would take) but she would do her best to mould it, because she wanted a happy ending.

She wasn't quite sure what a happy ending would entail, though. Did she mean love? Was it keeping the Tattler going? Maybe she meant both.

The pair of them settled into their seats, sipping their coffee and sharing the chocolate. It was all gone by the time the lights went down, as was often the way, before the opening credits rolled. Feeling thirsty, Juliette fished a bottle of water out of her bag and offered some to Oliver who took a sip, then handed it back. Maybe she was reading too much into that simple gesture, but it felt cosy somehow. She felt like they were a proper couple, as though they had known each other and had been together for far longer than they had. Being with him made her insides fizz, yet made her feel incredibly at ease at the same time.

When his arm crept around the back of her seat and rested on her shoulder, she snuggled into him, her eyes on the screen, enraptured by the music, the dancing, and the story itself. Oliver was right, it was almost like being in the theatre and watching a live performance. It was probably better, because the screen gave her close-ups the dancers' faces, and she knew from past experience that if you were in the back of an auditorium you wouldn't get to see nearly as much.

Darn it, she was crying. She couldn't help herself, it was such a sad story, and when she began to sob in a most unbecoming manner, Oliver's grip on her shoulder tightened and he pulled her closer to him. She felt his soft breath on her face and his lips on her forehead, and when his hand cupped her cheek and he brushed away the tears with his thumb, she cried even harder.

Gently, he tilted her chin, lifting her head, and his lips found hers. And suddenly there they were, sitting in the dark with the magnificent music of Swan Lake swirling around them, snogging like a couple of teenagers. Oh my God, she thought, they should get a room.

With a gasp she pulled away, as the realisation of how badly she wanted him struck her.

'What's the matter? Are you all right?' Oliver asked.

'Oh yes, I'm more than all right.'

'Are you sure?' The concern in his voice was palpable and it sent a warm glow right through her.

'I'm sure. I think we'd better go.' The lights were lifting and people were shuffling into their coats and making their way down the steps towards the exit.

'Do we have to?' he asked. 'I could stay here all night.'

Juliette giggled. 'I can't,' she said. 'It's not terribly comfortable. I prefer a bed.' She clapped a hand to her mouth when she realised what she'd said and a glow suffused her cheeks.

'So do I,' he said, and his voice was deep and slightly hoarse. He cleared his throat, and added in a more normal tone, 'Preferably one with an electric blanket in it, these days.'

It was exactly the right thing to say. She hadn't meant it to come out the way it sounded. Or maybe she had, but she instantly regretted it. She didn't want him to think she was suggesting they sleep together. Not yet, anyway. She had to get to know him a whole lot better first. But that was the ironic thing – she felt she knew him already, and not just from the past. She felt like she'd known him forever, and it was quite a wonderful feeling.

He got to his feet, and she was grateful he'd given her the reprieve.

'Have you really got an electric blanket?' she asked. She thought they were only for old people.

'No, I haven't. But the older I'm getting, the more

the thought appeals.'

'I know what you mean. I can't believe I used to put fashion ahead of comfort.'

'I can't believe you wear heels. Surely they can't be comfortable?'

She looked down at her feet and the little ankle boots she was wearing. The heel was a small one. 'I usually wear higher ones than this for work. These are more for pleasure.'

They'd stepped out into the foyer and as they did so he stopped and turned to face her. 'It certainly is pleasure,' he murmured, and her heart skipped a beat.

She didn't want the evening to end, but neither did she want to invite him back for coffee, because she had a feeling she knew exactly how that would pan out. She wasn't quite ready for it. She wanted to savour these early stages of their growing romance, because once she'd taken him to her bed, they could never be recaptured. Besides, she quite liked the anticipation. It was giving her goosebumps and making her feel all tingly inside.

'Do you fancy going somewhere for a nightcap?' he asked. 'We could have a lemonade and share a bag of crisps.'

His eyes were twinkling down at her, and she found him irresistible. 'Good idea, but I get to choose the flavour of crisps.'

'I think we can do slightly better than that. How about we grab some fish and chips, and eat them in the grounds of the cathedral?'

'You know how to show a lady a good time, don't you?'

'Oh yes, I certainly do. I'll even buy you a can of pop, if you're lucky.'

Juliette couldn't help laughing. One minute he was all highbrow and taking her to see a famous ballet, the next minute he was suggesting sitting on a park bench with some fish and chips and a can of cola. She found it fascinating. She loved that he didn't seem to take himself too seriously. It was refreshing. He could have suggested one of the fancy wine bars, as it was still early enough for them to be open. But he hadn't. He'd suggested the polar opposite. And once again his suggestion was perfect.

There were quite a few people about – city centres never became totally quiet, and the night was still relatively young – but within the cathedral grounds it was quite serene. Overhead the sky was a blue-black void, dotted with stars, and there was a chill in the air which hadn't been there earlier, but it still wasn't cold, and the opened wrapper of steaming fish and chips on her lap was keeping her warm. As was the man by her side.

He was sitting close enough for their thighs to

touch, and she could feel the heat of him through her jeans. The hot salt and vinegar chips weren't the only thing warming her from the inside.

She was surprised to discover how hungry she was, and she polished the lot off, washing it down with cold, fizzy cola. She hadn't done this in years, possibly not since she was a poor student, and fish and chips was a treat on a Friday night.

Finally, though, they were both done, their supper eaten, and it was time to go.

With reluctance Juliette stood, and brushed herself down. Oliver had already taken the rubbish to the nearest bin, and she was feeling a little bit lost as to what to do with herself.

She wanted to kiss him again, but she had a feeling she wouldn't know how to stop. It was probably best if they just walked back to their cars and went their separate ways.

There was always tomorrow. There was no need to rush anything. They had plenty of time ahead of them.

They held hands as they walked back to the car park, talking about nothing in particular, and when they arrived at their respective vehicles he kissed her again, with just enough passion to make her long for more, but not too much so she lost herself. It was perfect. *He* was perfect.

And as she drove back to Ticklemore, she was already looking forward to the next time she'd see him again. She had a good feeling about this, about *them*. The future was definitely looking rosier.

CHAPTER 14

OLIVER

So much for concentrating on Otis's biography, Oliver thought, as he unlocked the door to his flat and shucked off his jacket. He should have been working this evening, if he was to stand any chance of meeting this new deadline. But he hadn't been able to resist seeing Juliette, and he had absolutely no regrets whatsoever. Unless he counted the regret that he would now have to stay awake most of the night to finish the chapter he was currently working on.

Oliver was well aware that although he might find politics interesting, not everyone did, therefore he needed to inject a little oomph into the dry facts of the events if he wanted to appeal to a wider readership, so he went into the spare room switched on his computer and began work.

However, his thoughts kept circling back to

Juliette, and not just to her, but to the newspaper, too. They might be separate entities, but he could see how much the Tattler meant to her and he was determined she should make it work, if that was what she wanted.

He recalled the conversations about the Tattler's demographic, and that she needed to make it more relevant to younger people, so with that in mind, he was unable to resist a little research. Not the research he should be doing, but instead research about what interested people in their twenties and thirties, and he wasn't talking about the latest TV reality show, or fashion, either. He meant serious issues like climate change and sustainability, mental health, body image, and also subjects like trying to get a foot on the property ladder, starting a family – things he hadn't considered in a long time. Of course he thought about climate change and mental health, but starting a family or climbing the property ladder was a thing of the past.

But these were all relevant issues to young adults, and he wondered if Juliette was the best person to write about them. It needed to be someone their own age. Someone who understood exactly what they were going through, someone who they could relate to. Juliette may well understand, hell she might even be an expert, but she wasn't one of them.

Her daughter, however, *was*. Juliette had told him

Brooke was studying journalism and publishing, and that she used to help out with the Tattler. It may have been only delivering it, but he knew what kids were like. They were little sponges, and she had probably absorbed far more about her mum's job and the newspaper business than she realised.

He wondered how Juliette would feel if he was to suggest Brooke did some work on the side. He suspected Juliette was quite territorial about the Tattler, and he fully understood. She'd had sole input for such a long time without any input from anyone else, that bringing someone else in, even to write a feature or two, might go against the grain. But he had a gut feeling this was what was needed, and his gut feelings weren't often wrong.

Writing features wasn't the same as reporting the news. It was more like magazine writing; more articles rather than reporting on what happened yesterday or the day before, or last week. There was a difference, but he didn't see any reason for the two not to be compatible. The Times on Sunday did it brilliantly, with the newspaper itself reporting on the news, and the glossy magazine inside displaying the features.

The Tattler couldn't hope to get anywhere near that, but what it could do was to display the news at the front and more magazine-like articles towards the middle, with the back and last pages being reserved for classified ads and sport. He shook his head – he still wasn't sure about tug of war being an actual sport. But then again, maybe it was in Ticklemore.

With Brooke writing for the younger end of the market, there needed to be a balance in the middle. Juliette was perfectly able to take care of the older interests, as she'd clearly demonstrated, but there was the young-family part of society, too, and the only thing he'd noticed in the Tattler which might appeal to that particular group was an advert for a mother and toddler session. He might be doing the paper a disservice, because he'd only seen the one edition, but somehow he suspected not.

He flipped over a page in his notepad and scribbled some more, the ideas coming thick and fast. He knew from experience this kind of brainstorming session would lead to a whole lot of stuff that was useless, and even sometimes downright ludicrous, but it could also lead to things which would be of real benefit.

Before he showed it to Juliette, he would tidy it up, which meant trawling through and making a separate list of the less feasible ideas. He'd also make another two lists, the first with definites and the second with maybes. She had probably thought about, and considered, many of them herself and had perfectly good reasons for not implementing them, although he was still certain the app was a good idea. It would take some doing, because he didn't know how to start one up, and he made a note to check that out. And another note to think about a website. He knew the Tattler didn't have any money, so it had to be a free hosting site and there were quite a few companies out there who offered it. The one thing he thought it necessary for her to buy, was a suitable domain name and an associated email address.

Feeling suddenly weary, he looked at the time. Goodness gracious, it was four a.m. already. He had planned to do quite a few hours work before he went to bed, but not this kind of work. He eyed the pile of political tomes sitting on the end of his desk, and grimaced. He should have been working on his manuscript, not on the Tattler, but he was having far too much fun.

He undressed slowly, his mind filled with images of Juliette, and he realised why he'd been so eager to sit at his computer this evening. It was partly to do with the pressing deadline he was under, but it also had something to do with him not wanting to go to bed and lie there thinking about her.

He'd wanted to make love to her tonight, but he'd had the impression she wasn't ready. He wasn't sure he was, if he was honest. If he slept with her, it wouldn't be a simple tumble in the hay; it would be something much more significant. He knew this deep in his heart, and he needed to make sure he was totally certain about it before he did something both of them might regret.

He'd never been the type of man to love 'em and leave 'em. He'd never had one-night stands, and he'd never had an extra-marital affair. He liked his relationships to mean something and, if after a few weeks or months they didn't, he ended them. There hadn't been very many to end, though. Few made it that far. It wasn't that he was inexperienced, far from it, but he wasn't a Jack-the-lad, either. He never had been.

Perhaps he might be thinking things too deeply, or reading too much into it, but what he felt for Juliette was different to anything he'd ever felt before, including his ex-wife. It was deeper, more profound, and he realised although he hadn't known Juliette very long (not in the ways which truly mattered), time didn't seem important. What was important was the way he felt about her, and the way she felt about him. If her kisses, if her response to him was anything to go by, then she felt the same. He hoped so, because he didn't think he could bear it if she didn't.

He debated whether to have a more serious conversation with her, to put a few feelers out as to where she thought their relationship might be going.

He wouldn't call it love, not yet, but there was a very real possibility it could be, and he was certainly falling for her. Therefore he needed to know if she was falling for him, or whether he should back away now, before he ran the risk of being seriously hurt.

But he was also frightened that if he instigated such a conversation, she'd run away screaming, that he would frighten her off, and he couldn't bear it if that happened either. He wouldn't be able to live with himself if he thought he'd driven her away by being too premature.

He had to try to think of this as a fine whisky, he told himself. It needed to be aged, it needed to be treated with care, and not be supped before it was ready. What this relationship needed was time.

Unfortunately, he didn't have a great deal of that at the moment, but that would change. This biography would be written eventually, and he didn't plan on rushing into the next one. Even if he did have something else lined up, he could negotiate a decent length of time until any first draft was due in.

Over the past few years he'd managed quite tight deadlines, but that was simply because he didn't have an awful lot else in his life to occupy him. Now the boys were grown, they were quite content to only see him now and again. He would love to see more of them, but that was the way things were between them, and he had to accept it.

Oliver wondered how much Juliette saw of Brooke now she was in university. It must be hard for her, he mused. She'd been on her own with her daughter for so long, and now Brooke had effectively flown the nest. She was a young woman, with a life of her own, and he just hoped she'd make time for Juliette. He could see how proud Juliette was of her daughter, and the love that shone in her eyes when she spoke about her. Maybe she would be happy at his suggestion that Brooke wrote a few features. Or maybe she wouldn't. He wouldn't know until he asked.

It was now four-thirty in the morning and he still hadn't closed his eyes.

Restlessly he got up, fetched himself a glass of water, then went back to bed. This was hopeless. He needed to get some shut-eye so he was fresh when he started work again tomorrow. And this time he did mean work, the kind that paid the bills, not the fun he'd been having earlier by conjuring up things for the Tattler.

There he was again, going round in circles, his thoughts honing in on Juliette and her newspaper, like a comet spiralling towards a sun. He just hoped he didn't suffer the same fate and burn up in her atmosphere.

At five-thirty Oliver admitted defeat and got up

for good. It was light, the birds were making a racket outside and a new day had begun. He should be feeling exhausted, but what he felt was invigorated.

It was too early to call Juliette (although he dearly wanted to) so he settled down at his desk again, this time vowing to do some actual work – because the sooner he finished this damned book, the sooner he'd be able to devote more time to the woman he was falling in love with.

CHAPTER 15

JULIETTE

Juliette ended the call, and put her phone down on the desk with shaking fingers. Ralph had an answer for her. He wanted to see her later today, and she was incredibly apprehensive about it. She wasn't sure why, because she suspected this would be his second move, and the price he was asking for his newspaper still wouldn't be within the realms of possibility for her. She just needed to keep her cool and not show him how much she wanted it. After all, she wasn't buying anything physical. What she was buying was the name, the reputation, and the goodwill of the newspaper. How could you put a price on that? The only guideline, as far as she could see, was how much she could afford and how greedy Ralph was. It was a fine balancing act, and she was pretty certain she'd slip and fall at any moment.

She picked her phone up again, and stared at the screen for a while before making a decision.

'Oliver? It's Juliette.'

'I know.' His soft chuckle carried over the airwaves, and made the hairs on the back of her neck stand up. Even his voice was sexy.

She felt ridiculously pleased he'd recognised her, until she realised he would have put her name in his phone next to her number. Obviously.

To cover her embarrassment she said, 'Ralph called. He wants to meet today. I know it's short notice and I understand if you're busy—'

'I'm not busy. What time and where?'

'Oh, wonderful, that's great. Um, if you come to the Tattler's office we can meet there, and I'll drive us to Trudge Manor. He wants to see me at 11.40.'

Oliver snorted. 'That's a very precise time. He's playing mind games.'

'Oh, I hadn't thought of that.'

'That's the sort of odd time you get in a doctor's surgery or a dentist. Most people I know would schedule meetings on the hour or the half-hour. He wants to make you think he's so busy that he could only give you a few minutes in between other more important things.'

'That might be true,' she conceded. 'He's quite wealthy, and the Trudge-Smythe family own lots of businesses.'

'You would have expected him to have got one of his minions to do this for him,' Oliver said, his voice thoughtful.

***

Juliette was a bag of nerves when she saw Oliver walking up the street later. She had her head out the window and was watching for him, but she quickly withdrew it when he came into view, not wanting to seem too eager.

She arranged herself at her desk, her pen in hand, leaning slightly back in her chair, and trying to look like she was musing on something important. Then she realised how daft she was being, and popped to the little loo to check her hair and makeup instead. She was just coming out of it when she heard Oliver knock and walk in. Talk about being wrongfooted, she thought. Emerging from the toilet wasn't the look she had been aiming for.

Oliver didn't seem to mind. He strode over to her, gathered her in his arms and kissed her. For a fleeting moment Juliette considered suggesting they not bother going to the meeting, before common sense took over and she ended the kiss by dragging herself out of his embrace (very reluctantly) and stepping back.

'If we carry on like this, we're never going to get to Trudge Manor,' she told him.

Oliver shrugged. 'Suits me, but then again I'm being selfish.' His gaze swept up and down her body, and he added, 'Very selfish, indeed.'

Juliette knew she was blushing. 'Stop it. You'll have me all flustered.'

His amused gaze made her blush even harder. 'I like seeing you flustered,' he said, 'but right now you're looking far from it. You're looking extremely professional, cool, and confident.'

His words lifted her spirit, even though she felt the exact opposite inside. She was glad he thought she looked professional, as she had been tempted to wear a summery dress this morning but had changed her mind at the last minute. Instead, she had donned a navy skirt suit, with a navy and cream blouse, and navy shoes. When she looked in the mirror she'd thought she looked like a banker, and not simply the editor of a provincial, non-descript rag.

She remembered a successful female journalist, not long after Juliette had first embarked on her own career, telling her that appearances were everything. Many of her male colleagues could get away with dressing scruffily, but if women were to be taken seriously, they had to look the part. Juliette had taken the advice to heart, and made sure she looked like a stylish business woman at all times.

When she'd got the job at the Tattler, she'd invested in some new suits and had carried on the tradition. Today she was very glad she had.

'You scrub up quite well yourself,' she told Oliver, admiring his suit, shirt and tie. He looked even more handsome and distinguished than he had when he wore jeans, although he looked pretty darned good in both.

'And you look as if you're going to kick some ass,' Oliver said, smiling. 'You always did look like you meant business.'

His eyes were full of admiration, and Juliette revelled in it for a moment before she pulled herself together. She needed a clear head for the meeting, and Oliver wasn't doing much to help her keep on track and focused.

As if sensing this, he turned away to gaze around the room. 'Have you got a figure you're not prepared to go above?' he asked her.

She nodded and told him what it was.

'Okay, that sounds reasonable, not that I know much about buying newspapers. How do you want to play this? Do you want me to sit menacingly in the background, glowering, or do you want me to pretend to be your "financial advisor"?' He finger quoted the words, and Juliette smiled.

'I don't think Ralph would believe me if I said that was what you are. He knows how much he pays me, don't forget.'

'What do you want to introduce me as?'

'I'll just tell him your name and leave the rest to his imagination. If he asks outright, I'll tell him the truth, but I'm hoping he won't. It'll be much more fun if he has to wonder who you are and what you're doing there.'

'Right, shall we go?' Oliver asked, and Juliette took a deep breath.

She could do this. She had faced far more difficult situations, and for the most part had come out of them unscathed. What was the worst Ralph could do? Set a figure far too high so she'd walk away, that's what, and they'd either renegotiate, or that would be the end of it.

She shouldn't let herself be intimidated by a man like him, but she couldn't help it. He had money, power, and influence, and—

'He's just a bloke,' Oliver said, and her eyes shot to him in surprise. Were her thoughts so obvious? 'The trick is to imagine him naked,' he added.

Juliette shuddered. 'Please, no, you've put that image in my mind now and I don't think I'm going to get rid of it. Yuck.' She picked up her bag and pointed at the door. 'Out, before you do any more damage. If I start giggling halfway through the meeting because I'm imagining his man-boobs and his paunch, I'll blame you.'

She was still trying to rid herself of the image of a starkers Ralph Trudge-Smythe, when she brought the car to a halt on his weed-free gravel drive.

Ralph Trudge-Smythe did a double-take when the housekeeper showed them into the same room in which Juliette had met with him the last time. Today he only had the one man with him, and Juliette felt like shouting "snap!", and she had to hold back a giggle. It was due to nerves, but it wouldn't do to show it. She might be doing him a disservice, but she got the impression Ralph would smell out weakness in the same way a shark would smell blood in the water.

This time he was standing in the middle of the room, Merton Berrow hovering next to him. He was a quick learner was old Ralph, Juliette thought, realising he didn't wish to be outmanoeuvred in his own home again. He came forward before she was hardly through the door, holding his hand out and shaking hers, his grip firmer than it needed to be under the circumstances. Juliette was determined not to wince; during her journalism years, she recalled how her hand would often be sore from the overenthusiastic handshake of people who wanted her to know her place, women as well as men. It was petty and pathetic, but she didn't show her reaction. In contrast, Merton's handshake was brief, barely touching her fingers.

She turned slightly to indicate Oliver, who was standing behind her. 'I hope you don't mind me bringing someone,' she said. 'This is Oliver Pascoe; Oliver, this is Ralph Trudge-Smythe, the current owner of the Tattler.'

Ralph raised his eyebrows in silent acknowledgement when she said the words "current owner", and Juliette lifted her chin.

The three men shook hands, and Ralph gestured towards the sofas. Like armies facing each other across the field of battle, Ralph and Merton Berrow sat together on one sofa, Juliette and Oliver together on the other, with the coffee table between the two opposing parties. Its surface was bare, except for a single copy of the Financial Times which Juliette deliberately ignored, guessing Ralph had placed it there as a reminder to her of just how small and insignificant the Tattler was in comparison.

He needn't have bothered, because she knew that already. However, it might be small and insignificant in the scheme of things, but not to her and not to Ticklemore. And if he considered it to be so insignificant, then he should be giving it to her for a song and not making her jump through hoops for it.

'Shall we get down to business?' Ralph asked, looking from her to Oliver.

Oliver didn't say a word.

Juliette took a steadying breath. 'I think we should; we are both busy. In fact, I'm surprised you wanted to bring me all this way when a simple conversation over the phone would have sufficed.' She knew he'd understand her meaning – she was hinting he obviously had more time on his hands than he was letting on. These mind games were rapidly becoming annoying, but she recognised the need to play them, so she mentally rolled up her sleeves and prepared to do battle.

Ralph's eyes narrowed slightly, and she guessed she'd hit home. She also had the feeling she was playing with fire, because the next words out of his mouth was a figure lower than the one he suggested before but still far too high for her meagre budget.

She sat frozen for a moment, wondering how she should respond, then she felt Oliver's breath in her ear as he whispered, 'We need to pretend to consider it.'

Trying to keep her tone and her expression neutral, she said to Ralph, 'Do you mind awfully if I have a quick chat with Oliver?'

'Be my guest,' Ralph said, and she could have sworn she saw a smirk playing about his lips.

'I think we'll take it outside,' she said, and got to her feet, Oliver swiftly standing, too. 'Talk amongst yourselves,' was her parting shot as she walked out into the magnificent hall.

Conscious there may still be eyes on her, Juliette led Oliver into the centre of the marble floor and whispered, 'What do we do now?'

Oliver put a hand on her arm and gave her a reassuring squeeze. 'What do you want to do?' he asked.

That was easy. 'I want to refuse.' She didn't have any choice.

'Then that's what we'll do. The amount he's asking for the Tattler is too high anyway, and you've already told me your upper limit. Could you match this new figure if you had to?' he asked.

She shook her head. 'Not a chance.'

'Well then, we walk away.'

Juliette and Oliver re-entered the room and took their seats once more.

Juliette crossed her legs daintily at the ankle, folded her hands in her lap, and offered Ralph and his advisor a bright professional smile. 'Thank you, but we'll pass.'

It was Ralph's turn to huddle and discuss. He

didn't leave the room, however; instead, he gestured to Merton Berrow and they both went over to stand by the window.

Juliette didn't take her eyes off the pair of them, and even though they had their backs to her, she could see their reflections in the glass. But neither one was giving anything away. Even though she could see their mouths working, she couldn't make out what they were saying.

When they sat back down a couple of minutes later, Ralph gave her another figure, and Juliette resisted the urge to sigh. For goodness' sake, couldn't she just tell him how much she was able to pay and see if he'd accept it? That was what she wanted to do, but she knew he'd only consider it an opening amount on her part and he'd expect her to increase her offer.

She was silent for a moment, then she rose and held out her hand.

Ralph blinked, and he got to his feet too, his own hand reaching out to grasp hers, a small twitch of his lips growing into a smile. He clearly thought a deal had been struck.

Juliette took far too much pleasure in wiping the smile off. 'Thank you for your time, Mr Trudge-Smythe, but I don't think we'll be doing business. Good day to you both.'

She slipped her hand out of his and watched his expression harden. 'I will, however, discuss it further with Mr Pascoe, and if anything changes, I'll be sure to let you know.'

Ralph shot Oliver a sour look. 'I'm not prepared to take anything less for it,' he said, his attention resting on Oliver and not on her.

'So be it,' she replied calmly. 'I'll be sure to send you a complimentary copy of my new paper as soon as it's up and running,' she added and watched as his startled gaze switched from Oliver back to her.

She took a small amount of satisfaction from his realisation she intended to carry on with a newspaper for Ticklemore with, or without, the Tattler's name on it.

Relishing her tiny victory (it wasn't really a victory, was it?) Juliette inclined her head graciously, turned on her heel and marched out of the door. Once through it, she carried on her march, the housekeeper darting out from somewhere to open the large front door for her and Oliver, and only slowing when she felt the crunch of gravel underneath her heels. Heels and gravel didn't mix well, and she was forced to take her time as she made her way to the car.

She heard Oliver's footsteps following closely behind her, but she didn't dare look at him for fear she would give something away in her expression.

Something she didn't want anyone else to see.

They both got in and buckled up their seat belts, and only then did Juliette let go of some of the tension she was holding.

'Phew, I seriously didn't enjoy that,' she said.

'I don't think Trudge-Smythe meant you to. You did brilliantly, though,' Oliver said. 'But it might not have been a good idea to bring me along as I seemed to have antagonised Ralph. I get the feeling he thought he might have struck a deal with you if I hadn't been there.'

'I expect that's *exactly* what he was thinking,' she said. It's annoying how some men don't believe women are capable of making their own minds up,' she added, crossly.

'It's probably the way he was brought up. He's in line to inherit his father's title, isn't he?'

'Yes, his father is a baron and the title is hereditary. To think that one day he'll be sitting in the house of Lords!' Juliette shuddered. 'What do you think will happen now?'

'You told him you were carrying on with the newspaper whether it bears the Tattler's name or not, so I should imagine he's weighing up the cost of folding the business – which to be fair, isn't all that great – against the potential amount he might gain from you, were you to come to some agreement over price.'

'I hope so,' she said, pulling out onto the road and heading towards Ticklemore.

Trudge Manor was only five miles away, and it didn't take them long to return to the village, much to Juliette's disappointment.

'Do you fancy a spot of lunch, before you leave?' she suggested. It was the least she could do, considering he had jumped into his car at a moment's notice to accompany her to this meeting. She was thankful he'd made it at all, considering how short a time he'd had to get from Birmingham to Ticklemore.

'That would be lovely,' he said. 'I'm not quite ready to go home yet.'

Juliette wasn't ready for him to return to Birmingham at all today, but she could hardly tell him that without sounding as though she was suggesting he spent the rest of the day with her. He probably had stuff he needed to do, without holding her hand all the time. But lunch was a necessity, or that's what she told herself. They had to eat, didn't they? Therefore, they might as well eat together.

Bookylicious was busy as usual, and it looked like they were going to have to wait for a table to become free. Whilst they were waiting, Juliette and Oliver perused the menu and the specials written up on the chalkboard behind the counter.

She made her choice but when she turned to Oliver to ask him what he fancied, she spotted Hattie heading towards them.

'Oh, God,' she muttered under her breath. Maybe coming here wasn't such a good idea after all. Perhaps they should have gone to the Tavern – the only thing she'd have to endure there were Logan's questioning looks. Hattie was never content with just looking. Ever. She'd invariably say something.

'So, this is your young man?' Hattie said as she sailed up to them. She was wearing an apron over the top of an orange dress with purple stars over it, her tights were yellow, and she had a pair of green Crocs on her feet. It was a bit like meeting a talkative rainbow.

'I'm Hattie,' she announced to Oliver, and stuck her hand out.

'Oliver,' he responded, taking it. 'Nice to meet you.'

Hattie wasn't on her best behaviour today as she said, eyebrows raised, 'I'm assuming you have a last name?'

'It's Pascoe. What's yours?'

'Jenkins.'

Juliette closed her eyes briefly. The sooner she got Oliver out of the café the better for all concerned.

'Are you here about the Tattler?' Hattie asked.

'Erm...' Oliver shot Juliette a helpless look and she felt his discomfort.

'Yes, he is,' Juliette interjected. 'How about we have something to go?' she suggested to him. 'It's busy in here today.'

Hattie tapped her on the shoulder and pointed to a free table. 'You can sit there,' she said. It sounded more like a command than an invitation.

'No thanks, Hattie, we'll order something to take out.' Juliette was firm.

Hattie sniffed. 'Please yourself, but I'll have you know I've called a meeting.'

'Of what?' Hattie had called meetings before, when they were trying to set up the Christmas Toy Shop. Several members of the local community, herself included, had come together to enable the Toy Shop to get off the ground. But there hadn't been a meeting since the place had opened before Christmas.

'Of Team Tattler, of course,' Hattie announced.

'I don't understand,' Juliette said.

'You wouldn't, would you, what with you having your head turned by this handsome fella here. You need to get your mind out of the bedroom and into the office,' Hattie said. 'Us residents have got a vested interest in keeping the Tattler going, and if you're too busy thinking with your—'

'Thank you, Hattie, that's very kind of you,' Juliette

interrupted hurriedly, before Hattie said something which would embarrass everyone in the café – except for Hattie; she was never embarrassed. She called a spade a spade, and woe betide anyone who tried to tell her it was a shovel. Unfortunately, being so truthful didn't always go down too well, and Juliette was pretty sure the rest of the customers didn't want to know what Hattie thought Juliette was thinking with.

Or maybe they did, Juliette realised when she took a quick look around the café and saw how many pairs of eyes were staring curiously in her direction. Oh God, she was never going to live this down.

'What is the meeting about?' Juliette asked, dread sweeping over her. Hattie was a force of nature and when she decided on a course of action, it would take a stronger person than Juliette to turn her away from it.

'The Tattler, silly girl! What do you think I meant? For goodness sake, youngsters these days,' she said to no one in particular.

First Juliette's mother made her feel about fourteen, and now Hattie was doing the same. Juliette might not have minded so much but she was past the halfway mark when it came to getting a telegram from Buckingham Palace. She was hardly a youngster. She was an adult in charge of her own destiny, her own future. Whatever that might be…

'You need some help, missy, whether you realise it or not,' Hattie told her emphatically. 'And we're going to give it to you. Be in the Tavern this evening at seven o'clock sharp. Don't be late, or we will do this without you.'

'How on earth can you do this without me?' Juliette demanded.

Hattie tapped the side of her nose. 'You'll have to be there to find out, won't you.' She turned her attention back to Oliver. 'Are you going to accompany her? I think you should, by the look of you.'

Oliver opened his mouth to ask what she meant, and Juliette shook her head frantically at him praying that he wouldn't. He did.

'What do you mean "by the look of me"?' he asked and Juliette closed her eyes again.

Dear God, why was this happening?

She opened them in time to see Hattie's face wreathed in a broad smile, her eyes disappearing into the folds of her skin.

'Because you love her, that's why,' the old woman said. A muttered, 'Blimmin' idiot,' followed. Then, louder, 'I hate it when I have to point it out to them. You think they'd be old enough to know this for themselves.' And louder again so everyone in the café-cum-bookshop could hear, 'Life's too short to pussyfoot through it. You both need to get a wriggle on; you're not getting any younger.'

Oliver's face had taken on the look of a deer startled by headlights. The poor man didn't know what to do with himself.

Juliette did. 'We'll take two of those, and two of those, she said to Maddison, who was behind the counter, her mouth hanging open as she watched the proceedings. Juliette fumed; Maddison was Hattie's employer – couldn't she control the woman? Even as she thought it, she knew the answer. Hattie couldn't be controlled by anyone, and Juliette suspected she'd always been like it but now she used her advanced age as justification.

Face burning, Juliette shoved a ten-pound note at Maddison, grabbed the bag of goodies, took Oliver's hand, and dragged him towards the door. As she shot through it, Juliette heard Hattie shouting after them, 'Remember, seven o'clock in the Tavern. Don't be late!'

Juliette knew she'd have to go, but all she could think of right now was how Oliver must be feeling, because she'd seen the momentary flash of surprise on his face. together with the burgeoning realisation in his eyes when Hattie had told him he was in love with her.

She just hoped this wasn't going to ruin everything, because it had been going so well up until now.

CHAPTER 16

OLIVER

Oliver had never been so thankful to leave a café in all his life. What was wrong with that woman? On the outside Hattie looked like a nice, if somewhat eccentric old lady with her colourful clothes and her silver-grey hair caught in a bun at the nape of her neck, but when she opened her mouth there was simply no filter whatsoever.

And what was it she'd said about him falling in love? Was it that obvious? He couldn't believe anyone could tell just by looking at him. He hoped to God Juliette hadn't been able to; he didn't want to be walking around with an expression on his face that declared how much he was falling for her. What would she think of him?

Juliette appeared to be just as embarrassed. She couldn't get him out of there fast enough, and he guessed it was because she was mortified by what Hattie had said.

On the other hand, there was the possibility the love comment had totally passed her by, and maybe she had been more concerned with the meeting Hattie had called and hadn't heard a word.

He'd told Juliette she needed the community behind her if she hoped to make a go of the Tattler, but he'd anticipated she needed to persuade people and to make it worth the villagers' while. He hadn't imagined a little old lady dressed in glaringly bright clothes would grab the bit between her teeth and take matters into her own hands.

Juliette put their lunch on the desk and, without looking at him, disappeared into the little room at the back of the office. Shortly the aromatic smell of coffee wafted out and soon afterwards she brought out two mugs, placed them both on the desk, and took a seat. He dropped into the one opposite and opened the paper bag containing the sandwiches, lifting his out. He unwrapped it, but didn't make a move to eat it.

They'd hardly said a word to each other since leaving the café, the silence uncomfortable and awkward. The earlier easiness between them had evaporated like morning mist in a valley, and he was beginning to wonder whether it had been there in the first place or whether he'd been imagining it.

There was nothing else for it, he decided – he had to address the elephant in the room. 'About what Hattie said...' he began.

'Which bit? Hattie says a lot.' Juliette unwrapped her sandwich and took a small bite, chewing slowly. She didn't look as though she was enjoying it.

Once again, Oliver wondered if she'd heard Hattie say that he was in love with her. Because if she hadn't, and he said what he was about to say, things were going to get even more embarrassing than they already were.

Yet again, his mind was filled with jumbled thoughts. Had she heard Hattie but was pretending she hadn't to spare his feelings? Or maybe she had heard and was pretending she hadn't because she didn't feel the same way?

Damn and blast! When had dating become so complicated? He couldn't remember having all these second thoughts and self-doubts when he was dating his ex-wife.

He took a deep breath and came right out with it. 'The bit where she said I was in love with you.'

'Ah, that bit.' Juliette was studying her sandwich with great intensity. 'Hattie doesn't know what she's talking about. She gets these fanciful ideas...'

'That's the thing,' he interjected. 'It's not fanciful.'

Juliette shot him a quick look from underneath her hair, before her attention returned to her sandwich. He wished he knew what she was thinking. Was she hoping he'd go away? He prayed not; because what Hattie had said was true, sort of. He was well on the way to being in love with Juliette.

'I like you a lot,' he said, wincing at how inadequate those words were.

'Oh.' Juliette's voice was small, and she finally put her sandwich down, with only the one bite taken out of it. She picked up her coffee instead, and took a sip.

'I more than like you,' he persisted, wondering if he should stop talking right now.

'I like you, too.' Juliette's voice was slightly more confident. 'But you needn't, you know… say anything…'

'I know,' he said, 'but she's right. I'm seriously falling for you.'

Juliette raised her head and looked him in the eye. 'You've not fallen yet, then?'

He shrugged. 'I might have.' He might as well acknowledge it to himself, rather than dance around the subject. He was a mature man; at his age he should be able to come clean about his feelings.

'I think I've fallen for you, too.' Juliette was still hesitant about looking him in the eye, and he understood this was as awkward for her as it was for him.

It shouldn't be; falling in love shouldn't be this tricky.

Suddenly he sat up a little straighter – tricky indeed! It was only tricky because he was making it so.

'OK, now we've got that out of the way,' he said, 'let's just see how it goes, shall we? I care for you, I believe you care for me, so let's leave it there for the time being.'

He saw her relax a little, some of the tension dissolving from her shoulders and her brow clearing. She had enough on her plate at the moment what with trying to buy the Tattler, without him declaring his undying love. His emotions hadn't got that far yet, but the way they were going, he'd arrive there shortly. Talk about a whirlwind romance; they had barely come back into each other's lives, and here they were, almost at the point of saying those three little words. But not quite.

He was being cautious when he'd said, "let's see how it goes". It was too early, too soon, and everything was moving too fast. Deciding to park it there for the time being, at least until he could get things straight in his head, he changed the subject.

'What do you think they are going to talk about in this meeting tonight?'

Juliette's eyes narrowed as she thought about it. 'I have absolutely no idea. But I do know when Hattie gets an idea in her head, she runs with it. Take Alfred... If it wasn't for Hattie's sheer bloody-mindedness and determination, all the toys he'd made would be in a skip by now. It was all down to her that the Ticklemore Toy Shop got off the ground at all. Goodness knows what she's got in mind for the Tattler.'

'It might be a good thing,' Oliver observed. 'I said you needed the community behind you.'

'Yes, and I'd come to the same conclusion. It just worries me that I don't know what she's planning.'

'I take it you are going to go along to the meeting?'

'Of course; even if I didn't want to go, I wouldn't dare miss it.' She hesitated and he guessed what was coming next. 'I know it's an imposition and you've probably got things you need to be getting on with, but I'd love it if you came with me.'

Oliver would love it too, but there was that damned deadline looming. She must have been able to read his refusal in his face, because she quickly looked down, her sandwich claiming her attention once again.

'I'd love to go with you,' he began, and was just about to let her down gently, when he thought what the hell! 'In fact, I will, but I need to pop back home first.'

She looked sheepish. 'Sorry, I've taken up enough of your time already.'

'That's not what I meant. I have a deadline for this manuscript, and it's been moved forward, so I could do with getting a couple of hours work done. I need to pop back home for a bit, but I'll be back by seven, if that's OK with you?'

A smile lit up her face, and he knew he'd made the right decision.

'That will be wonderful, but I've got an idea. Do you have to go home? Are all your files on your computer, or do you backup to some kind of cloud?'

Oliver was surprised. The Tattler didn't even have a website, yet she was quite happily talking about cloud storage.

'Yes, I back up to Google,' he said. 'I tend to work exclusively with Google docs, because it's easier to share with my editor when it's his turn to do his bit.'

'If that's the case, do you have to go home? You could always stay here,' she suggested tentatively.

Oliver could see how much it was costing her to ask and he realised she was scared he might refuse. It was a sensible idea. Even if he hadn't wanted to spend the rest of the afternoon with her, it made sense for him not to drive all the way to Birmingham and back again. He usually managed the journey in an hour or so, but that still meant it would take two hours by the time he did the round trip.

'It's a good idea,' he agreed, 'but I can't work off my phone.' And there was only the one computer that he could see in the little office.

'That's OK. I can pop home and fetch my laptop. Is that all right?'

'Definitely. We'd better finish our lunch, if we're going to get any work done,' he pointed out, indicating their barely-touched sandwiches.

He was relieved to see Juliette pick hers up and begin eating with gusto. His own appetite returned with a vengeance, and he realised just how hungry he was. But looking at her, he wasn't quite sure whether it was his food he was hungry for, or her.

Right now, if given the choice, he'd happily kiss her until it was time to go to the meeting.

Her eyes met his and she paused, the remains of a sandwich halfway to her mouth. He wondered what she was seeing on his face, and he half-hoped she was seeing what Hattie had seen. But she carried on eating, and the moment was lost.

They polished off their food, and Oliver washed out their mugs while Juliette went to fetch her laptop.

He wondered where she lived. Ticklemore wasn't very big, but there was nothing to indicate that she lived in the village itself. However, when he quickly glanced out of the window, it was to see her walking in the opposite direction to where she parked the car, and he guessed she must live fairly near.

Just over ten minutes later she was back, carrying her laptop case, and he wondered whether he had passed her house when he'd driven into the village. There was so much they didn't know about each other, so much they had yet to learn, and the first thing he wanted to know was where she lived. He was excited to think of all the discoveries he could make; he intended to know her inside and out, from the tiniest detail to the biggest.

As soon as she came back into the office, he gently took the laptop case out of her hand and drew her to him. Work could wait for a moment, at least.

Kissing wasn't probably the best prelude to getting to grips with his latest biography, but he hadn't been able to help himself. And she didn't seem to be complaining either, as she matched his passion.

Eventually though, they had to break it up, otherwise the whole afternoon would slip away and neither of them would get anything done.

She removed the laptop from its case, opened it up and logged in. He appreciated her trust; people's phones, tablets, and computers were quite personal things, sometimes with information on them they wouldn't want anyone else to see. But he had no intention of prowling through her files, or her search history, or anything else for that matter, as all he wanted to do was to get online and begin work.

They sat either side of the desk for the rest of the day, both of them tip-tapping away, sometimes uttering little noises of satisfaction or irritation, depending on what they were doing.

They broke for coffee about halfway through the afternoon, and Oliver took the opportunity to ask her something that had been intriguing him for some time.

'Why hasn't the Tattler got a website? You do a lot of things by computer, so I would have thought the newspaper would have an online presence.'

'I have considered it, and it's sort of been on my to-do list, but to be honest I thought if the newspaper had a website with news and features and articles and stuff, people might not see the point in buying the paper itself.'

Oliver could see where she was coming from, but that wasn't necessarily the case. Broadsheets and tabloids alike had an online presence. Most of them displayed the headline along with a few sentences to get the reader hooked, but if a person wanted to read further they had to subscribe to the paper. That was one of the things he'd suggested to her, a subscription service, but first of all the paper needed a complete overhaul anyway. From what she'd told him, its readership was slightly on the older side, which meant some of them might not use the internet at all. His own parents didn't, although his dad did have a smartphone.

Oliver smiled to himself when he thought of the number of times his dad had called him in a panic because he'd done something to his mobile and couldn't work out what, asking Oliver to pop around and sort it out for him.

To be fair, they were in their eighties, and most of their lives had been lived without the sometimes dubious presence of highly sophisticated electronic devices. Not like today, when babes in arms could find their way around an iPad better than some computer programmers.

After the short break, Oliver and Juliette returned to their respective tasks until five o'clock, when she slumped back in her seat and let out a sigh. 'That's it,' she said. 'I'm done for the day.'

'Do you normally work these hours?'

'I do, sort of. Because I do everything myself, I usually come in at about half eight and work through till about one, five days a week. In the afternoons I'm often out and about scouting out stories, interviewing people, and sometimes touting for business. It's getting more and more difficult to get advertisers on board though. What about you?'

'I don't have any set hours, although I do tend to work in the evenings and sometimes into the night. It depends whether I'm in the flow or not. Sometimes the words come easy, sometimes they don't.'

Juliette smiled. 'I know that feeling,' she said. 'I tend to be a morning person, my words flow better then, which is when I come in and write everything up.'

'What's your favourite part about running a newspaper?' Oliver himself had never entertained the idea of climbing up the ladder. Once he'd reached the point where his features often hit the front page, he didn't want to go any further. For him, the story and the writing was everything. He didn't want to be involved in management, or have any additional responsibilities. He had been perfectly content being a journalist, and getting out and about, talking to people. Sitting behind a desk all the time wasn't his thing.

Or it hadn't been. He was doing that more and more as the years went by, now that he'd swapped one form of writing for another. He still interviewed people though and did lots of research, some of which involved visiting archives and sometimes libraries. That was the fun part. The grunt work was getting the words out of his head and onto paper.

But the best bit was when he held his newly-released book in his hands for the first time. Always in hardback, the books were chunky and solid and they had pride of place on his bookshelf.

'D you want to carry on, or can you stop now?' Juliette asked him.

'I'm done. I can pick this up tomorrow.' Or more likely, he would pick it up later this evening after he came home from Ticklemore, as he planned on working long into the night. He should be exhausted after the very poor night's sleep he'd had, but once again he wasn't. He felt more alive being with Juliette, than he'd felt in a long time.

He knew it couldn't last, and he would undoubtedly crash and burn at some point, but not this evening; this evening he had a meeting to go to, with a beautiful woman by his side.

'Are you hungry?' she asked. 'I think we should eat before we go out.'

Oliver assumed she meant popping to the pub and having a meal there before the meeting started, but Juliette had something else in mind.

'I could cook us pasta?' she suggested.

'At your house?'

Juliette laughed. 'Where else would you expect me to cook you dinner?'

'I thought you might cook here,' Oliver said,

having not thought at all.

'You've seen the kitchen area,' Juliette replied, wryly. 'It has a kettle and a microwave. I won't be doing much cooking in there.' She got up and came around to his side of the desk, perching on the edge of it.

She hadn't changed out of the suit she had worn to Trudge Manor, and the straight skirt rose up slightly as she sat, showing off her trim calves and a very shapely knee.

'Finish what you're doing, then we'll go,' she told him.

Oliver quickly clicked out of the Google document he'd been working on, and shut the laptop lid, then unplugged it from the mains and stowed it in the bag next to his chair.

'Ready when you are,' he said, wanting nothing more than to take her in his arms again, but he held himself back.

Juliette, on the other hand, had no reservations. As soon as he was on his feet, she slipped off the desk and when she kissed him, she took his breath away.

It was some considerable time before she broke away and said cheerfully, 'We'd better get a move on, otherwise we won't have time to eat before the meeting.'

'I suppose we'd better,' he agreed, picking up the

laptop case – but food was the last thing on his mind.

Juliette led the way along the high street, past the Tavern at the end, and turned into a side-street lined with hand-hewn stone-built cottages, sporting slate roofs, some of them still with their original sash windows. Most of them had plant pots and window boxes outside filled with fresh spring flowers, and the whole street looked cheerful and welcoming, and delightfully old fashioned.

Juliette halted outside a house about halfway down the street and took a bunch of keys out of her pocket.

So this was where she lived? Oliver spent a moment giving the outside of the building a quick once over. It was just as pretty and as well-kept as the others in the street (not that he expected anything less) and he thought it quite charming.

Inside was just as lovely, with what appeared to be the original tiles on the floor in the hall, dado rails halfway up the walls, a wooden staircase with a carpet runner down the centre, and bare pine doors.

She led him into an open plan kitchen, living room and dining room, and he saw that the kitchen part was an extension and was surprisingly modern. With soft white units below and pale grey ones on the walls, the room was flooded with light from big glass doors at the end and skylights above.

It was so very her – an intoxicating mix of new

and old. He hadn't known the old Juliette terribly well, but he thought he'd known her well enough. This new Juliette was an enigma, which he couldn't wait to delve into.

He put the laptop on the floor next to a small desk in the corner of the dining area, and followed her into the kitchen.

She began taking things out of the fridge and cupboards, and he asked if he could help.

'No, you just sit there and have a glass of wine,' she said. 'I know you're driving later, but one won't hurt with dinner. I've only got white, is that OK?'

It was, and Oliver gratefully took the glass and began to sip slowly from it.

They chatted as she cooked, him wishing she'd let him help because he felt a bit like a spare part. He wasn't used to anyone cooking for him, and although he was quite enjoying the experience, he still felt he should be helping.

It didn't take long for Juliette to magic up a big bowl of steaming tomato pasta and some garlic bread, and when they sat down to eat she offered him a hunk of parmesan cheese and a grater. As soon as their respective bowls were suitably garnished, (she'd even put a sprig of parsley on the top) they settled down to eat, munching away in companionable silence.

'What's happened to bring your deadline forward?' she asked, after they'd finished eating and were clearing the dishes away. 'I thought these things were planned months in advance.'

Crikey that wasn't something he could answer honestly. 'Yes they are, but the publisher had an opening in their schedule,' he lied, 'so I was asked if I wouldn't mind filling it.'

Juliette would know all about deadlines, and the speed at which stories could break. What she couldn't know, and what he didn't want her to guess, was the real reason for his new deadline.

She sent him a sympathetic smile as she stacked the dishwasher. 'How do you feel about that? I remember how awful it was when your editor told you they wanted a piece yesterday. They never used to give you enough time, did they?'

'No, they didn't,' Oliver agreed, thinking he wasn't being given enough time now, either. But that was something he'd just have to suck up. 'I'm not too pleased, to be honest,' he admitted, 'but it pays the bills, and if I put my mind to it, I can get it done.'

Juliette said, 'I feel awful, asking you to the meeting tonight when you've got so much to do. Why don't you get off? You can be home in an hour or so, and you'll have the whole evening ahead of you.'

'I'd prefer to spend it with you.' He wondered if

she was having second thoughts about him accompanying her.

'And I'd prefer you to be there, but I don't want to get in the way of your work.'

'Why don't you let me worry about that?' he suggested.

'Are you sure?'

'I've never been so sure about anything in my life,' he said sincerely, looking her straight in the eye.

They shared a slow meaningful smile.

'Good, I'd love to have you with me. Do you want to come upstairs?' she asked.

'Excuse me?' Was she suggesting what he thought she was suggesting? If so he wasn't sure—

'I'll show you where the bathroom is, so you can freshen up,' she clarified, a mischievous twinkle in her eye.

Oh, that's what she meant. He felt a bit of an idiot for thinking such a thing in the first place, but he didn't think he'd have the strength to reject her offer, even though he would have wanted to – he didn't envision their first time being a quickie before they had to dash out for a meeting. He wanted to take his time, to cherish her, to show her how much she meant to him…

Thankfully he hadn't said "yes please" and headed off up the stairs at a rate of knots.

But, dear God, a part of him had wanted so badly to do precisely that!

CHAPTER 17

JULIETTE

Juliette's tummy was full of butterflies as she led Oliver into the Tavern. She spotted Team Tattler immediately, sitting at a table in a corner of the room. The membership had grown in size since the last time, with Sara and Zoe also in attendance. The only two people missing was Logan, who was currently behind the bar, and Father Todd.

Juliette came forward, greeting Hattie first with a kiss on the cheek.

'I was beginning to think you weren't coming,' Hattie grumbled.

Juliette checked the time and saw it wasn't quite seven yet.

'She's not late, it's just that we've been here ages,' Alfred explained, and Hattie gave him a nudge.

Juliette kissed him on the cheek too, and said,

'Lovely to see you, Alfred. How are you keeping?'

'Not so bad,' he told her with a grin and a sideways look at Hattie.

'And how is the workshop going?' she asked.

Hattie leapt in before Alfred could answer. 'We haven't got time for this. We've got a newspaper to sort out. Now, you'd better introduce your young man, then we can get started.'

Juliette rolled her eyes (she heard Hattie mutter, 'I saw that,' but she ignored her) and went around the table.

'This is Nell, who runs an antique shop in the village,' Juliette told Oliver and blew her friend a kiss. Nell waved. 'Sitting next to her is Silas; he's an artist and runs the Gallery. You've met Hattie.' Juliette pulled a face and Hattie pulled one back, sticking her tongue out. 'Next to her is Alfred, who makes the toys, along with his assistant, Zoe.' Juliette smiled at the teenager sitting on the other side of the old man. Zoe was sipping a fizzy drink and looking cross about it, and Juliette wondered when she would turn eighteen.

'This is Sara, Alfred's daughter, who manages the Toy Shop, and her husband, David,' she continued. They both gave her and Oliver a smile. 'And this lovely pair are Benny and Marge Everson. Benny is the chairperson of the Allotment Association and

Marge is heavily involved in the local Women's Institute. Logan over there,' Juliette jerked her head towards the man behind the bar, 'was also part of Team Toy Shop. Will he be joining us?' she asked Hattie.

'He better had; he's getting a round of drinks in.'

'The only person missing is Father Todd,' Juliette told Oliver. She turned to Hattie again. 'Anyone know where he is?'

'I'm here,' a voice behind her replied, and Father Todd bustled up to the table, slightly red of face and rather breathless. He dropped into one of the three vacant chairs and let out a huff. 'Sorry I'm late, a bit of an emergency in the church hall involving mice and a Madeira cake.'

Juliette smiled vaguely, hoping he wouldn't go into any further detail. She wasn't all that keen on mice and the thought of one creeping around a cake and perhaps nibbling on it made her skin crawl.

'Oliver, this is Father Todd; there's no need for me to explain what he does.' She turned back to the table, glancing around at everyone. 'And this is Oliver Pascoe,' she announced. 'He's a colleague of mine from way back, when I used to be a journalist and he's very kindly offered to help.' He hadn't actually offered, she'd asked, but she didn't see the point in splitting hairs.

She took a seat and Oliver did the same, and just as they were settling themselves down Logan strolled across with a tray full of glasses, Scarlet, one of the barmaids, following behind carrying another. As soon as the drinks were distributed, Juliette introduced Logan and Oliver, then Hattie called the meeting to order.

'Ladies and gentlemen,' the elderly woman said grandly, getting to her feet. 'I've gathered you here today because you've done it once for Alfred.' She indicated the gentleman in question, giving him a beaming smile. 'And I'm sure you can do it again. Juliette has been informed the Tattler is to close. Ticklemore will no longer have a newspaper.'

Juliette went to say something, but she felt Oliver's hand on her knee, so she subsided.

'Are we going to let this happen?' Hattie asked, forging ahead without waiting for an answer. 'No, we are not! The Ticklemore Tattler has been around for as long as I have, longer actually. It's part of our heritage, and it's an important part of the village. I, for one, don't intend to let it close. Now,' she rubbed her hands together and glared at them, 'what are we going to do about it?'

Benny was the first to speak. 'I thought Juliette owned the Tattler,' he said.

Juliette shook her head. 'Unfortunately, not. I do

everything else, apart from own it. It's owned by the Trudge-Smythes.'

'It is? I'm not sure many people know that,' Benny observed.

Silas spoke up. 'And I'm not sure there's anything we can do about it closing,' he pointed out. 'If the Trudge-Smythes own it and want to dissolve the business, we can't exactly stop them.'

Alfred laughed. 'You *have* met Hattie, haven't you?' The rest of the table joined in with the laughter, including Silas. Everyone knew what Hattie was like when she got going.

'Silas does have a point,' David said.

Juliette hadn't had all that much to do with David. The only thing she knew about him was that he was Sara's husband and Alfred's son-in-law. Sara was a former head teacher in a primary school. Juliette wondered what David did for a living or whether he was retired, too, but she didn't like to ask. Anyway, it didn't matter, he was here and he was supporting her in her fight for the Tattler, and that was the only thing that mattered. Although, a little part of her hoped he had a good business head on his shoulders, because she had a feeling they were going to need it.

Juliette spoke up. 'I made Ralph Trudge-Smythe an offer to buy it off him. We are in negotiations.'

Nell, who was aware of most of what had been

going on because Juliette had kept her up-to-date (she'd not mentioned much about Oliver, though) asked, 'How is that going?'

'Not brilliantly, if I'm honest,' Juliette admitted, picking up her wine and taking a hefty slurp. 'He laughed at me at first, then he came up with a figure that was simply ludicrous. I've met him twice and the second time the amount he wanted for it wasn't all that much lower. I've left it with him, it's up to him now; there's nothing more I can do. I'm hoping he's going to come back to me with a lower figure, but even then I suspect I won't be able to afford it.'

'Can you just carry on in your front room?' This was from Zoe. 'I mean, all you need is a computer and a printer, and you can set those up anywhere. It's not like you have to have his permission to keep the Tattler going.' There was silence around the table, and Zoe looked from face to face. 'Do you?'

'Yes, I think she does,' Silas said. 'If she wants to continue using the name "The Ticklemore Tattler", I suspect she'll have to purchase it. I don't know much about it, but the last thing we would want is for her to keep the name going and for somebody to object.'

'By somebody, you mean this Trudge-Smythe person?' Zoe asked.

'Yes, him.'

'Where's his father?' Marge asked. 'I thought he

was the big cheese, not the son.'

Hattie jumped in. 'Haven't you heard? He's got heart problems, so he's turned over all the businesses to Ralph.'

'That's a pity; he's an OK bloke,' Father Todd said. 'I must pop in and see him, and ask if there's anything I can do.'

'I'd wait until the son wasn't around if I were you,' Juliette said with a slightly bitter note in her voice.

'Is he that bad?' Nell asked.

'Hmm,' was all Juliette said. She was crosser with herself than with Ralph, if she was honest. It wasn't his fault the newspaper was on its uppers. It was hers. She was the one in charge; she should have taken more care of it. But his attitude still stank.

David proved he did have a business head on top of his quite broad shoulders after all as he asked, 'Why does he want to dissolve the business in the first place?'

Juliette was a little embarrassed to say, but she felt she had to share the reason with them. 'Because it's not making a profit. I believe it's only barely covering my wages.'

'Do you know how long this has been going on?' David asked.

'I suspect for quite some time.' She seriously needed to have a look at the accounts.

'He's probably making a wise financial decision,' David said, and although Juliette knew he was right, she wanted to stick her tongue out at him, much like Harriet had done to her earlier.

Logan, who had been silent up to now, said, 'First of all, we need to analyse why it isn't making a profit, because until we know the reason, we can't move forward with helping Juliette.'

Hattie piped up, 'I can tell you why it's not making a profit – it's because none of you buggers bother to buy it. Or advertise in it.'

Sara said, 'You're wrong there; Juliette ran a piece on the Toy Shop subscription boxes only last week.'

Hattie shot back, 'I bet you didn't pay her for it!' She glared around at everyone. 'And how many of you have taken out an advert lately? None of you, I'll wager.'

Everyone looked sideways at everyone else.

Silas was the only one who spoke. 'Advertising costs money.'

'So does running a newspaper,' Hattie retorted.

'Apart from advertising, do you have any other revenue streams?' David asked Juliette, and she shook her head sadly.

'Only from the sales of the newspaper itself.'

'I take it that sales are in a steady decline?' the man asked.

'Yes, fewer and fewer people are buying newspapers.'

'That's what we have to do,' Hattie declared. 'Make more people buy it.'

'Easier said than done,' Juliette observed. 'It's generally the older generation who buy newspapers – the younger ones tend to get their news online.'

'I've only ever bought a newspaper when I was job hunting,' Silas stated.

'You certainly don't need a newspaper for that these days,' Sara said. There was a grumbling agreement around the table.

'What about the classified ads?' David asked.

Juliette sighed. 'There aren't many of those, either. If you want to sell a car, you tend to go to sites like Auto Trader or eBay. As for other things, there's eBay again, Facebook Marketplace, Gumtree, and that's just off the top of my head. An eBay advert, for instance, could be seen by hundreds of thousands of people. A little classified ad in the Tattler would only be seen by a few hundred. I can't compete with that.'

'So don't try,' Hattie said. 'Why do people read a newspaper at all?' She glanced around each face in turn.

Zoe put a hand up. 'Because they're old, and don't have a proper phone?'

Sara harrumphed at her. 'Don't be cheeky, and

there's no need to put your hand up, you're not in school.'

Juliette bit back a smile. You could certainly tell what Sara's profession used to be, she thought, as the woman's teacher-voice came out.

'It's true,' Juliette said, agreeing with Zoe. 'Most of the people who buy the newspaper, as I've said, tend to be the older generation. Some of the younger ones who are invested in the community and who want to know what's going on in the village, also buy it, but then again there is a Facebook page dedicated to Ticklemore and that's gaining traction.'

'But doesn't that mean people have to go to all kinds of different places to get the information they want?' Marge asked.

'Good point, that's exactly it. But if you only want one piece of information, you're going to go to the best place you can get it from, and that would probably mean you'd only visit one site,' Nell pointed out.

'It only works if you know what you're looking for,' Marge argued. 'For instance, if I wanted to know whether the council was planning on bulldozing the allotments and building a shopping centre on it, I might not find the information on Facebook. Besides, if you didn't already know about it, you wouldn't go looking for it. You'd see it if you read the paper, though.'

Juliette shrugged. It was true; she had been known to haunt the local council offices, to discover such juicy titbits. It reminded her of when she used to be a political correspondent.

'Those kinds of things tend to get out, anyway,' Marge carried on, 'but sometimes not until it's too late. At least with the Tattler you get everything you want in one place.'

'The problem is,' David said, 'people have to make an effort to go and buy a newspaper. They might pick up a copy in a shop along with another purchase, but there aren't many people who'd make a deliberate visit to a shop to buy one. Is it delivered?'

'It used to be when my daughter was younger,' Juliette replied, 'but not anymore. I can't afford to pay a papergirl or boy; although I do pop some copies in through certain people's letterboxes. You know Mrs Selway? She hasn't been able to get out for years, so I always take her a paper.'

'That's very kind of you,' Hattie said, staring at her shrewdly. 'But I bet you don't charge her for it.'

Juliette looked away. What was she supposed to do? She just slipped a copy through the letterbox and left it at that. Occasionally, she had been known to knock on the door and have a cup of tea with the old lady, but even then there was no mention of payment on either of their parts.

'You can't run a business on charity,' Hattie scolded.

Silas pulled a face. 'If there aren't enough people buying newspapers and there aren't enough people placing adverts, then it might be the best thing if the newspaper was to fold.' He sent Juliette an apologetic look and mouthed, 'Sorry.'

In some ways she agreed with him, and if things didn't change that's what would undoubtedly happen, whether she bought the Tattler or not. 'Which is why I brought Oliver in,' she said.

Oliver gave her leg another squeeze under the table. His hand was warm, and although the contact was brief, it made her quiver.

'I've had an idea,' he said tentatively, and Juliette could tell he was reluctant to speak. He looked at Sara. 'You gave it to me when you talked about subscription boxes.'

'Did I? Are you saying you want me to pop a newspaper in with every box we send out?'

It was a great idea, Juliette thought for a second, then her face fell. Actually, it wasn't such a good idea after all, because those subscription boxes could be sent anywhere in the country. Why would anyone want to read the Tattler if they weren't from Ticklemore or the surrounding area? None of the little human-interest stories she liked to include, and none of the classified ads or local adverts would be relevant to those people.

Oliver carried on speaking. 'It would only work if the newspaper carried mostly stories and features which would appeal to a wider readership.'

Juliette looked at him. It was almost as though he'd read her mind. He gave her a reassuring smile.

'How much do you charge for the subscription boxes?' David asked Sara.

'They're not cheap,' Sara said. 'Everything we sell is handmade and handcrafted.'

'But the subscription is guaranteed, so it must be worth doing,' David pointed out.

'Yes, that's true,' Sara said.

'When I was talking about subscriptions,' Oliver said, 'I wasn't talking about subscription *boxes*, I meant a subscription to the newspaper itself.' He went on to explain, finishing up with, 'At least Juliette would have some kind of a known income for the year, and I realise that although people might not always renew the subscription, if it was on direct debit and the amount wasn't great, they may well let it run.'

David was looking thoughtful, and for a little while no one spoke as they all digested the information. It was Alfred, who had said very little up until now, who hit the nail on the head.

'That's all well and good, but people have got to be able to read it on their phones and whatnot,' he said. 'That's what people want these days. Actual newspapers are a thing of the past.'

'I wouldn't want to subscribe to a newspaper,' Zoe said. 'Not a real one. I don't like the feel of them.'

Everyone turned to look at her.

'What do you mean?' Juliette asked.

'I don't like the feel of newspapers and I won't touch one if I don't have to. The black stuff comes off on your fingers. Ugh.'

'You're weird,' Hattie said to her, but there was affection in her voice.

'My mum says that,' Zoe agreed.

'Do you think other people feel the same way about newspapers?' Juliette asked, mystified.

Zoe shrugged. 'Nah, it's probably just me. But I don't read magazines either, and they haven't got the same icky feel. I prefer to use my phone. It's always there, innit?'

'What do you read?' Sara asked. 'Facebook posts?' There was a slight undercurrent of sarcasm in her voice.

'Facebook is for old people,' Zoe said. 'Like you.'

Juliette looked away, trying to suppress yet another smile. Sara had asked for that. When she got herself under control, Juliette said to Zoe, 'What do you read exactly? I'm genuinely interested.'

'I do sometimes read the news on my phone. And books. I've got a Kindle app.'

There was silence.

Oliver smiled, 'I was coming to that. What the Tattler needs is an app.'

Marge and Benny were looking a little bewildered. 'What's an app?' Benny asked. 'I've heard of it, but I'm not sure what it is.'

'It's short for application,' Zoe explained. 'Basically, when you download an app you download a little piece of software that tells you certain things, or allows you to do certain things. Like, the Facebook app.' Zoe sent Sara a derisive look. 'It takes you straight to the site on your phone or your tablet, without having to go to the internet and log in. It sends you notifications too, so you know when someone mentions you, or if someone posts something you're interested in.'

'Oh.' Marge's face cleared. 'I thought it had something to do with Apple.'

Hattie snorted. 'Even I know what an app is.'

Alfred patted her hand. 'Now, now, Hattie, don't be mean. Not everyone is as computer savvy as you. I didn't know what an app was, either.'

Hattie looked contrite. 'Sorry,' she muttered. She quickly perked up. 'Okay, then, how does an app work when it comes to newspapers?'

Everyone turned to Zoe. 'I'm not an expert,' she said, 'but lots of people use apps. Some are free, some you have to pay for.'

David was nodding. 'There's Juliette's subscription, right there,' he said to Oliver.

'Exactly,' Oliver said. 'She can have a subscription for the physical newspaper itself, and another subscription to allow readers to get the Tattler via the app. She will be appealing to both ends of the market in terms of age.'

'Oi! Just because I'm old,' Hattie said, 'doesn't mean to say I would buy a newspaper instead of reading it on my phone.'

'Get off your high horse, Hattie,' Alfred said. 'That's not what he meant, and you know it. Anyway, it's not just an age-thing, because some younger people must like to read a real newspaper, surely?'

'Agreed,' David said. 'But if you want to appeal to a wider audience and a wider customer base, you've got to make it accessible to everyone. I know newspapers are accessible by simply going into a shop and purchasing one, but not everyone can be bothered to do that, or will think of doing it. They might very well think of downloading an app, though, if it's not too expensive and you make it worth their while.'

'But that's the issue, isn't it?' Father Todd said, joining in with the conversation after a long silence. 'I'm sorry to say, Juliette, but there's not a lot in the Tattler that would make young people sit up and take notice.'

Harriet asked, 'What do you mean by *young people*? Because your definition and mine might be poles apart.'

'I'm talking about people of Zoe's age and maybe a decade or so older. They are the future of Ticklemore; they should be the future of the Tattler.'

Juliette was glad everyone was arriving at the same conclusion as her, as it reinforced what she'd already thought.

'Juliette?' Oliver's voice was quiet, and he sounded a little uncertain. The rest of the people around the table fell silent as they waited for him to continue.

'You did say Brooke was taking a journalism and publishing degree, didn't you?'

Juliette nodded. 'Yes, but…'

'What do you think she would say if you asked her to write a piece for every edition of the Tattler? What would *you* say?'

Juliette didn't know how to respond. Writing for the Tattler wasn't what Brooke had in mind when she'd applied to do her degree. Juliette guessed her daughter had visions of working for the Times or

Private Eye, or something equally famous.

Oliver carried on, 'You'd have to pay her, of course. Maybe just a nominal sum, but then she could legitimately say on her CV that she is employed by the Tattler, and she'd have a bank of evidence when she applied for a job. That's got to be worth something. And on your part, she'd be able to write about things which affect her age group. Like the difficulty getting your first job, or worry about exams, for instance. I'm sure there are lots of other things that I can't think of off the top of my head.'

What he was saying was doable; set up an app, and have some things written by her daughter in every edition. It was a start…

While she was mulling it over, David jumped in with some practicalities. 'Can anyone here write an app?' he asked.

Everyone turned to Zoe. Her eyes widened and she shook her head. 'I know they're often written in Java, but don't ask me how. I work better with my hands than my head.'

She held her hands out, and Juliette could see a couple of blisters and the odd nick from some woodworking tool or another. Zoe was very good indeed at working with her hands, Juliette conceded.

David carried on, 'The first thing we need to do, is to find out a bit more about apps. I can do that if you like and I'll come back with a report next time we meet.'

'Good man,' Hattie said. 'And you, Juliette, you'll ask Brooke, yes?'

Juliette nodded. 'Zoe how about you? You're bound to have some things I can use in the paper.'

Zoe blushed. 'I ain't got nothing to say,' she said.

'I'm sure you have. How about you tell me what it's like to be an apprentice? And then perhaps we could do a whole feature on it, and I could contact somebody in the college, your tutor maybe, and—'

'I don't want to be rude, but I don't like writing,' Zoe interrupted.

Juliette smiled at her. 'Don't worry – you do the talking, I'll do the writing. And you can have full approval before it goes to print.'

'Or to app,' Hattie said, chuckling. 'What I think you should do, Juliette, is carry on the way you are for the moment, but prepare a whole load of new stuff for the paper's new look. What do you think?'

'I think that's a cracking idea,' Juliette said, and there were murmurs of agreement all around the table.

'Right, that's it,' Hattie said. 'I've got some homework for all of you. David, you've already got yours, Juliette you've sort of got some in that you need to talk to Brooke, but this is your baby, so I expect you'll be doing an awful lot more. I want everyone to go away and think about how the Tattler could be improved. And I don't mean the quality of writing – there's nothing wrong with that – what I'm talking about is bringing it bang up to date, and having a newspaper fit for the twenty-first century.'

Zoe piped up, 'That's the problem – newspapers aren't fit for anything.'

Father Todd said, 'They're not environmentally friendly, especially now you can't wrap your fish and chips up in them. What are they good for after you've read them?'

Hattie banged on the table. 'Order, order! We know this, and we know how wasteful chopping down trees is just to print a few words on, only for them to be discarded the next day.'

Silas said, 'Everyone should be recycling any newspapers they buy.'

'But that's not a problem, if you don't buy a newspaper in the first place, because you wouldn't have to use all the resources to recycle it,' Zoe said.

Juliette jumped in. 'Zoe, I want you to be not only an ambassador for apprenticeships, but also for making the Tattler more environmentally friendly. We've still got to consider those people who like to read a physical copy of a newspaper, and especially those who can't access the internet. I'm aware that as time goes on those readers will probably get fewer, and fewer, as the younger generation gradually turns into the older one, but I can't do anything about that right now. I have to think about my readers, and the circumstances they're facing today. Therefore, I feel I need to continue to run both versions side-by-side, a physical copy and a virtual one.'

'Here, here.' That was Benny banging his empty glass on the table in response, and making Logan wince.

'Does anyone have any questions?' Hattie asked. 'Juliette, before you and your young man disappear, I need the pair of you to think about what would happen if Ralph Trudge-Smythe doesn't want to sell it to you.'

Oliver stepped in. 'We have been thinking about that, Hattie, and it's possible, in fact entirely probable, that Juliette will continue to run a newspaper even if it's no longer called the Tattler. It will be a shame, but it would be more of a shame if the local newspaper disappeared for good. The format might change, and some of the features inside might change, but the essence will still remain, and that is to provide information and service to the community of Ticklemore.'

'Here, here!' Benny banged again, receiving an elbow in his ribs from his wife, who hissed, 'Have you been drinking?'

Benny held up his empty glass. 'Of course I have; you've seen me do it.'

'I only saw you have the one,' Marge said with a frown. She turned on Logan. 'What did you put in his drink?' she demanded.

Logan got to his feet and backed away, shaking his head. 'Don't you involve me in this. I served the man what he asked for.'

Marge shot her husband a filthy look.

'Come on,' said Juliette, pulling at Oliver's arm. 'I think it's time we made a move; we've got a lot of work to do. Thank you, everyone. I really do appreciate your help. It means an awful lot to know I have my friends and Ticklemore behind me.'

Hattie said, 'Same time next week, please.'

It wasn't a request it was an order, and Juliette knew most people would comply for fear of the repercussions if they didn't. Hattie might look like a little old woman on the outside, but she was far from one on the inside.

Juliette and Oliver were just about to leave when Juliette felt a tap on her shoulder. She turned to see Hattie standing behind her, so close that Juliette could have bent down and given her a kiss, so she did so anyway. 'Thank you,' she said.

'I haven't finished yet,' Hattie declared. 'I've only

just got started, but what I really need to know is, how much did Ralph Trudge-Smythe expect you to pay for his silly newspaper?'

'A minute ago you were extolling its virtues,' Juliette laughed.

'Yes, well, I wouldn't want to see it fold, but on the other hand I don't want to line his pockets, either. The Trudge-Smythes have got enough, and he should be ashamed of himself, and so should his father for letting it happen.'

'I'm not sure Lord Trudge-Smythe knows anything about it. And if he did, he might not want to get involved. He has let his son take over, and what would it look like if the minute Ralph did something somebody didn't like, they went running to Lord Trudge-Smythe, and he stepped in and overruled him?'

'I don't care; Lord Trudge-Smythe should have brought Ralph up to be a bit more considerate of other people's feelings. And of history. You think he'd know better, living in a mansion like that, chock full of all kinds of antiques and historical stuff. I've a good mind to—'

'Let's wait and see what he comes back with shall we?' Oliver said and Juliette was grateful for the voice of reason.

'How much *does* he want you to pay?'

Hattie was persistent, Juliette acknowledged. She looked around to make sure none of the others were listening, and bent down to whisper in Hattie's ear.

Hattie let out a gasp and clapped a hand to her mouth. 'That much?! The cheeky git.'

'It is a bit, considering he's planning on shutting it down. But I put a shot across his bows, because when I said no, I also told him I'd let him have a complimentary copy of the new newspaper, so he knows damn well I'll go ahead, with or without him.'

'Good for you. I've still got a good mind to—'

'As much as you'd like to help, Juliette's got to fight her own battles over this one,' Oliver said. 'It wouldn't look good if you stepped in; Juliette and Ralph need to come to an agreement between them, or not at all.'

Hattie didn't look happy about it. 'Keep me informed, please,' she instructed and Juliette nodded.

Once they were outside, Juliette heaved a deep sigh. 'Sorry about that, they can be a bit full-on when you meet them en masse,' she said.

'They seem like a great bunch. You've got some good people behind you.'

'Yes, I have, haven't I?' she agreed. She hadn't realised until now, just how supportive they were. She knew they had been there for Alfred and the Christmas Toy Shop, but for some reason she didn't think it applied to her. After all, the Tattler was a business, and she was employed. Alfred's situation had been a different kettle of fish – what he did, what he was *still* doing, had been for a good cause, because even now a percentage of the profits made by the Toy Shop was given to charity.

The rest of Team Tattler filed out of the pub (apart from Logan), smiling goodnight or giving her a squeeze.

When Juliette and Oliver were finally alone on the pavement, she turned to him. 'Thank you for coming tonight, I really do appreciate it.'

'It was my pleasure,' he said. 'Juliette…? I'm glad you got back in touch.'

'So am I.' She hesitated, wondering if she should invite him back for coffee, but she didn't want him to get the wrong idea.

As much as she wanted to, she wasn't going to take him to bed yet. It might never happen at all, she conceded. It would all depend how things panned out between them. She wanted an emotional, loving connection, before she took the physical one up a notch.

'I'll walk you home,' Oliver offered. 'Don't worry, I don't expect to come in for coffee,' he chuckled.

Juliette blushed yet again. She couldn't understand it; she never used to be a blusher but now it seemed she was doing it all the time. He was having that kind of an effect on her.

He took her hand in his, as they strolled along the pavement. His fingers were warm on hers, and he gently swung their joined hands together.

When they reached her house, he stopped. 'Goodnight, Juliette,' he murmured, before bending his head to kiss her soundly.

When he let her go, she almost changed her mind about asking him in, but she managed to keep herself together.

Although, as she lay in bed later, the other side of it stretched emptily next to her, the sheet cool and unwrinkled, and she wished she'd had the courage to ask him to spend the night. Not just because she found him incredibly attractive and sexy, but because she genuinely liked being with him and enjoyed his company.

The thought of him not being in her life now filled her with mild panic and the more she imagined it, the more panicked she became, until she finally realised she hadn't just fallen for him, she was *in love* with him.

And now she was faced with the very real worry that he didn't feel the same way about her, and the awful thought kept her awake long into the night.

CHAPTER 18

OLIVER

Oliver yawned and stretched, trying to ease the ache in his back after sitting hunched over his computer for too long. He was tired and his eyes felt scratchy, and he didn't know how much longer he could keep this up. This deadline was going to be the death of him. He was getting far too old to work into the early hours of the morning night after night. Not without sleeping until midday at least.

But he'd only had a couple of hours sleep last night, and he was at it once again, working on Otis's biography. At least he had the rest of the day to himself, even though he would dearly have loved to see Juliette. They hadn't made any plans to see each other again, although Oliver suspected he was included in the invite to the next Team Tattler meeting. He had texted her goodnight as soon as he got in, sending her kisses and hoping she slept well.

He didn't follow his own advice though, and now he was paying the price.

Oliver hadn't eaten much either; very little in fact since the meal Juliette had cooked last night. He'd drunk endless cups of coffee, but no real food. It was time he got some carbs into his body otherwise he might keel over, so he wandered into the kitchen, scratching his head and running his hands over his face, feeling the rasp of bristles under his palms. He could do with a shower and a shave, too. But first, food.

He didn't cook, he'd never been able to, but he knew how to shove things in the oven, so he took a frozen meal out, pierced its plastic film, popped it on a baking tray and put it in. He'd have a break for a couple of hours, maybe take a little nap, then start work again.

Oliver couldn't quite see the finish, but he could sense it. It wasn't too far off. He could make a tentative outline of the final chapter, which would consist of Otis's victory in being declared the next party leader, and the ultimate victory of being voted in by the people.

But although Oliver knew the procedure and he knew how the events would pan out, he didn't know the detail and that would be down to Otis himself. He guessed the guy was going to be extremely busy in the coming months, but he had insider knowledge as he'd been around when Grantham Bridges became Prime Minister. Oliver needed Otis to describe it in great detail, as if he was the one who had become Prime Minister five years ago and not Bridges. Otis could probably almost taste victory, and Oliver guessed the man would have no trouble imagining it or portraying what it might feel like.

It was a bit of an odd way to write a book, to send the manuscript off to his editor, the copy editor, and the proofreader, all without the final chapter being written. But it couldn't be added at this point, could it, just in case Otis didn't get what he wanted. They couldn't produce the book and have it ready to go, because what if something went wrong?

The phone rang and when Oliver looked at the screen, he saw it was his editor. Talk of the devil…

'Clifton, how are you?' he said as soon as he picked up the call.

'Busy, busy, busy,' the man on the other end of the phone said. 'More importantly, how are you?'

Oliver knew Clifton wasn't inquiring after his health or his wellbeing; his editor wanted to know how the manuscript was coming along.

'It's almost there,' he said. 'I've still got some things to iron out, and the final chapter to outline. But I'm warning you, it *will* only be an outline at this stage. I'm not going to write it completely until I know for sure.'

'Yes, well, best laid plans and all that,' Clifton said.

'What if he doesn't get in?' Oliver wanted to know.

'We'll just have to pray he does.'

'If he doesn't, we'll have to change the title,' Oliver warned.

'That's easy enough to do, but what we're going to call it I've no idea. I don't want to think about that. It would certainly affect sales if he doesn't make PM.'

Oliver didn't need to be told that. He knew full well that writing a biography about a newly elected Prime Minister would do so much better than publishing a biography of someone who'd nearly had it but didn't.

'When are you going to send me the first draught?' Clifton asked.

Was that a hint of worry his voice? Oliver didn't blame him. He was worried too. The timeframe for this book was ridiculously tight, and he vowed he'd never allow himself to be put in this position again. He didn't like having to rush things. He was meticulous, and he was worried that haste wouldn't make this his best piece of writing. Biographies might be factual, but that didn't mean to say they shouldn't have the same world-building qualities fiction portrayed. The book still needed to be engaging – not merely a list of dry facts, otherwise he may as well write a shopping list and be done with it. He wanted the reader to become immersed in Otis's life, almost as if they were living it themselves. And so far, Oliver didn't think he'd achieved that, because he didn't know Otis well enough, even after all the hundreds of hours he'd spent poring over everything and anything he could discover about the man.

'I'll have it for you soon,' Oliver promised; he didn't cross his fingers, although he felt like it. 'I do need to have another meeting with Otis soon, though, and I'm still not happy about the way everything has been brought forward.'

'I'll arrange it and get back to you.' He heard Clifton's heavy sigh. 'I'm not happy with the deadline move either, but you know the reasons for it. It all ties in with the next general election.'

'Couldn't it come out a few months later?' Oliver also felt like sighing.

'Look, I didn't want to say anything, but there might be another horse in this race,' Clifton said, 'So time is of the essence.'

Oliver said, 'I don't understand.'

'There are rumours that someone else is writing a biography on Otis.'

'But surely it won't be officially sanctioned by Otis, will it?'

'No, this is more like a warts-n-all version, from what I've heard,' he added.

A shaft of unease stabbed Oliver in the chest. Warts-n-all didn't sound good. It could mean this unknown author had discovered a few things that Otis wouldn't want to be revealed. Oliver suspected Otis had at least one skeleton in his closet, although he didn't know for sure, but what if someone else also suspected? Or what if this someone else knew of several other skeletons, all crammed together quite cosily until they spilt out, unleashed on the world in a competing biography? It would certainly steal his own book's thunder. And stealing its thunder, meant readers would purchase the other one, rather than Oliver's.

Should he tell Clifton his suspicions about Otis and Juliette?

As soon as the thought crossed his mind, he dismissed it. If somebody else revealed Juliette's secret, that was one thing. If Oliver revealed it, it was something else entirely. He wouldn't do that to her; he *couldn't* do it to her.

But should he prepare her for the possibility her secret might be about to come out? He *should* tell her – but what if he was wrong? This new biography might have no mention of an affair with Juliette, or with anyone else.

Oliver knew he'd have to tell her at some point that he was working on Otis Coles's life story to date, but at the moment he didn't quite have the courage. It wasn't a secret, yet he was keeping it secret from Juliette. It was for all the right reasons, he argued silently, knowing that the only person he was fooling was himself.

If he told her, he worried he'd risk jeopardising their growing romance. He couldn't even begin to wonder how she'd feel, knowing the man she was dating was writing about the man who had fathered her child, which no one was supposed to know about

She'd be looking at him and wondering if he knew. Wondering if Otis had told him, and she might even ask him outright whether he intended to put it in the book.

On the other hand, she just might withdraw from him, cutting off all contact because of the fear he would do precisely that.

Or, of course, he could be totally and utterly wrong about his suspicion that Otis Coles was Brooke Seymour's father.

But he was pretty sure he wasn't. The timings added up, and he had a hunch he was right.

Guilt that he wasn't sharing such vital information with her made him pick up his phone once again, as soon as the call with his editor ended.

But instead of speaking to her, he sent her a text.

I enjoyed last night.

It took only moments for him to receive a message from her.

So did I.

In one fell swoop his heart rose from his boots and soared up into his chest. Dear God, he didn't even have to hear her voice for him to be affected by her. He didn't think he could stand this much longer. Such swings of emotion were alien to him; he wasn't used to them and they terrified him.

Yet it made him feel so incredibly alive at the same time. More alive than he could remember being in his whole life.

To think a couple of text messages could get him so worked up.

I wish I could see you today, but I have work to do. He pressed send with a smile on his face.

So why aren't you working instead of texting me?

Because I can't help myself. What are you doing?

I should be working too.

So why aren't you? he parroted, chuckling as he sent the question, enjoying the banter between them.

He imagined her in the Tattler's office, sitting at her desk with the afternoon sun streaming through the window. He wished he was there with her, like yesterday, but although it had been fun he hadn't been able to concentrate as well as he should have done, distracted by her nearness. There was also the little niggling fear that she might stand up, come around behind him, and see the words on his screen, and that hadn't sat well, either.

He needed to be at home to write Otis's biography. He needed distance from Juliette in order to do that, both physically and emotionally, because he found it slightly distasteful that he was writing about the man who had got her pregnant. And he was also forced to admit he was jealous.

The revelation was quite disturbing – he'd never been jealous in his life. He'd been envious, nearly always over someone else's writing ability, but he'd never been jealous in the possessive meaning of the word. He wanted Juliette all to himself, even her past, which was quite honestly pathetic. They were both over fifty, and of course each of them had a past. But he wished things had been different back then, for both of them.

He gave himself a shake, recognising how silly he was being. The past was the past and it should stay there. It had made her the woman she was, and for that he had to be grateful, but that was the end of it.

It was easier said than done though, wasn't it?

He ate his food quickly, barely tasting it, and headed back to his office, aka his spare bedroom. But when he sat down at his computer, instead of carrying on with his manuscript he found himself on the internet, Googling ridiculous things like how to run a newspaper app effectively, and getting all kinds of silly hits.

He managed a few more hours work, off and on; possibly more off than on, if he was being truthful, but every time he tried to get back into the zone with his manuscript, he found himself thinking about Juliette. Her lovely face kept popping into his mind, and he kept hearing her soft laugh, feeling the warmth of her lips on his, the taste of her, the scent of her.

He struggled on until it began to get dark, then he gave up, recognising he wasn't going to get any more work done today.

There was something else he wanted to do, something that couldn't wait.

He had a quick shower, threw on a pair of jeans and a sweatshirt, stuffed his feet into some trainers, grabbed his car keys and his wallet, and headed out of the door.

It was already dark when he left Birmingham and it was getting quite late by the time he arrived in Ticklemore, but he didn't care how late it was, he just prayed she was at home.

As he pulled up outside her cottage, he noticed the glow of light behind the curtains. Aware it didn't mean anything, as she might have left the light on so she didn't have to come home in darkness, he nevertheless felt more hopeful on seeing it.

Heart hammering, he walked up her short path and rang her doorbell. It seemed an age before he heard a noise and realised she was indeed in.

He heard the sound of a key in the lock then there she was, standing in front of him dressed in silky pyjamas in a soft shade of dusky pink, with her hair slightly tousled, devoid of makeup, and looking more beautiful than he could remember seeing her.

This was what he wanted, he realised; to wake up next to her every morning with her looking as delectable as this. Minus the surprised expression. Her eyes widened as soon as she saw him, her lips parted and she was about to say something, but he stepped forward and gathered her into his arms.

Then he lost himself in her kiss for a wonderfully long time.

He finally became aware they were standing on her doorstep and he reluctantly withdrew his lips.

Her eyes were soft and dreamy, her lips a plump pink from his kiss, and he thought she might be breathing as heavily as he was.

'Come in,' she said, throatily.

There was nothing he would have liked better, but that wasn't why he was here. This wasn't a booty call; this was an "I'm missing you" call, and "I just wanted to let you know how I feel" call.

He retreated and shook his head. 'No, I won't come in. I just wanted to let you know I was missing you. And I wanted to kiss you.'

Juliette's expression was utterly bemused as she watched him get back in his car, and he gave her a wave before driving off.

Suddenly, he laughed to himself, joy coursing through him.

He had an inkling she felt exactly the same way as he did, and it made him want to sing with happiness.

CHAPTER 19

JULIETTE

'I don't like playing games,' Ralph Trudge-Smythe announced when Juliette picked up the phone the following morning.

'Neither do I,' she replied calmly. 'What can I do for you?'

'I'm a busy man, I've got better things to do with my time than mess about with a paltry newspaper.'

'Wonderful.' He had managed to insult her twice in the space of one sentence. 'We're both busy people, Mr Trudge-Smythe. What do you want?'

'It's not me who wants something, it's you.'

'I didn't think we could reach an agreement,' Juliette pointed out, gritting her teeth and hoping he couldn't hear her frustration in her voice.

'I'm prepared to give it one more go. If you can meet my asking price, that is.'

'And what is this new asking price?' Her heart was thumping, and she felt a little light-headed. She wasn't cut out for this.

'I'll be back in Ticklemore the week after next. I'll get my secretary to make you an appointment.'

She honestly didn't think she could wait that long. Time was slipping away from her, so she said, 'I'd like this sorted well before then. Can't you tell me over the phone?'

'I prefer face-to-face meetings.'

'OK, so I'll come to you. When and where?' She crossed her fingers and hoped he wasn't in Mauritius.

'London.' The way he said it, it sounded like the most important place in the world, and that she was far too provincial to even think about visiting.

'That's good, I'm going to be in London tomorrow, anyway,' she lied. 'If you can free up five minutes of your time, I'm sure I can juggle my meetings around to accommodate you.'

'Oh.' Ralph Trudge-Smythe sounded surprised. 'I'll see what I can do.'

Juliette thought the line had gone dead and she was just about to shout "hello", when she heard a click and he came back on.

'Apparently, I can fit you in at 11:45.'

He gave her the address and she hastily scribbled it down, and as soon as she got off the phone, she looked up the train times and worked out how she would get from the station to his office.

Her heart rate had slowed slightly, but it soon started galloping away again when she realised this was a perfect excuse to ring Oliver.

'Hi,' she said softly.

'Hi, to you, too.' His voice thrilled her. 'This is a nice surprise.'

She was inordinately delighted that he sounded pleased to hear from her.

'I've got some news,' she said. 'I'm meeting Ralph Trudge-Smythe tomorrow. He has another figure in mind.'

'What time?'

Juliette was sure she heard disappointment in Oliver's voice and she wondered what had caused it. 'Around about noon.'

'Damn. I've got to be in London tomorrow, otherwise I'd come with you.'

'What time are you travelling down?' she asked.

'I've got a lunch meeting, so sometime in the morning.'

'Then we can travel together,' she announced.

'Are you going to London, too?'

'So am I. Ralph said he wouldn't be in Ticklemore until the week after next, and I think I surprised him when I said I had to go to London tomorrow, so I could meet him there if we could find a suitable time.'

'Were you really going to London?'

'No,' she replied, cheerfully. 'But I am now.'

'Shall we meet up? Actually, I've got a better idea. Why don't I drive to yours, and we can travel down on the train together?'

'You'd do that?'

'Yes, I would.'

She believed him, especially after what he'd done last night by driving all that way just to kiss her. It was the leaving bit which had made the biggest impression on her. He could have come in and spent the night. She had certainly wanted him to, but he'd refused, and she'd fallen in love with him a little bit more because of it.

She said. 'Why don't we both meet in Worcester and catch the train together from there? It's only about forty-five minutes from Hereford by train; I'm not sure how far it is from Birmingham, though.'

'Hang on, a sec. I'm going to put you on speakerphone.'

She heard him tapping away on a keyboard.

'There's a train from Worcester at about eight-fifteen,' he said. 'Is that too early for you?'

'I'll have to be out early anyway if I want to catch a train from Hereford, because it goes via Newport and it takes forever. That's the problem with living out in the sticks. I'll meet you at the station at eight. How does that sound?'

When Oliver agreed, Juliette felt like jumping up and down and waving her hands in the air.

After a few endearments, they finalised their travel plans, and Juliette decided to ring Brooke. It looked like today was going to be a day for phone calls.

'Brooke, sweetheart, how are you? I hope I'm not interrupting anything?'

'I'm between lectures,' her daughter said in a soft voice. 'I'm in the library.'

'Are you okay to talk?'

'Why, what's up?'

'Nothing's wrong,' Juliette said. 'I've got a proposition for you – how would you feel about doing some work for the Tattler?'

Brooke was quiet for a second then she asked,' Are you serious?'

'Utterly. A lot has been going on in the past few weeks, but the main thing is the Trudge-Smythes want to close the paper down and I'm negotiating to buy it.'

'That's cool.' Suddenly her daughter sounded worried. 'You don't expect me to give up my degree to come and work for you, do you?'

'Of course not, don't be silly. I do want you to work for me, however,' Juliette said. 'The newspaper is stuck in a bit of a rut.'

Brooke laughed before quickly lowering her voice. 'You don't say! Don't you mean the Grand Canyon?'

'Very funny. Not.'

'What is it you want me to do?'

'Write a feature for every edition.'

'What about?'

'Young people things.'

Brooke laughed again and Juliette heard her being shushed. 'That's a bit vague,' her daughter said. 'And a bit random. Why do you think that's a good idea?'

Juliette explained her vision for the future of the paper and how Team Tattler was now involved. She could almost hear Brooke roll her eyes when she said, 'Oh, God, Hattie's involved? Good luck.'

Juliette knew Brooke meant it in the nicest of ways. Hattie was one of her most favourite people – she used to sneak Brooke an extra cookie or sliver of cake whenever she went into Bookylicious.

'Was this Hattie's suggestion?' Brooke asked, and Juliette very nearly told her it was Oliver's, but she stopped herself.

Over the phone wasn't the best way to inform Brooke there might be a new man in her mother's life. Although "new" wasn't quite right – Oliver wasn't new to Juliette, and by saying he was a new man, it made Juliette sound as though there had been hordes of men in the past, when there hadn't been any at all.

When (if) she told Brooke, she intended to sit her down and have a serious discussion with her – because by the time that happened things would be serious between her and Oliver. By the speed at which their relationship was progressing, Juliette anticipated the talk with her daughter wouldn't be too far away, and her heart skipped a beat; she just wished she knew what Brooke's reaction would be.

'Mum, are you still there? Hello?'

'Sorry, er, something came up. Um, where were we? Oh yes, writing features. If you can – and there's no pressure, so please don't feel you have to – I'd love for you to write some pieces on things concerning people your age.'

'Such as?'

'I don't know – you tell me?'

'The economy, climate change, crime rates… things like that?'

'Yes, but make sure it's from your perspective, not what you think Tattler readers want to read. Write it so your friends would want to read it.'

Brooke sounded excited. 'I'll do some market research and ask the students on my course,' she said. 'When do you want the first one?'

Juliette told her there wasn't any rush. She had so

many other things to do before the new-look paper was ready to go, although the deadline might well be less than three months away if she and Ralph couldn't reach an agreement and she had to publish it under another name. Because if she did that, she'd want the new paper to be totally different from the Tattler. If she could carry on with the Tattler, it would give her a little bit of leeway.

Feeling suddenly energised, she spent the rest of the day sketching out some of the features that would go in the newspaper and coming up with several more ideas.

By five o'clock she was exhausted. It didn't help that she was aware she was spending too much time on the new newspaper and not enough time on the old one. No matter what happened in the future, she had a paper to get out next Friday and not an awful lot to put in it. She should get started on it, but not tonight.

Instead, she dialled Nell's number. 'Are you up for me cooking you some supper?' she asked.

'You know me, I never turn down a free meal. With the twins in uni, I don't often bother to cook for myself. I know I should, but I'm too lazy. Is there anything in particular you want to see me about, or do you just fancy my scintillating company?'

'A bit of both. There's nothing wrong, but I'd like

to bounce some ideas off you, and I feel as if I haven't seen you in ages.'

'That's because you haven't; you've been far too busy with "that young man of yours",' Nell laughed, as she quoted Hattie.

'He's not my young man,' Juliette protested.

'You could have fooled me,' Nell said. 'What time do you want me to come over?'

They arranged a time and Juliette had only just got home a short while later when she heard a knock at the door. She was busy grilling a couple of lamb chops, and she yelled for her friend to come in, stopping long enough to give Nell a hug, before turning her attention back to her cooking.

Nell sniffed appreciatively. 'It smells lovely. What are we having?'

'I'm grilling us some lamb chops, and we are going to have sauteed rosemary potatoes, roasted vegetables, and cauliflower cheese to go with.'

'Is there dessert?'

'I think I have some lemon sorbet in the freezer, will that do?'

'It will do splendidly,' Nell said. 'Is there anything I can do to help?'

'Thank you, but it's all under control. There's wine in the fridge if you want to pour us both a glass.' Juliette couldn't help thinking of Oliver doing the exact same thing, standing where Nell was standing now, and she felt her heart give a little squeeze of excitement.

She couldn't wait for tomorrow, and she was pretty certain the anticipation was because she would be seeing Oliver again, and not because she was meeting with Ralph, or even visiting the capital – something she hadn't done for some considerable time.

After Nell had taken a long swallow of wine, she said, 'You wanted to bounce some ideas off me?'

Juliette opened the oven door and steam billowed out. Carefully, so as not to burn herself, she removed the tray of vegetables that she had sprinkled with olive oil and a little bit of salt and pepper, gave it a shake and put it back in, then she turned to face Nell.

'I'm going to see Ralph tomorrow. He has yet another figure for me.' She snorted. 'I doubt if this one is going to be any more affordable than the last, but whatever happens, the newspaper is my life; it's all I know, and I fully intend to keep it going.'

Nel laughed. 'I don't think you're going to have any choice in that, not with Hattie behind you.'

Juliette picked up her wine and drank some. 'You're right; the woman is unstoppable. I hope I'm like her when I get to her age.'

'I don't see why you can't be like her now,' Nell

said. 'Why do you have to wait until you get to eighty before you write your own destiny?'

'I was talking about her energy and enthusiasm,' Juliette said.

'And I was talking about the way she embraces life. She knows what she wants, and she goes for it. The question is – what do you want, Juliette?'

'I want to keep running the newspaper,' Juliette said without hesitation. 'Whether it's the Tattler or whether I have to call it something else.'

'Is that the only thing you want?' Nell was gazing at her shrewdly, and Juliette squirmed a little.

'Maybe not.'

'Then you should go after that, too.'

'It's early days, yet. But I am seeing Oliver tomorrow. I said I'd go to London to meet with Ralph and Oliver has got a meeting in the city, so we are catching the same train down from Worcester.'

Nell stared at her over the top of her glass. 'You really like him, don't you?'

'Yes, I do.'

'Good for you, girl, it's about time.'

'What do you mean?' Juliette knew exactly what Nell was referring to. 'I've been far too busy to think about the opposite sex.'

'Sounds like you're even busier now,' Nell pointed out, 'and from the look in your eyes the opposite sex is all you can think about. Well, one of them anyway.'

Juliette willed herself not to blush, but it didn't work. She could feel the heat in her face, and it wasn't from the grill, either.

'About those ideas,' she said changing the subject. 'I've spoken to Brooke and she's thrilled to be writing some features for the paper. I've left it with her and I'm sure she'll come up with some brilliant pieces of writing.'

Nell topped up their glasses. 'That's good news. What else?'

They discussed Juliette's ideas long into the night and she felt that chatting to Nell had been very constructive.

But throughout the whole evening, when she should have been totally concentrating on her friend, or at the very least on her impending meeting with Ralph, her thoughts were on Oliver, and she couldn't wait to see him again.

CHAPTER 20

OLIVER

Oliver had almost expected Juliette not to be at the station, which was silly considering he knew she had to go to London today, the same as he did. So when he saw her on the platform his tummy did a funny little roll and the butterflies in it began playing a game of tag.

My God, she was gorgeous, he thought. Dressed from head to foot in black, apart from a flash of pink at her neckline, her face lit up when she saw him, and he could feel a big answering grin on his own.

Oblivious to the other passengers, Oliver rushed over to her and kissed her thoroughly. When they pulled apart, he took a tissue out of his pocket and dabbed at her smeared lipstick.

Juliette pointed to his face. 'You've got a bit there, and there.'

He scrubbed at it. 'Is it gone now?' he asked.

She nodded. 'Remind me to repair my makeup before I meet with Ralph,' she said. 'I don't want him to think I've been dragged through a hedge backwards.'

'You look wonderful. I don't know what you're worried about.'

'When I put on one of my power suits and have a face full of makeup, I feel like I'm donning some kind of armour,' she told him.

Oliver wondered if it was a bit like the All Blacks, wearing their rugby kit and smearing their faces with paint. Actually, he wasn't quite sure whether they did that anymore, but he understood the concept. Certain clothes made you feel and act in a certain way, which was why he was wearing his suit today. He couldn't hope to compete with Otis Coles in the threads department, because his clothes weren't hand-made, but it was fairly decent quality, and he'd had it a while and felt comfortable in it. Besides, he had a suspicion Otis's gentleman's club wouldn't let him in if he was wearing jeans and trainers.

When the train arrived and they got on, Juliette slipped off her woollen coat, folded it carefully and he stowed it in the overhead rack for her. She popped her handbag on the floor down by her feet, and settled back in her seat. Oliver had opted to sit opposite, so he could see her face.

'It suits you,' he said. 'The pink.'

Now that she'd taken her coat off he could see the flash of colour was a fuchsia-pink blouse. It contrasted dramatically with her black tailored suit. She looked like she meant business. He sincerely hoped she did.

'I wish I could come with you,' he said, 'but I'm meeting—' He stopped suddenly before continuing, '—with my editor.' He felt bad lying to her, but neither did he want to be evasive and say something like "the man I'm writing a book about". It just seemed a bit odd, so it was better to tell a little fib.

'Where are their offices?' she asked.

'Oh, I'm not meeting him there, I'm meeting him at Rochford's.'

'Rochford's?' Then she got it. 'That's a rather exclusive gentlemen's club, isn't it?' she said.

'It is.' He didn't want to say an awful lot more, for fear of giving himself away.

Juliette smirked at him. 'I'm surprised they let the likes of you in,' she teased.

'So am I! They do allow guests though, as long as they are dressed appropriately. You never know, I might even be fed.' He sincerely hoped so, considering Otis had invited him for lunch.

'I hope the publishing company is picking up the

tab for that one,' Juliette said. 'Otherwise you might have to take out a second mortgage.'

Oliver didn't have a mortgage on his property. He'd bought his flat outright when he made the decision to quit journalism and turn his hand to another form of writing. He'd sold his tiny flat (it was about the only thing he could afford after the divorce) and moved out of London. Property prices were so much better outside of the capital, yet he still wanted to continue to live in a big city. Now though, seeing Ticklemore and the way the villagers had rallied around Juliette, he wasn't so sure he'd made the right decision.

They chatted all the way into London and the journey seemed to fly, but once they arrived at Paddington station it was time to go their separate ways.

Or so Oliver assumed.

When they both headed for the Circle Line, he asked, 'Where are you meeting Trudge-Smythe?'

'He's got offices in Little George Street,' she said.

'That's not far from where I'm going. Rochford's is in Parliament Square. Shall we let each other know when we're done?'

Juliette gave him a sad smile. 'I'm pretty sure I'll be finished before you. I'm anticipating my conversation with Ralph will only be a five-minute thing. I'll let you know when I'm finished, and text you which cafe I'm sitting in.'

Oliver suspected what she said was correct, Although, he could never tell with Otis; sometimes the man was effusive and wanted to chat and was quite content to let an hour or so go by, and at other times he was brisk and Oliver was expected to be concise and quick.

He had no idea how today was going to pan out. He supposed it all depended on whether Otis had enough support in the ranks of the backbenchers. If things were going well on the takeover front, Otis might very well be in an expansive mood. If things were going badly, Oliver's meeting with the potential new Prime Minister might be far swifter than he hoped.

Oliver kissed Juliette briefly, this time on the cheek, conscious of her newly-applied lipstick. Besides, he didn't want to ruffle her, because she was focused on the meeting with Ralph Trudge-Smythe.

'Good luck,' he told her as they parted ways. She was probably going to need it, but he hoped she didn't.

He wanted nothing more than for her to be happy, and if buying the Tattler made her happy, then he prayed she would succeed.

CHAPTER 21

JULIETTE

It had been wonderful travelling down on the train with Oliver, because he'd taken her mind off her meeting with Ralph. She knew if she'd been on her own, she would have bitten her nails to the quick with worry.

She hated uncertainty; not knowing what was going to happen with the newspaper was driving her to distraction. In a way, she just wished Ralph would put her out of her misery and tell her he wasn't selling. Then she could move forward, and she could also save herself a substantial amount of money. It wouldn't be too hard to start afresh, she knew. It would be very easy, especially with the backing of the villagers behind her.

But she desperately wanted the Tattler's name to continue.

She sighed. This was all getting a bit much. Her previously predictable and safe existence had been turned on its head, and she wasn't sure she was up for it. Ever since she learnt the Tattler was to close, she'd had difficulty sleeping, as the thoughts kept whirling around in her head. Although, most of them seemed to involve Oliver and didn't have a great deal to do with the newspaper at all.

What a time to be having such thoughts, when she was on her way to meet the man who was supposed to be selling the business to her. She needed to focus. She could do this, she knew she could. After all, she'd been doing it for years, albeit not as well as she might have done. She was a journalist, not a publisher, but since she had taken over management of the Tattler, she had been both. It was journalism she loved, writing articles, writing features, telling people's stories. The publishing part she had learnt along the way. Now that she'd learnt how to do it once, she knew she could learn to do it in a different format. The essence was the same, it was just the delivery which might be different.

She could do this, she repeated to herself from the tube station to the street where Ralph's London office was located. She found the correct building and stopped outside it, to look up the red-brick facade. Engraved plates outside listed the companies within, and she saw his was on the third floor.

She made her way upstairs and when she arrived she took a moment to compose herself, fishing a small mirror out of her bag and checking her makeup. Her cheeks were slightly flushed, but satisfied she passed muster, she made her way into the reception area.

The offices were larger and grander than she'd imagined, although she wasn't exactly sure what she'd been expecting. Giving her name to the receptionist, she took a seat. She'd made sure not to be late, and neither was she too early, not wanting to seem eager, so it was with grim amusement she watched the minutes tick by and realised Ralph must be deliberately keeping her waiting.

Nearly twenty-five minutes passed before a young man appeared and said, Miss Seymour? Follow me.' He turned sharply on his heel, not waiting to see if she was following.

Narrowing her eyes, she got to her feet and strolled nonchalantly after him. When he arrived at a door and halted, she took a tiny bit of satisfaction that he had to wait for her to catch up, before he knocked and opened it.

'Mr Trudge-Smythe?' he said. 'I have Miss Seymour for you.'

She entered, expecting to see Ralph behind his

desk, but instead he was standing near the window and a woman was helping him with his jacket.

Juliette hesitated.

'I'm running late,' Ralph announced. 'You can either come back, or you can walk with me. I have a luncheon appointment.'

Juliette swiftly gathered her thoughts. 'That suits me better,' she said. 'I, too, have somewhere I need to be shortly.' She glanced pointedly at her watch. 'I didn't anticipate being kept waiting, so I was just about to say you had better be quick, because I don't have much time. We can talk business in the lift, and if we've not reached an agreement by then, you can call to rearrange.'

He looked a little taken aback, and the woman who had been helping him put his jacket on sucked in a quick breath. Juliette had no idea who she was or the reason for her being in the room. Why Ralph wasn't able to put his arms in his own sleeves baffled her, before she realised this was probably all done for effect, to make him seem important. Juliette didn't need to be told that; she already knew he would be Lord Trudge-Smythe one day – he didn't need to display his power or his wealth to someone like her.

A thought occurred to her, as the woman opened the door for them. Maybe he'd been living in his father's shadow for so long that now that he was more or less free of it, he felt he needed to make sure everyone was aware. Including himself. This might be as much for his benefit as for those around him, and Juliette was fairly sure she'd hit the nail on the head. In a way, she almost felt sorry for him; it was a similar situation to Charles and Queen Elizabeth. Juliette bet neither of them had anticipated her reign going on for so long.

It didn't excuse Ralph's obnoxiousness though, and she was determined not to let him see how she was affected by it or by his position. He might own the newspaper, but he didn't own her. And the sooner he realised it, the better the pair of them would get on. Not that she wanted to get on with him, because once he had either shut the newspaper down for good, or signed a contract handing it over to her, she never wanted to see him again.

It looked like the woman was going to accompany them down in the lift, as she walked past holding a notepad and pen. Juliette smiled at her. It was rather remiss of Ralph not to introduce them. This woman could be his wife for all Juliette knew, although she suspected not. She could be a senior member of his staff, or someone who made his tea. To be honest, someone who could provide Juliette with tea whenever she needed it, would be senior indeed as far as she was concerned.

The woman didn't smile back; instead she kept her eyes firmly on the little digital display which informed those waiting for it where the lift was now. It seemed it was on the ground floor, and they would have to wait for it to come back up.

Getting fed up with playing these ridiculous games, Juliette said, 'What is your latest figure?'

Ralph snapped his fingers and pointed at the woman.

Juliette made a face – what was all that about?

The woman glanced at her, eased a sheet of paper from between the pages of the notepad and handed it to Juliette. She took it, this time without the smile, glanced at the figure written on it and tried not to let her dismay show. Ralph had come down considerably, but not enough, nowhere near enough. She still wasn't going to be able to pay it.

She looked at him, her expression as blank as she could make it. 'Thank you. But I will be passing on this, too.'

'This is my final figure. It is the least amount I am prepared to accept for the newspaper,' he informed her.

'I understand.'

'Do you want to think about it?'

'I don't need to.'

'What about that Pasco fellow you had with you

the last time? Should you consult with him?'

Once again, she said, 'I don't need to. This is my decision, my business. He was there only to advise me.'

He hadn't been there to advise her at all; he'd been there for moral support, but Ralph didn't know that. She wished with all her heart Oliver was with her now. She felt like crying.

'I think you should take some time to talk it over,' Ralph insisted. 'I will be in Trudge Manor on the 25th. You can give me your answer then. But, as I've said, this is my final offer.'

The lift arrived and all three of them stepped in, the ensuing silence like a fourth person in the enclosed space. Juliette was acutely aware of it, but she didn't have anything further to say. Ralph had made his position clear, and she'd made hers just as clear. A few days to mull it over wasn't going to make the slightest bit of difference. At least she knew where she stood now and could plan ahead.

She'd share the news with Team Tattler in the meeting on Friday. Their next task could be to come up with another name for the Ticklemore newspaper. As the lift glided smoothly down to the ground floor, Juliette's mind was jumping about all over the place. Son of Tattler, Tattler Junior, Tattler Two, all popped into her head and were all swiftly ushered back out again. The title could not have the word "Tattler" in it in any way, shape, or form. Ticklemore Times? Ticklemore Tribute? Ticklemore Trumpet?

The lift pinged open and Ralph stepped out into the foyer, the woman hurrying after him. 'Will that be all, Mr Trudge-Smythe?' she asked.

Juliette didn't wait to hear his response. She began walking towards the main doors, then she hesitated and turned.

'Get your secretary to give me a call and let me know what time you'd like to visit the Tattler's office when you are next in Ticklemore,' she instructed. She wasn't going to put herself out any further for this man. If he wanted a final decision from her, when she'd already given it, then he could come to her. She was done with going to Trudge Manor, done with going to his offices in London, done with him.

She made her way outside, conscious of Ralph behind her. She could almost feel his eyes on her back and it made her distinctly uncomfortable. Once on the pavement she stopped, took out her phone, and pretended to take a call. He walked past her without a second glance, and she let him get far enough ahead, before she began walking in the same direction.

They were both heading to Parliament Square, and she hoped he didn't think she was following him, although he didn't bother to look around. Why should he? He had no idea she was behind him, and even if he had, she knew he wouldn't care. She was most likely out of his mind, never to be considered again. She honestly didn't expect his secretary to ring her, or for him to come to the Tattler's office. He would probably simply start the ball rolling on closing the business down.

Juliette arrived in Parliament Square, the figure of Ralph Trudge-Smythe a few yards ahead of her, and she looked around for a cafe or coffee shop, but all she could see was one small wine bar. It would have to do.

She glanced back at Ralph just in time to see him disappearing into a door above which was a very discreet sign: Rochfort's. There was no indication what it was, just a sign and a door. Idly, she wondered what the reaction would be if she tried to walk inside. She'd be turned away pretty sharpish, she knew, even though it was sexist to have a club only for gentlemen, especially when some of the members weren't "gentlemen" at all.

Juliette ordered herself a gin and sat on a stool at a tall table in front of the picture window, and texted Oliver to let him know where she was, then she pulled a pad and pencil out of her bag and got to work.

If this new newspaper of hers was going to get off

the ground, she had an awful lot of work to do, so she might as well begin now.

CHAPTER 22

OLIVER

Rochford's wasn't an entirely new experience for Oliver. He'd been there once before, years ago, and he hadn't liked it. If you imagined a gentleman's club – and he didn't mean the sort with strippers in them, although no doubt Rochford's had had one or two of those through its doors in the past – this was it.

There was oak panelling on the walls, it had wool carpets that were possibly four inches deep, and important men sat around in winged-backed armchairs either singly or in groups, reading newspapers or other documents, and sipped golden liquid from crystal glasses. The only thing missing was the smell of expensive cigars, although Oliver was sure there was a lingering aroma in the air from all those decades of smoking. Employees, all of them men, glided around discreetly.

Oliver had been questioned as soon as he stepped through the door, and he'd only been allowed to get this far because Otis had informed Rochford's staff he was expected. If he tried to turn up without his name being on a list, he would have been quietly ushered outside. This place was where the great and the good networked, and it was also the place where many a man went to escape his wife or his mistress, perhaps both, and they didn't let any old riffraff in.

The club had its own dining room with an excellent restaurant, Oliver knew, although he'd never eaten there. The one and only time he'd been allowed in, he hadn't even been offered a cup of tea. Now though, a member of Rochford's staff led him silently through the members' lounge and further into the depths of the club. He led him past the dining room, with a tantalising sniff of food emanating from it, and headed for one of the private rooms beyond. Oliver knew there were meeting rooms here, some of them large enough to comfortably accommodate twenty people, and some considerably smaller.

Oliver was taken to one of the smaller ones. Inside, a table had been laid for lunch, with a pristine white tablecloth, gleaming cutlery, chinaware with the club's crest imprinted on it, and crystal glasses. A waiter was already there, and he pulled out a chair for Oliver.

'Mr Coles will be with you shortly,' the man who had shown him into the room said, then he left. The waiter retreated to the side of the room and stood there with his hands behind his back. If his surroundings hadn't been so opulent, Oliver might have likened it to being put in an interrogation room with a police officer standing there to make sure he didn't try to hang himself with his shoelaces.

Thankfully, he didn't have to wait more than a minute or so before Otis was shown in by the same gentleman. This time, though, the staff member almost bowed as he left. Oliver hadn't been offered the same degree of deference, and he was slightly amused by it. Everyone knew great things lay ahead for Otis Coles.

Lunch was delicious, and Otis was quite good company. He regaled Oliver with a few tales, amusing ones – they weren't malicious – which Oliver was free to use in the book, if he so wished, Otis informed him.

Oliver knew that these funny tales, which were very often to the detriment of the great man sitting opposite him, were being shared with him for a purpose. Otis was trying to let him know he was just a man the same as any other, with the same human frailties and the same propensity to make mistakes.

The mistakes were amusing and none of them very

serious, which made Oliver wonder what the more serious ones might be. Otis would never tell him, and Oliver wasn't stupid enough to go digging. He was being paid to write an authorised biography, not an exposé, so he would tell Otis's story the way Otis wanted it told.

Occasionally it occurred to Oliver that he was selling out, that he was letting royalties get in the way of the truth. And that might very well be the case, but none of his other biographies, and he'd written six so far, had told the whole story. He wasn't in the business of tearing anyone's career apart, and if he didn't feel comfortable writing about someone because he'd discovered information that didn't sit well with him, then he'd have no qualms about walking away.

So far this hadn't occurred with any of his previous biographies, and it wasn't occurring with Otis's. He knew the politician hadn't got where he had without treading on a few toes or pushing a few people off ladders, and he was no saint, but Oliver had no reason to think the man was any worse than any of his peers.

And even if he was Brooke Seymour's father, it wasn't up to Oliver to divulge the information. It made no difference to how well Otis might or might not govern the country or lead his party. Otis's wife might well not know, and if she didn't there was no way he wanted to break up a marriage.

There was also the possibility he was totally wrong about Juliette Seymour and Otis Coles. After all, the rumour that Juliette had been seeing Otis *had* only been a rumour. All Oliver had to go on was the timing.

Dessert eaten, Otis suggested they retire to the members' lounge to enjoy their post-lunch coffee, and Oliver guessed Otis wanted people to see them together. He was perfectly happy for everyone to know his biography was being written, and approved of by him.

Oliver had anticipated an hour and a half for the meeting, and he wondered briefly where Juliette was and whether she had finished hers with Ralph. He was tempted to get his phone out, but mobiles were frowned on in Rochford's, and it would be bad form to do so.

He would just have to wait until he was outside before he could see whether she had sent him a text. He hoped things had gone well, but figured they probably hadn't. Ralph Trudge-Smythe might come from a wealthy background, but he wasn't a patch on his father. He was known for being ruthless, whereas Lord Trudge-Smythe was more altruistic. He had a greater sense of history then his son.

Ralph looked self-important and slightly smug too, Oliver thought, then he realised it wasn't an image in his head he was looking at, it was the real thing. Ralph Trudge-Smythe was in Rochford's lounge, and was looking very pleased with himself. Oliver wondered whether the man's satisfaction was a result of his meeting with Juliette, and once again he was tempted to check his phone.

Trudge-Smythe swiftly glanced around the room, before spotting Otis Coles. A smile spread across his face, and he walked towards Otis with his hand outstretched. He didn't notice Oliver.

'Otis, my dear fellow, how are you keeping? How do you think the vote is going to go this afternoon?'

Otis clasped Ralph's hand, his other patted him on the shoulder. 'Let's not talk business, eh? Not right now. There'll be plenty of time later.' Otis released Ralph's hand, and shot a quick glance at Oliver.

Oliver smiled at Ralph; Ralph didn't smile back. Instead, his eyes widened slightly and he looked from Oliver to Otis, and back again.

Oliver continued to smile. 'Mr Trudge-Smythe, nice to meet you again.'

Ralph didn't look like it was nice at all. His face hardened, and Oliver guessed he was wondering why the man who had accompanied Juliette Seymour to a meeting regarding the sale of a provincial newspaper, was now appearing to be quite pally with Otis Coles.

Oliver decided to rub it in. 'If you're here for lunch, I can recommend the salmon. It was superb, wasn't it, Otis?'

Ralph's eyes narrowed as he realised Oliver was making him aware he'd had lunch at the club and with Otis Coles to boot.

'I wasn't aware you two knew each other,' Ralph said.

Oliver said, 'I know a great many people.'

If Otis wanted to introduce him as the writer of his biography, then fair enough, but Oliver wasn't going to tell the man why he was here.

Neither, it appeared, was Otis. 'We were just finishing up,' he said to Ralph. 'If you'd like to give me five to ten minutes, I can have a chat with you later. *If* it's important,' he added.

A spot of colour appeared on Ralph's cheek, and from it Oliver surmised that firstly, the man was being dismissed, and secondly, the offer to speak with him later was dependant on whether what Ralph wanted to talk about was important or not. Oliver guessed it wasn't important at all; Ralph just wanted to be seen with Otis. It would do wonders for Ralph if everyone thought he had the ear of the upcoming leader of the party.

Ralph, though, wasn't good at taking the hint.

Realising Otis wasn't going to say anything further about Oliver, Ralph decided to ask outright.

'What are you doing here? Did you know I was meeting Juliette Seymour this morning? I suppose you advised her to turn down each and every offer I made to her.'

'We travelled down together,' Oliver said, 'and yes, I did know, but no, I haven't advised her. She is her own woman, and she can make her own decisions.' Shit, Ralph must still be asking too much, and his heart went out to Juliette as he realised the meeting hadn't been a good one.

Oliver was acutely aware of Otis Coles's reaction when he heard Juliette Seymour's name. The man had frozen in his seat; he made no movement whatsoever, and Oliver didn't think he even blinked.

Otis's expression was very carefully blank and Oliver could only imagine what must be going through the man's mind right now. It certainly confirmed Oliver's hunch that Juliette and Otis had known each other very well indeed.

It didn't, however, confirm that Otis was even aware Juliette had a daughter, or if the daughter in question was his.

'I find that hard to believe,' Ralph said. The two spots of colour had grown slightly and Oliver could see he was annoyed. No doubt he was wondering how Oliver was linked to Otis Coles, and whether he should be at all concerned.

'You can believe what you like, Mr Trudge-Smythe,' Oliver said mildly. 'If Juliette has informed you she's not prepared to pay the price you're asking for the Ticklemore Tattler, that is her decision. She's not been influenced by me.'

Oliver was beginning to feel decidedly uncomfortable. Although he wasn't looking at Otis, he felt the politician watching him with as much intensity as a hawk watched a mouse in the grass below.

'You travelled down with her, you said?' Ralph was flustered, and Oliver wished he would go away. This wasn't doing either of them any good. 'I wasn't aware you lived in Ticklemore.'

'I don't, I live just outside Birmingham.'

'Oh?' It was said with a sneer and Oliver didn't have to guess what Ralph was thinking.

'We met on the platform at Worcester station.' Oliver didn't want Otis or Ralph to think he was sleeping with Juliette.

The cogs whirred as Ralph thought about that. 'A bit out of the way for you isn't it? And for her.'

Otis finally spoke. 'I'm sure this conversation is fascinating,' he said, coldly, 'but can you save it for another time? I am rather busy, and I have business to finish with Oliver.'

Ralph had no choice; he was clearly dismissed but as he walked away Oliver could see his reluctance in the set of his shoulders and the slight drag of his feet. He clearly wanted to pursue this, just in case his dealings with Juliette had any influence on Oliver's dealing with Otis.

Oliver guessed he would sell his right arm to know exactly what that was.

'What was all that about?' Otis was lounging in his chair, his legs stretched out, one hand wrapped around his glass, the other resting lightly on the arm of the chair. He looked the picture of nonchalance, but Oliver could almost see the tension radiating from him like the lines of a child's drawing coming out of a picture of the sun.

'It's nothing, just a friend of mine who has some business with Ralph Trudge-Smythe.'

Otis looked put out. 'What sort of business?'

At that moment Oliver knew without a doubt that Otis Coles had had an affair with Juliette Seymour. Otis was too full of himself to be interested in anyone else's problems. If they didn't affect him, he didn't want to know.

Oliver's fingers were tingling; they used to get that way when he was close to a story. It was the adrenaline surging through him and he felt ultra alert, which meant he needed to be ultra careful. Otis Coles wasn't a man anyone wanted to cross if they could help it. Oliver had to make sure Otis didn't think he had any idea about Juliette's past.

'I used to know Juliette Seymour years ago, when she was a political correspondent. She dropped out of journalism when she had a baby and went back to the little village she grew up in. When Lord Trudge-Smythe needed an editor for the local newspaper, the Tattler, she was a logical choice. She's worked there for years, but now Lord Trudge-Smythe has handed over most of his business interests to his son, and Ralph wants to close it down. Juliette has been trying to buy the newspaper from him.'

'Hmm.' Otis took a sip of his brandy, the glass nearly empty.

Oliver had hardly touched his, wanting to keep a clear head, especially after the glass of wine he'd drunk with his lunch.

'I take it Trudge-Smythe is being a tad greedy?' Otis said after a pause during which Oliver wondered what he was thinking.

'I expect so. I've not been involved in the negotiations per se. Juliette only asked me along for moral support.'

'How well do you know Juliette Seymour?'

Oliver took a moment to answer. 'Fairly well, I

suppose,' he said. 'I haven't seen her for years and years, but we recently reconnected when Trudge-Smythe told her the newspaper is going to fold.'

He picked up his drink and took the smallest of sips. Otis was studying him intently, but Oliver pretended not to notice as he glanced around the members' lounge.

Otis put his glass down with a thud. 'I think we're done for today,' he announced abruptly and got to his feet.

Oliver was more careful when he replaced his own glass on the table, not wanting to break the expensive crystal. He held out a hand to Otis and they shook.

'I want to see the final version before it goes to print,' Otis told him. 'I want to see every single version there is.'

'I've almost completed the first draft,' Oliver said. 'It should be with my editor the week after next.'

'I want to see it *before* it goes to your editor.'

Oliver shrugged. 'That's not normally the way things are done.'

'I don't care. This is the way it will be done with my biography.'

'As you wish.' Oliver knew what Otis was getting at, but the question was, had Otis guessed that Oliver knew his secret? 'I suppose it can be done,' he said pretending to think about it. 'But you have to get it back to me within a matter of days, otherwise my editor is going to go berserk. The deadline is tight, you know,' he reminded him.

'You'll have it back within twenty-four hours. I give you my word.'

Oliver grunted. 'Good, because this is your book and your deadline. If it's late, I'll blame you.'

Otis gave him a hard stare, then his expression relaxed and Oliver exhaled gently. That was close; his humour had diffused the situation and Oliver was hoping Otis believed Oliver wasn't aware of anything between him and Juliette.

Otis gave him a hearty slap on the back. 'Good man, I'm relying on you. I know you have as much invested in this as do I.'

Oliver nodded. 'If I can get it done a little sooner, I will. I just want to add some of the things we've talked about today, and of course the final chapter can't be written yet.'

'Why not?' The tightness was back in Otis's face.

'Because it hasn't happened,' Oliver said. 'I've written a draft outline, but not the whole thing. I don't want to tempt fate.'

'Leave fate to me,' Otis said. 'Write the chapter. I don't want to see an outline, I want to see the final thing.'

'As you wish,' Oliver agreed.

It was only when he was on the pavement outside Rochford's, the door clicking gently shut behind him, that Oliver breathed freely.

Bloody hell, that was a close call. He'd been in worse situations in the past, but back then he had been paid to be in those positions. It was how he'd earned his living.

Not now though; these days he put food on his table by a different form of writing, and he had to be careful. Otis Coles had the ability to squash him like a fly.

That wasn't his chief concern, however. What worried him now was that if he hadn't been sure before, there was now no doubt in his mind that Juliette had dropped out of the London journalism scene because she had been pregnant with Otis Coles's baby.

And if Otis Coles hadn't known before today that Juliette had a child, he did now and he was just as capable as Oliver at getting the dates right. One thing was sure, Otis had displayed an uncharacteristic interest in someone who hadn't been around for nearly two decades and who supposedly meant nothing to him.

He would only do that if there was some reason for him to do so.

Dear God; Oliver prayed what Otis had

discovered today wouldn't harm Juliette in any way. Because he wouldn't be able to live with himself if that happened.

CHAPTER 23

JULIETTE

Juliette had a clear view of Rochford's, and she alternated between checking her phone and glancing at the door of the club. She had been sitting there for at least an hour, during which time she had ordered and eaten a light snack, then followed it up with a glass of mineral water.

She knew Oliver was having lunch at the club, so she thought she'd better eat even though she didn't feel like it. It would be quite some time before they caught the train back and she arrived home, and she wasn't sure whether anything would be served on the train. Even if it was, the likelihood of it being edible was very slim indeed. So she forced herself to eat some lunch, and afterwards she rang Nell to give her the news about Ralph's offer.

'Don't tell any of the others,' she said to her

friend. I'll let Team Tattler know myself at the next meeting.'

'It's a shame he's not being more reasonable,' Nell said. Juliette could hear genuine regret in her voice.

It was, but no matter what happened, whether she could manage to get another newspaper off the ground or not, she still had her friends, she still had her daughter and her mother, and now she sincerely hoped she had Oliver in her life, too. The Tattler was only a means to an end, to provide enough money for her to live on. Running a newspaper wasn't the only way to do that.

She glanced out of the window again, telling herself not to be too premature. She'd give this new publication her best shot, and if it didn't work so be it. She'd cross that bridge when she came to it.

There was still no sign of Oliver, so she called her mum just to hear her voice.

'I can't talk, dear; Marge has roped me into collecting blankets.'

'Why are you collecting blankets?'

'To send to Africa. Or is it the Amazon? I can't remember. Anyway, we're collecting blankets to send abroad, so I've got to go knocking on peoples' doors. I'm not looking forward to it, you know. I don't like disturbing people, but how else are they going to know?'

'Mum, I could write something in the paper,' Juliette offered.

'Oh, could you, dear? That would be wonderful. I didn't like to bother you.'

'You didn't think of it, did you?' Juliette asked.

Her mother's voice was slightly sheepish when she replied, 'No, I didn't.'

Juliette finished her chat with her mum and let out a heartfelt sigh. That was the problem, wasn't it? People just didn't think of the Tattler. Which was a shame, considering it had been around for over a hundred years. She'd have hoped it would be ingrained into Ticklemore society by now. Juliette had always assumed it was, yet if her own mother didn't think to ask her to include something in it, then why should anyone else?

Was it her fault, Juliette wondered. Had she not been proactive enough in the visibility of the publication? She suspected it might be the case. She needed to get out there more often, do her own door-knocking, finding out more about people and about what was going on around her. She thought she had a finger on the pulse of the village, but quite clearly she didn't, and that was the first thing she needed to change. Although how exactly she was going to do that, she hadn't thought yet. Maybe Oliver would have some ideas.

Just then the man himself appeared, Juliette saw, as the door to the club opened and he stepped through it. He took a couple of paces, then came to a halt in the middle of the pavement and checked his phone. Even from this distance she could see a smile spread across his face, and she hoped it was because he was reading her text.

He must have been, because he looked up, his eyes scanning the buildings around him, and then he saw her through the window. She waved and his smile widened even further as he made his way across the street to the wine bar.

She watched his loose-limbed easy grace, the way he was so confident in his own skin, and she felt inordinately pleased she was here with him today, despite her less than satisfactory meeting with Ralph Trudge-Smythe.

A movement behind him caught her eye and she absently glanced past him, wondering who else frequented the famous club.

Shock flashed through her. Oh my God, was that who she thought it was?

She squinted, peering through the glass. Yes, it was. It was Otis Coles, and he had just come out of Rochford's less than a minute after Oliver.

Shaking slightly, because she hadn't expected to see Otis at all and especially not coming out of the same building that both Oliver and Ralph had been in, a feeling of unease stole over her and she hoped to God the three men hadn't bumped into each other. That would be too much of a coincidence.

Although, when she thought about it logically, why wouldn't it happen? Otis and Ralph moved in the same circles. They were probably at the club several times a week when they were in London. It was just unfortunate Oliver happened to be there at the same time. She wondered if he had seen anyone else besides his editor. The person he was writing about had to be somebody important, she thought, if the rest of his biographies were anything to go by.

Before she could analyse the situation further, Oliver had entered the wine bar and was walking over to her. He took her hands in his and kissed her, immediately soothing her with his presence.

'Is everything all right?' he asked. 'I take it the meeting with Trudge-Smythe didn't go too well?'

'No, he got his secretary to give me this.' She shoved the piece of paper towards Oliver who took it, glanced at it, and threw it on the table. He didn't seem surprised.

'Didn't he speak to you himself?' Oliver asked.

'He did, but he had this woman with him the whole time. He was getting ready to go somewhere, to the club you've just come out of, actually. And he kept me waiting for nearly twenty-five minutes. He was running late, so he said. He made me walk with him. We got as far as the lift and he told his secretary – to be honest, I'm not quite sure who she was or what she does for him apart from helping him put his jacket on. She gave me that. I told him we wouldn't be doing business, but he said I should talk to you first and then get back to him. It annoyed me that he thought I needed to check with someone before I made my mind up. Anyway, he said he'll be in Ticklemore on the 25th and I was to give him my final answer then. He also said he wasn't prepared to come down any further.'

'That's that, then, isn't it?' Oliver said.

Juliette pulled a face. 'I suppose it is. I honestly didn't expect anything else, although I was praying for a miracle. How was your meeting?'

'Would you like another drink?'

'Yes, please, I'll have another mineral water.'

Oliver ordered then sighed deeply. 'It was OK.' He bit his lip and Juliette wondered what was bothering him.

'Is something wrong?' she asked.

'What?' He looked distracted for a moment before focusing on her. 'Everything's fine, why do you ask?'

'You appear to be a bit preoccupied.'

'Do I? I'm sorry, I don't mean to be. It's this

deadline… it's starting to get to me.'

'Isn't there anything you can do to push it back?'

'Not really.' He sighed again. 'It is what it is, and I'll just have to deal with it. I'm nearly there; I've just got the final chapter to write. I had hoped I could get away with an outline but O— oh, no, I have to write it in full.'

'I'm not quite sure I understand,' Juliette said. 'Wouldn't you have to write it in full anyway?'

'There's, um… some things are not quite yet finalised. I was hoping to write that chapter after they were.'

'OK.' Juliette thought he was being rather vague, but it was his business, not hers, so she didn't push it. It was up to him what he told her, and perhaps he was bound by some kind of confidentiality clause. He'd tell her when he was ready, she was sure of it.

They finished their drinks then made their way back to the station.

Juliette felt deflated, even though she'd guessed what was going to happen with Ralph. It was human nature to have some hope, despite knowing deep down it was pointless and fruitless.

Oliver seemed to be immersed in his own thoughts too, so the journey back to Worcester took place in relative silence. However, this time Oliver sat in the seat next to her so they were facing the same direction, and he slipped his hand into hers.

Now and again, he'd kiss her cheek or stroke her hair, and occasionally they'd have a little chat, but both of them seemed tired, and she was content to wallow in her thoughts, happy that Oliver was sitting next to her and keeping her company.

'What name are you going to give the newspaper?' Oliver asked when they were about halfway to Worcester.

'I don't know. I had a couple of ideas, the Bugler, the Times, but none of them seem right. The Ticklemore Tattler should be the Ticklemore Tattler, not the Ticklemore something or other. Nothing I've thought of seems right, but then again, I haven't paid it a great deal of attention. I'm sure something will come to me.' She knew she sounded a little despondent, but she couldn't help it. The day seemed to have fallen rather flat.

It didn't have anything to do with Ralph, or the Tattler, or Oliver's slightly distracted air.

It was because of Otis Coles.

Seeing him had knocked her for six, and had brought back a whole load of memories she preferred not to dwell on.

Confirming to him that she was pregnant hadn't been a conversation she had particularly enjoyed. Neither was her determination to keep the baby. She had also been determined about something else, too, and that was to never reveal the name of her child's father – she hadn't wanted to cause his wife or children any hurt. When she'd told Otis this, the relief on his face had cut her to the quick, yet he'd made regular monthly payments into her bank account to support Brooke, and for that she'd been grateful.

She just wished she hadn't seen him again today, that was all. She hadn't been prepared, and with so much going on in her life, it couldn't have come at a worse time.

'Are you sure you're OK?' Oliver asked when they were about five minutes away from the station.

'I'm sure.' She sent him a small smile. 'It's been a long day, that's all.'

'I know what you mean, and I'm sorry I haven't been much company on the way back.'

'You've been plenty of company,' she said. 'I'd probably be sobbing into a hanky if you weren't here.'

'Are you really that gutted?'

'I don't know. I'm feeling rather overwhelmed, if I'm honest. I keep swinging between wanting to give it all up completely and do something else, and wanting this new newspaper to make everyone sit up and take notice. I feel quite strongly that Ticklemore should have a newspaper and I'm the best person to make it happen, but... I don't know anymore. I'm wondering if I'm about to bite off more than I can chew.'

'You've been chewing on this for a long time now, and it hasn't choked you yet.'

'Yes, but I haven't been much good at it, have I? If I had been, the newspaper would be in profit.'

'It can't have been easy for you bringing up a child on your own and running the Tattler. Cut yourself some slack. It's only recently, since Brooke went to university, that you've been able to concentrate on anything other than her. Am I right?'

Juliette felt the sting of unaccustomed tears. He was right; she *had* found it hard even though her mother only lived a few doors away and she had some lovely friends.

Having to juggle work and motherhood had been difficult, and when she was in work she felt guilty about not being there for Brooke, especially during the school holidays; but when she was with Brooke and she should have been working, she'd felt guilty about that, too.

Of course, it had become easier as Brooke got older, but until this summer her child had been her number one priority. She still was and she always would be – she just wasn't here so much. Which left Juliette more time for herself.

But if she carried on with the newspaper, all her

time would be taken up with trying to get it up and running. She might be worse off when it came to the amount of free time she had.

Assuming everything was going to go ahead and she was going to continue to run a newspaper, she'd have to be strict with herself. She should try to stick to office hours, even though she'd be working from home. She would start work at eight-thirty and finish at five, and take half an hour for lunch.

Oliver brought her out of her thoughts. 'We're here,' he said, sliding out of the seat to stand in the aisle.

She followed him to the doors, where they waited for the train to come to a stop. Once out on the platform, they exchanged several kisses before they went their separate ways.

Juliette was sad to see him go, because he had been a comfort to her this afternoon, even though they hadn't spoken much. It hadn't been an awkward silence, but rather a comfortable one, despite both of them being immersed in their own thoughts for most of the journey.

He was an easy man to be with, steady and undemanding, yet with an undercurrent of something which she could only describe as passion.

He was a man she was almost certain she was in love with. But instead of filling her with trepidation, as she assumed it might have done, she was filled with hope and anticipation – because Oliver was a man she could seriously imagine spending the rest of her life with.

CHAPTER 24

JULIETTE

If she had been at home, Juliette would probably not have answered the phone to a number she didn't recognise. But she was in the office, and numbers she didn't recognise were par for the course.

Her mind was only half on the phone call, when she said, 'Hello, you've reached the Tattler, this is Juliette, how can I help?' The other half was on the layout for the front page of the next edition. The lead story wasn't quite as meaty as she'd like, so she was considering filling the rest of the page with something else, but she wasn't sure what yet.

'Juliette?'

'Yes, this is she,' she said, thinking the voice sounded vaguely familiar, and worry pricked at the corner of her mind.

Don't be daft, she told herself; she was jumpy

because of yesterday, that's all. The journey to London hadn't done her any good whatsoever, apart from being able to spend time with Oliver that she otherwise might not have done.

'It's Otis.'

No, it couldn't be; she didn't believe it. But even as she was denying it, she knew it was Otis Coles on the other end of the phone.

'Are you there?' he asked.

'I'm here.' Her voice sounded hesitant and slightly strangled. She cleared her throat. 'What do you want?'

'Are you OK?'

'Why shouldn't I be?' Her voice was stronger now, more confident, although she felt anything but inside. Why the hell was he ringing her? He hadn't contacted her in nearly nineteen years, and then it had only been a simple phone call to acknowledge she'd given birth to a healthy daughter and to reassure her he would provide for the child.

'Brooke will be nineteen in a couple of months,' he said.

'I know. Don't worry, I don't expect the payments to continue.'

'Is she well?'

'She's very well,' Juliette said frowning heavily. She'd assumed the payments would stop on her daughter's birthday, as per the promise he'd made.

That he would ring her to confirm, hadn't entered her mind. It was quite crass of him. Or was he worried she would continue to make demands on him? If so, that was even more crass.

'She's at Bath University,' Juliette added. 'Journalism and publishing.' Not that it was any of his business.

'Like mother, like daughter.'

'I bloody hope not,' Juliette said, and Otis laughed softly down the phone, then fell silent.

Juliette felt obliged to fill the void. 'A little bird tells me you're doing okay for yourself,' she said.

Another laugh. 'I suppose you could say that.'

'How does your wife feel about being the UK's next first lady?'

'She seems happy enough'.

More silence. Juliette couldn't for the life of her think why he'd called her out of the blue like this.

Otis asked, 'How are you doing? Financially I mean? Are you going to be all right for money when I stop supporting you?'

'It's not me you're supporting, it's Brooke. And you don't have to do that. You never did have to do that. I'm perfectly capable of—'

He cut across her. 'I know you are, but I hate to think of you struggling.'

'It's not easy raising a child alone, but I'm not

struggling.'

'I didn't think it would be easy, hence my financial help.'

'It came at a price.'

'What did you expect me to do? There were other people to consider.'

Juliette was immediately contrite. She'd known what she was doing; she had gone into the affair with her eyes wide open, and it wasn't fair of her to lay blame now.

'Look, the reason I'm calling, is I can always transfer some funds to you if Brooke needs any help in university,' Otis said. 'She's bound to have student loans or some other fees.'

Juliette was almost tempted to accept, but that wasn't what they had agreed and she had to learn to stand on her own two feet. Otis's financial help had been more than welcome, but Brooke was an adult now, even though she was still in full-time education. 'No, thank you, we'll manage.'

'I've heard the Tattler is about to fold,' he said abruptly. 'I also heard that Ralph Trudge-Smythe is asking too much.'

'You heard right.' Fleetingly, she wondered how Otis knew, before she remembered they were members of the same club and guessed Ralph must have mentioned it.

Then he said something that sent her reeling. 'What would you say if I suggested investing in it?' he asked.

Juliette nearly dropped the phone. As it was, she fumbled with it and heard him call, 'Juliette?'

'I'm still here,' she said. 'Are you serious?'

'Perfectly. I'm assuming he's asking more than you can afford, and I'm offering to make up the shortfall. No strings, no obligations, just a straight forward business transaction to enable you to purchase the Tattler. If that's what you want.'

'You haven't thought this through, have you? That's very unlike you.' She didn't give him a chance to respond before she ploughed on, 'It's a kind offer, thank you. But you've got to be careful about investing in a media outlet, especially if I decide to publish something which is detrimental to you.'

He didn't say anything and she knew what was going through his mind.

'No, not that,' she assured him. 'What I meant is, when you do get to be Prime Minister and you make a decision I don't like, I'm not going to be shy about printing it. It would do you considerable harm if somebody found out you'd invested in it, yet I was slagging you off.'

She didn't think she imagined his sigh of relief as he said, 'That's true. Thank you for being so thoughtful.'

The other reason she didn't want him to invest, was because she didn't want to be any more indebted to him than she already was. If she had to have an investor, she wanted to choose the person wisely and not out of sheer necessity. She couldn't think of anything worse than being answerable to Otis Cole.

'Will you be OK?' he asked her.

'Of course, I'll always be OK. I've got Brooke, and I'll have a newspaper, even if it isn't the Tattler.'

'And you've got a new love in your life.'

'How the hell do you know that?'

'I know a lot of things.'

'Stay out of my love life,' she said. 'It's no concern of yours.'

'*Love* life? So it isn't a casual fling?'

'I don't do casual flings, as you well know.'

'Sorry, I wasn't insinuating anything.'

'Good, I hope you weren't. Look, I have to go.' There wasn't anything pressing or urgent, but she couldn't stand talking to him any longer.

But even as she ended the call, there was a part of her that was touched by his offer. For all his faults, and no doubt he had many, Otis Coles had never gone back on his word to provide for Brooke, and now he was offering to help Juliette herself. He wasn't such a bad man. Was he?

CHAPTER 25

OLIVER

Since they'd returned from London Oliver hadn't spoken to Juliette much over the past couple of days, only swapping text messages with her. Both of them were busy, both of them had work which urgently needed completing. But tonight he was going to see her again, and he couldn't wait, even if some of that time would be spent in Ticklemore's pub, surrounded by members of Team Tattler.

This evening, Juliette was going to inform the villagers that the Tattler would be no more, and he knew how difficult it would be for her. As he pulled up outside her house, he vowed to do his best to help her get the new venture off the ground. It was going to be a hard slog, but he had every faith in her.

He opened the car and as he did so he saw Juliette fly out of her house, pulling her front door shut behind her.

'I'm not looking forward to this,' she said. 'I feel like I've let them down.'

'It's not just down to you,' he said, scooping her into his arms and holding her tight. He kissed her hair. 'I've told you before, people often don't know what they've got until it's gone, and that will probably be the case with the Tattler.'

'I know, but I do feel partly responsible. The success of the Tattler was down to me.'

'Not solely down to you, surely? Lord Trudge-Smythe should have been a little bit more hands-on, and not just let you get on with it. It was his business after all, not yours.'

'I still feel awful; he entrusted me with it and I failed.'

'You must stop thinking like that,' he told her sternly. 'This is a new opportunity for you, and you need to look forward, not back. And,' he said, 'It's now time for... I don't know, the Ticklemore Belter.'

He was relieved when she laughed.

'That's a dreadful name. Although I haven't been able to come up with anything better,' she said. 'I'm going to ask Team Tattler what they think, if they can come up with a new name. Although, I suppose we have to stop calling ourselves Team Tattler from now on.'

They walked towards the pub, catching up properly on the last few days as they did so. He'd missed her badly since their visit to London and he'd felt as though a part of him was missing.

He had it bad, didn't he, he chuckled to himself. The thought didn't dismay him. Instead, he felt incredibly lucky that the woman whose hand he was holding, appeared to feel the same way about him. Abruptly he stopped and drew her to him, and his lips found hers. They stayed there for a while, enjoying their closeness, until Hattie interrupted them.

'For God's sake get a room, but leave it til later, eh, because we've got business to attend to. Are you pair going to stand out here snogging for the rest of the evening, or are you gonna come inside?'

He released Juliette, trying not to laugh. 'I quite like her suggestion,' he murmured in her ear, as they made their way inside the pub.

'Which one?' She sent him a coy look.

'The first bit about getting a room.' His eyes met hers, and for a moment nothing and no one else existed.

'Yes,' she breathed, and her voice held a promise.

Excitement surged through him; it was time, he felt it deep inside. He didn't know how much longer he could last without making love to her. She was driving him crazy, the scent of her, the dewy expression in her eyes, the softness of her skin, the feel of her lips on his.

'Can we skip the meeting?' he croaked, his voice hoarse, not quite joking.

'I wish we could, but we can't, so man up and get on with it.' She elbowed him lightly in the ribs, and he groaned. He loved this flirtatious side of her, but he didn't think he could stand it for much longer.

Praying the meeting wouldn't go on forever, he took a seat next to Juliette and draped his arm across the back of her chair.

Hattie winked at him, and he could feel a slight blush warm his cheeks. Hoping no one else could see and guess what he was thinking, he turned his attention to the pint of ale placed in front of him, trying frantically to think about anything other than the woman at his side. Which wasn't easy, considering he could feel her warmth, and smell her delicate perfume.

He kept his eyes on her while she delivered her news, and listened to the groans and the mutterings around the table. Once it subsided, Hattie spoke.

'I thought this might happen,' she said. 'The son isn't anything like his father. Lord Trudge-Smythe wouldn't have let this happen, but it has, so we have to get on with it.' She gave Juliette a sharp look. 'You *are* getting on with it, aren't you? I'm assuming you're not throwing in the towel, but you are going to carry on the tradition of a Ticklemore newspaper?'

'I am, and the first thing we need to do,' Juliette said, 'is to think of a name. We obviously can't call it the Tattler, so I'm hoping everyone could come up with some suggestions, and we can discuss them at the next meeting. There *will* be a next meeting, won't there?' She looked a little panicked.

'Of course there will be,' Father Todd said. 'We've been asked to help, and help you shall have,' he declared.

'Here, here,' Benny cheered, until Marge shushed him.

The next hour or so was taken up with the ideas people had come up with for moving the now-unnamed newspaper firmly into the twenty-first century. David gave a report on exactly how apps worked, and how they could set one up themselves, and received a round of applause in return, and he and his wife paired up to try and see if they could construct one.

Oliver was relieved to hear that everyone had something to contribute, and he couldn't believe how the villagers had rallied around Juliette. It was refreshing, and also a little humbling – if he hadn't witnessed it with his own eyes, he wouldn't have believed such community spirit still existed. Gosh, he wished he lived in a place like this – it restored his faith in human nature.

The meeting drew to a close with a vow to meet again next week, same time, same place. Friday evening in the pub seemed to suit everyone, and as Oliver looked around at the faces of these new friends, he wanted to know a little bit more about them. Hattie and Alfred were an item, he knew, so was Benny and Marge – they had clearly been married for some considerable time. Oliver got the impression that Logan was single, and he thought both Nell and Silas might be too, although he wasn't entirely sure. Sara and David were married, and Zoe most likely had a boyfriend, but that was it, that was all he knew about them.

It suddenly occurred to him that he should be writing biographies about people like these – ordinary people, people who deserved to have their stories told for no other reason than they were kind, honest human beings. They weren't famous, like Otis Coles, but their lives were just as remarkable.

An idea lodged in his head and a surge of excitement shot through him; maybe his next work might be closer to home, so to speak. His next book wouldn't be the biography of a famous person, but the biography of a village. It was a thought, one which he put aside for consideration after the first draft of this damn biography had been shunted off to his editor, and he'd had time to draw breath.

However, all thoughts of his next work and his current one were blown out of his mind when Juliette leant in close and whispered in his ear. 'Are you ready?'

His heart leapt, and he looked at her. 'I am, if you are,' he said.

'Are you sure you don't want another drink?'

'What I thirst for won't be quenched by a pint of Old Grizzly Bear.' He got to his feet. 'I'll be back in a moment,' he said jerking his head towards the bar. He needed to settle up with Logan.

After Oliver had paid the tab, he turned around and almost bumped straight into Hattie. He put his hands out to stop her from falling over, saying, 'Oops, sorry, I didn't see you there.'

He stepped aside to let her pass, but Hattie didn't make a move. 'I want to talk to you,' she said.

'Now?' He didn't want to have a conversation with her right now, not with Juliette waiting for him.

'Yes.'

'OK,' he said, realising he didn't have much choice and giving in to the inevitable. 'What is it?'

'About the Tattler,' she began and furtively looked over her shoulder. 'How much did that man want for it this time?'

Oliver wasn't sure whether he should share the information with her.

Hattie must have guessed what he was thinking, because she said, 'If you don't tell me I'll ring him up and ask him myself.'

She would, Oliver knew. So he told her.

Hattie sucked at her teeth. 'Ooh, that's a bit more than I'd hoped.'

'It's a bit more than Juliette hoped, too,' Oliver pointed out.

'How much was she prepared to pay him?'

Oliver told her that as well, knowing she'd winkle it out of him sooner or later.

Hattie tapped her foot. 'I want you to keep this to yourself,' she said, 'But I'm going to have a chat with the troops. See if we can raise some funds. We might end up being a cooperative, mind you, but we'll cross that bridge when we come to it.'

'I'm not sure a cooperative will work. A limited company might, with Juliette holding the majority of the shares.'

'Hmm.' Hattie screwed up her face. 'David might know about that. He's a sensible fella. I'll sound him out. But I don't want you mentioning anything to Juliette until we know what's what.'

'I won't say a word,' he promised. 'But you're going to have to make this quick. Ralph Trudge-

Smythe is back in Ticklemore in just over a week, and he's given Juliette until then to make a final decision.'

'Right, young man, leave it to me, I'll see what I can do. Give me your phone number and I'll be in touch.

They swapped numbers, Hattie entering his nimbly on her phone. 'You'd better get back to your girlfriend,' she said to him, slipping her phone into the pocket of her cardi. 'Go on, skedaddle.'

Oliver shook his head in amusement. Hattie was a force to be reckoned with, but he had warmed to her, and he felt a warm glow in his heart when he thought about what she was prepared to try to do to save the Tattler.

He doubted she'd be able to pull it off, but he didn't care, it was the thought that counted. Hattie had a heart of gold, and he felt privileged to know her.

There was another woman he felt privileged to know, he decided, as he saw Juliette chatting to Benny and Marge and Oliver suddenly felt he was an incredibly lucky man indeed.

CHAPTER 26

JULIETTE

Oh my God, Juliette couldn't believe she'd done it! She had taken Oliver Pascoe to her bed last night and had thoroughly enjoyed every second.

She should be exhausted because they hadn't had a great deal of sleep, and when she thought of the reason, her heart did little skippy-skips against her rib cage.

They had finally dropped off to sleep, but after a couple of hours Oliver had woken her again, gently showering her with kisses, and they had made love once more before they finally emerged from her bedroom and went in search of sustenance.

'I can do you bacon and pancakes?' she offered. Coffee was brewing and the smell of it percolated her kitchen.

'Sounds wonderful. *You're* wonderful.'

When she looked at him, her stomach turned over with sheer unbridled lust. God, he was handsome. There was a hint of stubble on his chin, and his hair which was still quite thick but peppered with silver strands, was mussed. He'd got dressed, but his feet were bare and she thought how cute his toes looked peeping out from beneath the hem of his jeans. At the thought of what they'd done last night, Juliette's own toes curled inside her socks.

Over breakfast, where he fed her bits of bacon and she poured maple syrup over his pancakes, they decided Oliver needed to return to his own home for the rest of the day, because if he stayed with Juliette it would prove to be too much of a distraction for them both.

Juliette giggled. 'I think you're right,' she agreed. 'I couldn't bear the thought of you hunched over the laptop, with me sitting there, watching you. You wouldn't get a scrap of work done.'

'I realise that,' he said, 'And I must get this damn manuscript done and dusted. Once it's out of the way, I'm all yours.'

'I thought you were all mine last night,' she retorted archly, and his sexy chuckle made her insides flutter.

'What are you going to do for the rest of the day?' he asked, mopping up the last bit of syrup with a forkful of pancake.

'Considering I'm going to be working from home for the foreseeable future,' she said, 'I'm going to turn my dining area into more of an office. The table is one of those that you can shrink down, so I'm going to do that, then sort out my desk. It's a bit cramped in the corner at the moment because I rarely use it. But as it's going to be my new workspace, I need to make sure there's room for a bigger desk, and maybe a filing cabinet.' She nodded. 'Yes, definitely a filing cabinet. I'll probably need another set of drawers as well, so I'm going to have a little play with the space and see what I can come up with.'

'Sounds like a good idea. Wish I could stay to help.'

'I wish you could, too.' She didn't want him to go, but she knew he had to. Besides, some time apart would give her the opportunity to reflect on their relationship, and on the wonderful night she'd spent with him. A little distance wouldn't be a bad thing today.

Just as he was about to leave, there was another moment where she felt sure she was going to drag him back upstairs to bed, but she controlled herself with some difficulty and pushed him out of the door. She didn't want to be the one responsible for him missing his deadline. She knew he wouldn't blame her for it, but she would blame herself.

'Go,' she told him and, with many more kisses and promises to speak later, he finally went.

Juliette was surprised how empty the house was without him. It was a different kind of emptiness to that which she'd experienced when Brooke had left for university. This was more visceral, she felt it deeper in her bones. It was as though he was supposed to be here, and she almost mourned his departure, no matter how fleeting his absence would be.

They'd agreed to meet up tomorrow for lunch. She was going to go to his, and she was looking forward to it immensely. He was going to take her to a pub near where he lived, which was renowned for its carvery, and she couldn't wait.

It wasn't the food that excited her, though – it was the thought of seeing where he lived. It was a bit hard this feeling of knowing him, but not knowing him. The man he had been when they'd first met, was different to the man he was today; not totally, but in subtle ways. She wanted to see where he lived, to gain greater insight into him. And to take him to bed, of course.

Further down the line, she knew that if their relationship continued, at some point he'd meet Brooke. He'd probably meet her mother before that though, as there was no doubt Audrey would pop in when he was here. Thankfully she hadn't turned up last night because that would have been embarrassing indeed. There was also the possibility of Juliette meeting his sons, and she was filled with mild alarm at the thought. This little bubble, just the two of them, was perfect. Once they started introducing other people into the equation, who knew how the dynamics might change. She just hoped her mother wouldn't embarrass her, and that Brooke would approve. Because if she didn't, Juliette didn't know what she would do.

The very fact that she was thinking of introducing Oliver to her daughter at all, was telling in itself. It showed how deep her commitment to him already was. She didn't make a habit of jumping into bed with men. The last one had been Brooke's father. And neither did she think she was another notch in Oliver's bed post. If what he'd whispered to her last night in the darkness of her bedroom was true, he felt the same way about her as she did about him.

Get your head out of the clouds, she told herself, and do something constructive, realising if she carried on daydreaming about him the day would slip away from her.

After telling herself off, she grabbed a duster and the vacuum cleaner and began work in the dining area, moving furniture around and experimenting with how the space looked. She didn't want to get rid of the seldom-used dining table altogether, because in the back of her mind she was hoping that one day she, Oliver, and Brooke would eat a meal or two at it together.

This morning the pair of them had perched on stools at the island in the kitchen to have their breakfast, but she didn't want to eat every meal there. That was the problem with open plan living she decided, after an hour of shunting furniture around. The living-cum-dining-cum-kitchen had distinct areas, but none of them was cut off from the other. They all sort of blended into one.

She could always try to make her office space in the dining area more separate by the position of the dining table itself, and maybe one of those double-ended bookcases which could be used as a divider. The more she thought about the option, the more she liked it. Something in pine, something light so it wouldn't intrude on the room.

Having arranged the desk to her satisfaction, Juliette decided to open her laptop and have a look online for some shelving. While she was at it, she could spend the rest of the day sorting out some files and creating backups.

It might not be morally right to use the Tattler's

contacts and so on, but she'd worked hard for those and it wasn't as though Ralph Trudge-Smythe was going to need them. What she was doing couldn't be compared to a lawyer taking clients away from the company he or she currently worked for to take them to another, for instance.

Although all the files were stored on the Tattler's computer, she diligently backed up everything to Google Drive which she could access from home, so the first thing she needed to do was to transfer everything into her own Google account. She would make a new one when she decided on a name for the new newspaper, but for now her own would have to do.

She supposed she could delay transferring the files until a new name had been decided, but she was reluctant to do so because she had an awful feeling Ralph might shut the newspaper down without waiting the full three months. He'd be well within his rights for the paper to cease trading immediately and he was petty enough to do just that.

It would probably take some time to copy everything over, but she had the rest of the day, and it would be the sensible thing to do.

Her laptop was still in its case because it hadn't been used since Oliver had sat in the Tattler's office working on his manuscript the other week, so she took it out and plugged it in. Before she sat down to work, she made herself a cup of coffee, smiling when she thought of Oliver sitting on the very stool she was sitting on now, as she waited for the coffee machine to work its magic.

She smiled even wider when she returned to her office chair, clicked on the Google icon on the tool bar at the bottom of the screen and realised Oliver was still signed in. Even after such a short amount of time in her life, he seemed to have touched every part of it and she was reminded of him again as a tiny photo of him popped up in the corner.

His drive with all his folders was displayed on the screen, and she was just about to log him out and sign into her own Google account, when a name on one of his folders leapt out at her.

One of the files was entitled *Otis Cole*.

Juliette let out a gasp. Abruptly her veins were filled with ice and her heart clenched. She had a horrible churning in her stomach and her mouth was suddenly dry. Why did Oliver have a folder with *Otis's* name on it?

A dreadful suspicion began worming its way into her mind. Was Otis the subject of Oliver's new biography? If so, how much did he know? Did he suspect anything?

With shaking hands, and knowing she shouldn't

but unable to prevent herself, she clicked on the folder to display its contents.

And she realised her instinct was correct – Otis Coles *was* the subject of Oliver Pascoe's new book.

She swallowed, nausea making her feel faint. There were several questions she desperately wanted the answer to, but only one of them was tearing her heart apart.

Was Oliver only dating her in order to discover the truth?

CHAPTER 27

OLIVER

Oliver wasn't a wealthy man, but he had some savings behind him. It wasn't a great deal, but maybe it would be enough for what he had in mind.

He wasn't sure when the idea first came to him, but gradually it had worked its way to the forefront of his thoughts, and now that the idea had occurred to him, he didn't seem able to think of anything else. Juliette's happiness was becoming increasingly important to him, which was why he was sitting at his computer and had logged into his bank account.

It was a bloody big decision, investing in a failing newspaper, but he had every faith in Juliette. He knew she could turn it around if she put her mind to it, and with Hattie and the rest of the villagers behind her, he was certain she could make a go of it.

The only issue was that Juliette mightn't be too

happy about what he was about to suggest. It was one thing dating her, it was quite another offering to be a sort of silent partner in her new venture. He may be better off waiting to see what Hattie could come up with. Juliette might be more disposed to several Ticklemore residents owning a small number of shares of the business, rather than one person owning a substantial chunk of them. Especially when that person was sleeping with her.

"Sleeping with her" was not the right way to describe what had happened between him and Juliette last night. For one thing, they hadn't done much sleeping (his whole body glowed when he thought about what they *had* done), and for another thing it just sounded too casual, too flippant. What he felt for her was hardly that. Last night had been amazing – *she'd* been amazing – and he seriously didn't want to do anything to jeopardise what was developing between them. Or should he say *developed*, because he was certain of his feelings towards her. It was time to admit he was in love.

It had taken him by surprise. He hadn't expected to find love again, and he certainly hadn't gone looking for it. He'd been content enough with things as they were, throwing himself into his work the way he always had done. But since Juliette had come back into his life, work didn't seem as important anymore.

Especially with what he knew about Juliette and Otis Coles. It was knowledge he wished he didn't have and it had soured the manuscript-writing process somewhat.

But that wasn't the whole picture when it came to his attitude to writing right now. He had a feeling that no matter what he'd been working on, his enthusiasm for it would have waned in direct correlation to how his feelings for Juliette were growing. He was consumed by her. Nearly every thought he had was about her. It was slightly terrifying and blissfully joyful at the same time.

Which was why he was worried about ballsing it up. What he was about to suggest would tie them together for some considerable time. He wasn't sure she was ready for that. It might be a case of too much too soon, as far as she was concerned. He knew she felt something for him, he could tell, but whether it was enough to go into business together was a whole different matter.

Confused about what to do for the best, he picked up his phone.

Hattie might be eccentric but she had a heart of gold; look at what she'd achieved with Alfred and the Ticklemore Toy Shop. Thinking it a good idea to sound her out, he called her.

'What's wrong?' Hattie demanded, without

preamble when she answered the phone.

'Why should there be anything wrong?' Oliver asked, bemused.

'I don't know, but I can feel in my water that something isn't right.'

'Excuse me?' Why was she talking about water? Did she have a leak?

'Never mind, what do you want?' she asked.

Oliver shook his head. She was definitely eccentric all right. 'I want to run something past you, and I want your honest opinion. I think I might be able to make up the shortfall between the amount Ralph is asking for the Tattler, and the amount Juliette is able to pay. What are your thoughts?'

'Hmm. I'm not sure. How does Juliette feel about it?'

'That's the thing, I haven't told her.'

'I can see why you wouldn't – just how serious is it between you?'

Crikey the woman certainly knew how to cut to the chase. 'I honestly don't know.'

'It's one thing her taking you into her bed, it's another thing her taking you into her business,' Hattie stated pragmatically.

'Yes, you're right. This is what's worrying me. We've only just started dating, and I'm concerned as to how she'd react to my suggestion.'

'I suppose it'll depend on how much she trusts you, how much she wants to purchase the Tattler, and whether she can see your relationship lasting.'

Hattie had hit the nail on the head. All three points were valid, and he wasn't certain about any of them. He trusted Juliette implicitly, knowing she would do her best to make the Tattler a success, but he wasn't sure whether she wanted it badly enough to have him for a partner, no matter that he'd be one of the sleeping variety; he grimaced at the pun. As for their relationship lasting, no matter how much he hoped it would, it wasn't a given. Especially since neither of them had declared their love. Perhaps that should be the next step, for him to offer her his heart before he offered her his money? And under normal circumstances he would, but he was conscious that time was of the essence. Ralph Trudge-Smythe would be back in Ticklemore in a few days and Juliette only had until then to give him her final answer.

'Why don't you leave it a little while?' Hattie suggested. 'I've sounded out a few people, and some of them are willing to invest and I've still got a couple more to talk to.'

'Will it be enough?'

'I'm not sure. It's not looking brilliant, to be honest. People are pledging what they can. My only hope is that they see it as an investment, and not a lost cause. They won't be throwing their money away, and Juliette may be able to pay them back with interest at some point in the future.'

'I don't think any of us have thought this through, have we? We can't expect people to hand over their savings without getting something drawn up legally, and we don't have time for that.'

'But that's what you are prepared to do,' Hattie pointed out.

'That's different.'

'Because you love her?'

'Yes,' he admitted. 'And because I know Juliette; she wouldn't allow the Tattler to fail. 'Can you do me a favour?' he asked.

'It depends what it is,' Hattie said.

'Can you not mention anything to Juliette just yet? I've got a few ISAs and other things I have to sort out and I'll need to speak to my accountant, but I won't be able to do that until Monday. I should have a better picture by then of exactly where I stand.'

'Mum's the word,' Hattie said. 'But don't leave it too long, will you?'

'I won't, I promise. As soon as I'm able, I'll talk to Juliette and hopefully we'll have better news by the time Team Tattler meets again.'

He ended the call, and sunk back into his chair.

The more he thought about it, the more ludicrous

the idea was, but the more he was becoming increasingly excited. It was the perfect solution for Juliette. They could even draw up some kind of an agreement which meant he wouldn't have a say in the running of the Tattler. This would be her baby, not his, and he had no intention of interfering.

The only problem would be trying to persuade Juliette to see it that way; to make her trust him as much as he trusted her.

CHAPTER 28

JULIETTE

Juliette stumbled through the door of the Ticklemore Treasure Trove, almost knocking over a large vase, and she hastily righted it, before stepping into Nell's outstretched arms.

Nell hugged her tightly, patting her on the back, and Juliette sniffed loudly, tears trickling down her face.

The pair of them remained that way for a few moments, then Nell released her and moved towards the door, locking it.

'Are you sure you and Oliver are over?' Nell asked as she led Juliette upstairs to the flat where she lived above the Treasure Trove with her twin sons, who were also at university.

Juliette followed her into the kitchen and propped herself against a cupboard, as Nell reached into the fridge for a bottle of wine.

'I know a cup of tea is more traditional, but I think you could do with something alcoholic. Are you sure about you and Oliver?' her friend repeated.

Juliette dabbed at her cheeks with a tissue. 'I'm sure.'

'What went wrong? You two seemed perfect for each other.'

Juliette had thought the same thing. She hesitated; she wanted Nell's advice, but she couldn't tell her the full story without betraying Otis. She was also keenly aware that if anyone was to hear first it should be Brooke, not Nell, no matter how close they were.

'I'm sorry, I can't tell you, but all I can say is I've discovered something about him and I never want to see him again.'

'Please don't tell me he's married?'

'No, it's not that. It's something else, from years ago.' She had to be careful what she said – Nell it was an intelligent woman and she'd easily be able to guess, especially since Juliette had never revealed who Brooke's father was. Nell might even think it was Oliver himself.

'What's he said?' Nell asked.

'Nothing. I haven't told him we're over yet.' Her first instinct had been to seek Nell out. But without being able to share the full details, her friend wouldn't be able to offer any advice, Juliette realised.

'Don't you think you should? At least give him a chance to explain.' Nell was itching to hear the full story, but Juliette simply couldn't tell her, no matter how much she wished she had a shoulder to cry on.

'I don't think I can.'

'That's a bit harsh. Doesn't he deserve to tell you his side?'

Juliette didn't believe he did. Confidentiality clause or not, he should have told her whose biography he was working on, especially since he knew her connexion to Otis.

Or did he?

Despite her distress earlier, when she'd realised what he was working on, she had run a search for her name and Brooke's in his manuscript, but nothing had shown up. Maybe he didn't know, and it was a coincidence? After all, *she* had contacted *him*, not the other way around. If Ralph Trudge-Smythe hadn't told her he was closing the Tattler, Juliette would never have phoned Oliver Pascoe. Never once had Otis's name come up, and although she'd told him about Brooke, he'd never asked who her daughter's father was.

Could that be because he'd already guessed?

Oliver would be thorough in his research, she knew. She'd been aware there'd been rumours about her, and so had Oliver. She recalled their meeting in Birmingham when he'd quizzed her about why she'd left London. She'd told him the reason was her pregnancy. He would most certainly have joined the dots. But he hadn't mentioned it and he'd kept the identity of the man whose biography he was writing, a secret from her. Why?

Was it because he intended to include this information in the book?

She was going around in circles, making herself feel sick and dizzy with trying to second and third guess what might be going on.

Before she could say anything else, Ethan, one of Nell's twin sons came into the kitchen, heading straight for the fridge.

'Don't you dare,' his mother warned. 'You won't have any appetite for dinner.'

Juliette was mortified. 'Oh, I'm sorry, I didn't realise your boys were home.'

'Just the one – and I think that's only because he needs his washing done. He's kindly agreed to accompany me to dinner this evening.'

Juliette finished her wine in two swallows. 'I won't keep you.'

'Don't be daft. It's only five o'clock. We weren't planning on going out until seven.'

Juliette shook her head. She knew how precious

time with grown-up children was, especially if they were at university and their parents didn't get to see much of them. She would hate it if anyone intruded on her time with Brooke.

'I've got to get back. Thank you for being a friendly face, and for listening to me moaning,' she said.

'Any time you feel the need to talk, I'm here for you.' Nell waited for a second for her son to wander back out of the kitchen, his bare feet slapping on the tiles.

Juliette felt fresh tears prickling behind her eyes as she saw Ethan's toes peeping out from beneath his jeans. They instantly reminded her of this morning and Oliver.

It seemed such a long time ago, so much had happened since.

She said goodbye to Nell, the pair of them hugging tightly and Nell once again advising her to speak to Oliver.

Juliette wished she could share the reason for her heartache with her friend, but she couldn't. She'd just have to deal with this on her own; not even her mother could be told the truth.

'Juliette!'

As she left the Treasure Trove, Hattie called to her from the doorway of Bookylicious and Juliette's heart sank even further.

She didn't want to speak to Hattie right now. She didn't want to speak to anyone. It had been a mistake phoning Nell and dashing over to see her. It wasn't as though she had been able to pour her heart out to her, but she'd been in desperate need of a sympathetic face.

'What on earth is wrong with you? You look like somebody has died.' Hattie's hand flew to her mouth in sudden mortification. 'Oh, dear, please tell me no one has. It's not your mother, is it?'

'No, my mother is fine, and so is Brooke,' Juliette added hastily before Hattie questioned her further.

'What is it then? Are you upset because of the Tattler?'

Juliette closed her eyes briefly and took a steadying breath, before opening them again. She wanted to tell Hattie to mind her own business, but that would be cruel and mean. The old lady was only trying to help, and it was quite lovely that she cared enough to ask.

Before Juliette could say anything further, Hattie carried on, 'Lovely girl, there's no need to get so upset – a little bird told me you might be able to buy it after all.'

'What do you mean?'

Hattie glanced over her shoulder as if she expected someone to be listening in on their conversation. 'I'm not supposed to say anything and he did ask me not to, but I had a phone call from your Oliver earlier. He thinks he might be able to… what was his expression…? Never mind; what he meant was he could make up the difference between what you've got and what Ralph wants. Isn't that marvellous?'

Juliette didn't think the day could get any worse, but it so clearly had.

Hattie must have seen something in her expression, because she went on to say, 'Please don't tell him I told you. He asked me not to – he's not even sure himself yet whether he can manage the full amount. Oh dear, now I've gone and put my foot in it, haven't I?'

Juliette took another deep breath before she said, 'I'm glad you told me, Hattie. It's better to know these things, isn't it?'

'Promise you won't tell him I told you?'

Although Hattie was upset, Juliette couldn't promise anything. 'I'm afraid I'm going to have to. You see, Oliver and I are going our separate ways. I can't accept his offer.'

'Oh dear, it's nothing I've said, is it?'

The old lady looked distraught, and Juliette hastened to reassure her. 'It most definitely isn't.'

Unsure whether she could keep a grip on her emotions for much longer, Juliette gave Hattie a reassuring hug and promised to see her at the next Team Tattler meeting before making her escape.

White-hot anger joined her heartbreak. How dare he? Just a few hours ago she had been marvelling how he seemed to be infiltrating every part of her life. Now, though, she was absolutely furious he seemed hell-bent on taking over her newspaper.

She didn't wait until she got home. Instead, she came to a shaking halt on the little bridge over the river and dialled his number with trembling fingers.

He was only able to say 'Juliette' in that sultry voice of his, before she launched her attack.

'How dare you! I can't believe you'd do this to me. I trusted you. And now you go and do this. I never want to see you again, Oliver Pascoe. You can keep your sodding money, I don't need it. The Tattler doesn't need it. Stay out of my life!'

She ended the call abruptly, tears wetting her cheeks. Breathless sobs escaped her and all she wanted to do was to curl up in a ball and pretend these last few weeks had never happened.

The ringing of her phone made her jump and she looked at the screen. It was Oliver.

With a frustrated scream, she drew her arm back and flung her phone as far as she could. It entered the water with a splash, then was gone. There was no trace of it. It had disappeared as completely as she intended for Oliver to disappear from her life.

But he wouldn't disappear though, would he, not if he was going to expose her and Otis in his book. Soon the whole world would know, and the thought sent her reeling.

CHAPTER 29

OLIVER

Oliver stared at his screen. What the hell had just happened? He tried ringing Juliette again, but she must have turned her phone off. Bloody Hattie – he'd asked her not to say anything to Juliette, but only a couple of hours later she'd gone and done the very thing he'd asked her not to. And now Juliette was furious with him.

He had to explain; she must be thinking he wanted to take over the Tattler, when he so definitely didn't. If the thought of him investing in the newspaper made her this unhappy, he needed to tell her that was all it had been, a *thought* – he didn't intend to go through with it if she didn't like the idea.

But surely she could have just said "thanks, but no thanks", without getting so upset. Her reaction had been way over the top, and he couldn't understand why.

And now she was refusing to answer his calls.

There was nothing for it; he'd have to drive over to Ticklemore and speak to her in person. He had to get to the bottom of this and put it right. A sharp pain of anguish gripped his heart where minutes before it had been brimming with happiness. He was determined to sort it out. She'd got the wrong end of the stick somehow – goodness knows what Hattie had said to her.

Oliver was tempted to phone Hattie right now and give her a piece of his mind, but he didn't. He didn't want to upset the old lady; she only had Juliette's best interests at heart, and if something had got lost in translation, then it was his fault. He should have spoken to Juliette first. No wonder she was cross with him, but being cross was one thing, telling him she never wanted to see him again was something else.

He made the journey from Birmingham to Ticklemore in record time, desperate to see her. He was sick of telling Siri to call Juliette, and he was sick of getting the same unavailable tone. He must have called her thirty times over the course of the journey, and he was beginning to feel she must think he was totally deranged.

Maybe he was; the thought of never seeing her again hurt far worse than anything he'd ever experienced before.

Finally he arrived, and he pulled up outside her cottage, craning his neck to see if there was any movement. It wasn't yet dark enough for her to have switched any lights on, so he couldn't tell whether she was in or not. He prayed she was, because he didn't fancy wandering around Ticklemore trying to find her.

Gathering his courage, he pressed her doorbell, his mouth dry, and his palms damp, and he shuffled from foot to foot to stop himself from shaking. His heart was hammering, an answering throb pulsed in his temple, and his jaw ached from where he'd been clenching his teeth. He swallowed convulsively when he heard a noise from inside, and suddenly there she was, standing in the open doorway, looking as though she'd been crying.

She took one look at him and said, 'I thought I told you I never wanted to see you again.'

'I was only trying to help,' he began.

'I don't call prying into my private life helping.' She went to shut the door on him, and he stuck his foot between it and the frame, wincing as he did so. He prayed he hadn't broken anything.

'What do you mean? I'm not prying. I won't have anything to do with the Tattler; I'm just offering you a means to purchase it.'

She shot him a disbelieving glare. 'I hope you weren't too disappointed when you had a good look around my computer the other day. Did you honestly expect to find anything about Brooke's father on there?'

Shit. This wasn't about him offering to invest in the newspaper, he realised – she'd discovered he knew about her and Otis. Bugger. This wasn't going to be so easy to explain. He should have told her right from the start...

'Did you think I wouldn't find out that you're writing a biography about Otis Coles?' she demanded. 'If you put anything about Brooke or me in your book, I'm not going to be responsible for my actions.'

'Why would you think I'd do something like that?'

'Ha! Why wouldn't you? That would be a scoop, wouldn't it? It might help sell your bloody book for you.'

'I'd never do anything to hurt you. I wouldn't dream of putting it in. Besides, Otis wouldn't let me.'

'You've spoken to *Otis* about this? When? Where?' The penny must have dropped because she became even angrier. 'It was him you went to see in London, wasn't it?'

'Yes, but—'

'I hate you! Stay out of my life, stay out of Brooke's life, and stay away from Otis.'

'I can't, I'm writing his biography.'

'I don't care what you're writing, just stay away from me and stay away from my daughter. I can't believe you'd do this to me. I thought we had something. I loved you, damn it!'

Wait, what?

Oliver lurched back in shock and she used the opportunity to push the door shut. He had no choice but to remove his foot as she slammed the door in his face.

'Juliette!' he yelled through the letter box and rang the bell, keeping his finger on the buzzer. 'Please let me explain. Talk to me!'

'The only talking I'm going to do is to the police if you don't go away. You've got thirty seconds before I call them.'

He stepped away from the door disbelievingly. 'So this is it? This is the end of us?'

'Too bloody right it is.'

She'd just said she loved him – how could someone go from love to hate so quickly?

Having little choice, he walked slowly back to his car, his mind reeling. The only thought he could grasp was that she'd told him she loved him. And that she didn't want anything to do with him ever again.

CHAPTER 30

JULIETTE

Juliette slumped against the door, then sank to the floor and held her head in her hands. She tried to hold the sobs inside for fear Oliver might hear, but she couldn't help it. She'd told him to leave, had even threatened him with the police, but when she heard his car start and the sound of the engine gradually diminished, she realised she'd got what she wanted. He was gone, out of her life for good. So why was she feeling so awful?

Did Oliver honestly think he could keep it from her that he had written Otis's biography? She was bound to find out when the book was published, so when had he been planning on telling her? She'd not found any evidence he intended to expose her in the files she'd seen, but that didn't mean Oliver wasn't going to do it.

Dear God, what a mess.

She felt even more betrayed when she remembered he had met with Otis in London. No wonder Otis knew so much about her – it was Oliver who had told him.

But did Otis realise Oliver knew their secret?

She'd have to speak to him. If Oliver was intending to publish the information…

With her heart in her mouth she reached into the pocket of her jeans for her phone, before remembering she'd thrown it in the river.

Damn it – that was the only place she'd stored his personal number. She'd have to email him, instead. This couldn't wait until Monday when she could phone his office. Not knowing who might read his emails and praying to God this one wouldn't end up in his Spam folder or that a secretary would delete it, Juliette typed three words.

Oliver Pascoe knows

.

CHAPTER 31

OLIVER

Oliver's phone pinged, indicating he had a message and he lunged for it, hoping it would be from Juliette.

It wasn't.

It was a message from Otis Cole. **We need to talk. I'm sending a car for you.**

Bugger. Did this mean what he thought it meant? That Otis knew that he knew about him and Juliette? Double bugger.

The journey was a long one, and when Oliver asked the driver where they were headed, he was shocked to be told he was being driven to Otis's home in Surrey.

The man must seriously want to speak with him.

Otis was waiting and he didn't look happy. He was pacing up and down the length of his living room, his hand on his hips and a frown on his face.

'What do you know about Brooke Seymour?' was his opening line, even before Oliver was fully in the room.

'Um, she's Juliette Seymour's daughter, she's eighteen and she's studying journalism at Bath University. She's also helping out with her mother's newspaper,' Oliver added, not liking the direction the conversation was taking.

'And her father's identity? What do you intend to do with the information?'

Oliver stuttered. 'Nothing. I love Juliette far too much to do anything to hurt her. Neither do I want to harm your career. The past is the past – everyone makes mistakes. It might come out though, if you have any other skeletons in your closet.'

Otis gave a grim smile. 'I have no other skeletons.'

'Good. The public would probably excuse you having a love child from an affair twenty years ago, but anything more recent wouldn't do your career any good.'

To Oliver's surprise, Otis barked out a laugh. 'An affair?' He shook his head, his expression bemused.

'Are you denying you had an affair with Juliette?' Oliver demanded.

'Do you love her?'

The question took Oliver's breath away.

He looked at his feet. This was awkward. He didn't

want to discuss how he felt about Juliette with the man who she'd shared a bed with and who had fathered her baby. And it was typical of a politician to answer a question with a question.

'You do, don't you?' Otis pushed.

Oliver's head came up and he stared him straight in the eye. The love he held for her was nothing to be ashamed of. 'Yes.'

Otis let out a breath. 'I wasn't the man she had an affair with. I'm not the father of her child.' He scrutinised Oliver, his gaze sharp, and he seemed to arrive at a decision. 'What I'm about to tell you isn't for public consumption. I'm only telling you this because I see you care for her, and I get the feeling she cares for you. I don't want this to come between you.'

He nodded to himself, then he began to speak. 'Juliette met my brother on the same day she met me. Even if I'd wanted to chance my arm with her – which I didn't – it was clear she had eyes only for him. She was smitten as was he. I didn't condone it. He had a wife and two children, and God knows how the thing between them would have panned out, or whether it would have lasted, but he received his diagnosis and that changed everything.'

Otis sucked in a breath and blew it out again, his cheeks expanding. 'However, before Finley could break the news to her, Juliette told him she was pregnant. I suspect she mightn't have told him at all if she'd known about his cancer beforehand. She was devastated, but when she said she intended to keep the baby, he begged her to keep quiet about the child's parentage. He didn't want to put his wife and children through any more, you see. Neither did Juliette. Which was where I came in. I arranged for monies from my own account to be paid to Juliette for Brooke's upkeep. Finley and I agreed that Juliette shouldn't have to struggle, but he was unable to make arrangements for their child without his wife knowing.'

'You paid maintenance all these years for a child that wasn't yours?' Oliver was incredulous.

Otis shrugged. 'I don't care if you don't believe me. You can ask Juliette. She seems to think you know all about it anyway. She emailed me today.' He glanced at the clock on his mantelpiece. 'Yesterday, now.'

Oliver was flabbergasted. 'I've got it all wrong,' he admitted. 'But even if I hadn't and this biography of yours wasn't an authorised version, I still wouldn't have included it in the book.'

Otis studied him. Oliver maintained eye-contact without flinching; he was telling the truth.

'I believe you,' Otis said. 'I think Juliette may take

some convincing, though. You should have told her as soon as you had your suspicions.'

'I've made a complete hash of it, haven't I?'

Otis shrugged. 'You've been professional and not discussed your work. I like that. Do you want me to have a word with her for you?'

Oliver was quite affronted to think he needed help from Otis. He raised his eyes to the ceiling for a moment whilst he composed himself. He'd try to speak to Juliette again, to explain, but he had an awful feeling she'd continue to refuse to hear him out.

There might be something Otis could do, though. Not for him, but for Juliette.

'No, I'll fight my own battles, thank you. Juliette, however, can't fight one of hers. Any chance of talking some sense into Ralph Trudge-Smythe?' He might have burned his bridges with the woman he loved, but the least he could do was to try to make her dream of owning the Tattler come true.

'I take it you're referring to the newspaper she manages?'

'I am. I was going to offer to help her with purchasing it, but…'

Otis smiled. 'I'll see what I can do. Trudge-Smythe might be greedy, but I'm sure I can make him see sense. A bird in the hand is worth two in the bush, so they say. Anything he gets for that newspaper will be better than nothing. I suspect he doesn't like losing, and he certainly seemed to take a dislike to you.'

'Believe me, the feeling is mutual.'

'Pompous sod, isn't he?' Otis showed him out. 'Leave it with me. I'll let you know how I get on, and if Trudge-Smythe doesn't play ball, maybe we could come to some arrangement to help her out together. She needn't know anything about it.' He held out a hand and Oliver shook it. 'My driver will take you back. I hope you didn't mind me sending for you, but I thought it best to meet face-to-face and sooner rather than later.'

Oliver didn't mind at all. What Otis had shared with him gave him a different perspective on the man, and Oliver couldn't wait to get back to his manuscript. Although he had no intention of writing about what he knew, the new regard he held for the man would colour the whole book. Otis Coles wasn't as hard-nosed as Oliver had thought. The man was compassionate and honourable, and Oliver wanted to make sure this was reflected in the biography.

First, though, he had something more important to do.

He had to try to convince Juliette he loved her.

CHAPTER 32

JULIETTE

Two days had passed since Juliette had booted Oliver out of her life. Two long, very sad, very lonely days. Suddenly it seemed her whole life was falling apart. First Brooke had left for university, then she'd been given the news about the Tattler, then she'd fallen in love, and now she'd had her heart ripped from her chest.

And that last thing was exactly why she hadn't bothered with men for the past twenty years. Who wanted to feel like this? That's what love did to you – it built you up then trampled you back down. It was what Oliver had done to her.

She hadn't heard from Otis either, not since she'd sent him the email, and she was beginning to wonder whether he had received it. His personal mobile number had been stored in her phone, the one she'd thrown in the river; a new mobile had arrived today, and she was trying to find the courage to insert the SIM card and get it working, to see whether any of her contacts would be there.

She wasn't expecting any visitors to the Tattlers office this morning, so when she heard a tentative knock on the door she was surprised. 'Come in,' she called.

For a moment she almost hoped it was Oliver, and her heart leapt at the thought, only to plummet straight back down again when she saw it was Hattie. Which was just as well, because she didn't want to see Oliver anyway. She'd told him that in no uncertain terms, and it looked like he was respecting her wishes.

'What can I do for you, Hattie?' she asked.

'I just wanted to see if you were all right. You didn't seem to be when I spoke to you on Saturday evening.'

'I'm fine,' she said firmly, not meaning it, but that's what one said, wasn't it?

'I'm sorry,' Hattie said contritely. 'I didn't mean to let the cat out of the bag.'

Juliette looked at her blankly. 'What cat, what bag?'

'About Oliver wanting to invest in the Tattler. It was only a thought he had; he wanted to sound me out. I've managed to speak to a few of Team Tattler and some of them are able to invest, but not as many as I hoped. Times are hard, and it's perfectly understandable if people haven't got any spare money to throw around.'

Juliette had totally forgotten about it – her thoughts had been consumed with Oliver knowing about her and Otis.

'It doesn't matter.' She waved her hand in the air. 'It's not relevant anymore.'

'What's happened?' Hattie persisted.

'It's nothing to do with the Tattler, or with you,' Juliette hastened to reassure the old lady. 'Team Tattler will carry on, although under a different name, whether Oliver is part of it or not.'

'But I thought you two were an item?'

Sadly, Juliette said, 'I'd thought so, too.'

Hattie must have sensed she wasn't going to get anything more out of her so, after a couple more exchanges of pleasantries, she left, and Juliette was alone with her thoughts once more.

With sudden resolve, she picked up the new mobile phone and inserted the SIM card. It was time she stopped moping about and was more proactive. Besides, she had to know what Otis was going to do about Oliver knowing their secret.

Despite neither of them having had any contact with the other since shortly after Brooke's birth until Otis had phoned her the other day, these were unprecedented circumstances, and although she didn't want to, she decided to phone him.

She had no idea how Oliver's impending revelation would impact on Otis's private life or his political career, although she didn't see how anyone could take anything bad from his generosity. All he'd wanted to do was to spare his brother's wife and their children (now all grown up) the heartache of knowing that Finley had fallen in love with another woman, who had borne him a child. Was that such a bad thing? It had nothing to do with covering up the truth for any political gain. In fact, by doing so, Otis possibly had something to lose if someone had taken it the wrong way and thought Brooke was *his* daughter, and not Finley's.

Juliette froze and slowly closed her eyes before opening them again. The thought which had just occurred to her made her go cold all over. What if the truth Oliver thought he knew, wasn't the real truth? No one had known about her affair with Finley, because if they had it would have come to light before now. But Oliver was an intelligent guy; had he put two and two together and come up with six?

She'd left London before the birth of her child, and before Finley's death. It wasn't totally unreasonable for Oliver to think she'd left because she was pregnant with Otis's child. There was no reason to connect her and Finley.

Dear God, this was a mess. If Oliver claimed Otis had had an affair and that the woman in question had born him a child, how much more sensational would that be? It would certainly trump the truth. Was that what Oliver was planning to put in Otis's biography?

'Come on, come on, come on,' Juliette muttered to herself, her fingers stabbing at the screen as she went through the rigmarole of setting it up.

Finally, it was done, and she held her breath that all of her previous phone's details were downloaded. It seemed to take forever, but when she scrolled through her contacts, there was Otis's name.

It was one below Oliver's.

Her finger hesitated over the delete button. Then she pressed it.

Every trace of Oliver was now gone from her life; apart from her memories, and she was desperately trying to suppress those.

With a heavy heart she thumbed the phone icon and listened to the ringtone. The situation was even worse than she'd first thought when she'd sent Otis the email, and she didn't relish telling him her suspicions. He'd be furious, and it was all her own fault; if she hadn't contacted Oliver Pascoe, then none of this would have happened. That she didn't know he was writing Otis's biography, was neither here nor there. She'd reached into her past, dragged it into the present, and now it was biting her on the backside.

'Are you calling to thank me?' was Otis's opening remark.

'What? No! Thank you for what?' Then she realised what he was talking about. 'You haven't, have you?' If he'd put something in motion to invest in the Tattler, she was going to be furious with him.

'I had to. When I saw your email, I thought it best to talk to him in person.'

'Who?' She was feeling slightly sick.

'Oliver of course.'

'What have you done?' Dread wrapped its clammy tendrils around her, and she shuddered. Had Otis somehow managed to silence Oliver?

'Nothing,' he laughed. 'I talked to him, that's all. You've got it completely wrong, you know,' Otis continued, but Juliette interrupted him.

'I realise that now,' she said. 'Oliver didn't know about Finley – he believes *you* and *I* were having an affair. He thinks you are Brooke's father, and if he publishes that you'll have a hard time coming back from it, even though it's not the truth. Who would believe you? I'm sure there are ways and means of finding out that you've been paying for Brooke's upkeep ever since she was born. Otis, I'm so sorry this is happening.'

'It's not happening. Oliver won't be publishing anything I don't approve of.'

'But what happens afterwards? After the book is written? Surely he could do some kind of exposé?'

'You haven't got much faith in him, have you? He's not going to do that.' Otis's voice softened as he said, 'He loves you too much for that. Juliette, I told him the truth about you and Finley. I'm sorry, but I felt I had to put him straight.'

Juliette nearly dropped the phone in shock. Otis had always been adamant no one should ever know the name of Brooke's father. Now he'd gone and told the one man who could do the most damage to Finley's family.

'Why the hell would you do that?' she demanded.

'Because he loves you. Didn't you hear me the first time? Even if the biography he was writing wasn't the authorised version, he'd never hurt you like that. Has Brooke ever asked who her father was?'

Juliette thought that one of the hardest things had been when Brooke asked about her father, and Juliette had refused to tell her. Her daughter had gone through several years of asking every now and again, but had gradually fallen silent on the subject, and Juliette had been relieved. In the back of her mind, though, there was always the dread that Brooke might raise the subject again. And the older the child got, the more difficult it was to deflect her questions.

'I think it's time you told her,' Otis said.

'Is this because you don't believe Oliver will keep it to himself?'

'Not at all. Oliver made me realise what I did was wrong. For Brooke.'

'Why, what did he say to you?'

'He didn't say anything. Just this whole business – you living in constant fear of letting the cat out of the bag, Brooke not knowing who her father was… I should never have insisted you kept quiet about Finley.'

'You were doing it for the best of reasons, for his wife and his children.'

'But it wasn't the best for Brooke, was it? And you wouldn't be hating Oliver right now if I hadn't bought your silence.'

'Is that what you think? That I stayed silent because you supported Brooke financially?' Juliette was totally taken aback.

'Didn't you?'

'I can't believe you'd think such a thing of me. All you needed to do was ask. I don't want your money, I never have done, and you didn't have to buy my silence. My silence isn't for sale. It never was.'

'I'm sorry, I didn't mean to upset you, but other

women—'

'I'm not other women,' she interjected icily.

'No, I know that. So does Oliver. I haven't bought his silence, either. He's not going to mention it out of the goodness of his heart and because of his love for you. There, that's the third time I've said he loves you. Are you listening, Juliette?'

Juliette was, but she wasn't sure it was going to make any difference. She was too full of anger and feelings of betrayal to take it in.

'Oliver isn't the bad guy. I am,' Otis insisted. 'Hate me as much as you want, but don't hate Oliver. And tell Brooke the truth; she deserves to know. Just give me a day, please? I have to break the news to Finley's family.'

Oh, blast! Now what was she going to do?

CHAPTER 33

OLIVER

It was done. Oliver pressed the send button, and sat back with a relieved sigh. Otis had his manuscript two days ahead of the deadline Oliver's editor had set. He hoped Otis would be happy with it. He was done with it; he never wanted to see it again, although he knew he would have to because there would be endless rounds of edits to go through. But that was it for now, so he was free to concentrate on trying to win Juliette back.

The problem was, he hadn't come up with anything other than to try to talk to her again. And he wasn't sure that would work. He had a feeling no matter how much he protested about having no intention of putting anything about her into Otis's biography, she still wouldn't believe him. He didn't blame her. It was his own fault for not coming clean in the first place.

But if he had told her, she may well have walked away and he wouldn't have fallen in love with her. Despite his heart feeling like someone had driven shards of glass into it, he didn't regret one second he'd spent with her. He'd always have his memories.

He wondered if Otis had had any joy with Ralph Trudge-Smythe. He hadn't heard from him yet, but it was still only Thursday, and Juliette wasn't meeting with Ralph until tomorrow. It would be just like the man to leave it until the last minute.

As if thinking about Otis had conjured him into being, Oliver's phone pinged. It was a text from the great man himself.

Meeting at Trudge Manor, 2.30 today. Be there.

Oliver nodded to himself. It didn't look like Trudge-Smythe intended to play ball. Oh well, he'd told Otis he was willing to invest in the Tattler if it enabled Juliette to buy it, and he intended to stick to his word. Although Otis hadn't been able to make Trudge-Smythe come down on the price, he should have enough clout to ensure the man's silence. Juliette need never know that he and Otis had paid the difference.

CHAPTER 34

JULIETTE

This was absolutely pointless, and Juliette didn't know why she was here. She didn't owe Ralph Trudge-Smythe anything, although she did feel some obligation to his father. She felt very regretful that she'd let Lord Trudge-Smythe down.

There was nothing to say that Ralph Trudge-Smythe wouldn't have got rid of the Tattler anyway, she told herself, in a vain attempt to feel better. An old-style newspaper, from a little village on the Welsh-English border, was hardly up there when it came to displaying a grand portfolio of businesses. Maybe he would have closed it anyway, due to sheer embarrassment.

She was only going to Trudge Manor now out of a sense of duty and a need for closure. She wanted

Ralph to give her a final date after which the Tattler would cease trading.

She couldn't believe it was almost a week since she'd thrown Oliver out of her life. In some ways, it felt like only yesterday that she'd been snuggling up in bed with him. Yet it also seemed like a decade since she'd seen him last. Would this ache ever go away?

At least today would mark a new chapter in her life. From tomorrow she could move forward with her plans for the new newspaper. She was hoping someone could come up with a name for it tonight. And she also had to get her head around the need to speak to Brooke.

By now Finley's family would already know, and she half expected some contact from Otis, but there had been nothing.

Brooke would be nineteen in just over a months' time; that was when any and all monies from Otis would cease. With the truth out in the open on both sides, Juliette only hoped Brooke would understand why she'd withheld her father's name from her for all these years.

It was with a heavy heart that she got behind the wheel of her car and headed towards Trudge Manor.

CHAPTER 35

OLIVER

Otis's text hadn't given Oliver a great deal of warning, but after a frantic dash he thankfully arrived, anxious and on time.

The driveway in front of Trudge Manor was far busier than it had been the last time he'd visited, when there had only been two or three other vehicles. Today there were quite a few, including a couple of large trucks which looked suspiciously like removal vans.

'What's going on?' Oliver asked the housekeeper.

'Lord and Lady Trudge-Smythe are relocating to their house in Kent.'

'They have a house in Kent?'

'Oh, yes, it's been in the family for years. It's much smaller than this, and they've had it renovated to make it easier for his lordship for when things get too bad.' She lowered her voice. 'He will possibly be wheelchair-bound before too long,' she added sadly.

Oliver gave her his commiserations and wished Lord and Lady Trudge-Smythe the best.

He wondered what Ralf intended to do with Trudge Manor. It was a big old pile to simply be closed up, and he hoped it wouldn't fall into decay, the way so many grand old manor houses had done in the past.

'They're waiting for you in the drawing-room,' the housekeeper told him, and pointed at the door. 'Please excuse me, I've got such a lot to do, so just knock and walk in.'

He strolled across the marble tiled floor, dodging a couple of men carrying a rather grand sideboard, and hesitated outside the door she'd indicated, before knocking and opening it.

Three pairs of eyes turned to look at him. One of them belonged to Ralph, the other to his financial advisor, and the third pair belonged to Juliette. Otis was nowhere to be seen.

Oliver wanted the ground to open up and swallow him whole. Assuming Otis had told Ralph he was planning on paying the difference, did Juliette's presence mean she also knew about the arrangement?

'What are you doing here?' she demanded. Her

face was pale, and she looked aghast.

In one swift glance he took her in, and he was dismayed to see how tired she looked. She had lost her glow and her sparkle.

What the hell was going on? That she'd asked him why he was here, indicated she had no idea what he was planning. So why was Juliette here for a meeting which was supposed to be between him, Otis, and Ralph? Why—?

Damn! He clapped a mental hand to his forehead. He'd been so lost in his work, so desperate to get it done, that the last few days had rolled into one and he'd lost track of the date.

Damn and blast. Today was the day Juliette was giving Trudge-Smythe her answer.

'I assume he's here to join our meeting,' Ralph replied to Juliette, giving him a hard stare. 'Is that not the case?'

'No, it isn't,' she said frostily, and Oliver cringed at the ice in her voice.

'Why *are* you here?' Ralph echoed Juliette's question.

Oliver looked from Juliette to Ralph and back again. 'I'm sorry, Juliette,' he said. 'I was doing this for you.'

'Doing what?' she demanded.

'Yes, pray tell,' Ralph Trudge-Smythe said, and

Oliver could have sworn he heard Merton Berrow give a little snigger.

'I know you didn't want me involved,' he said to Juliette, 'but I knew you couldn't afford to pay the full amount.'

Before he could say anything further, Ralph barked out a wry laugh. 'It was you, wasn't it, who got our future Prime Minister to put some pressure on me?'

Juliette gasped and demanded, 'What on earth is going on?'

'Would you like to tell her?' Ralph said to Oliver.

'Do you honestly think I'm in a position to put Otis Coles under pressure?' Oliver asked, trying to evade the question.

Ralph shot him a very shrewd look indeed. 'I don't know; you tell me. You're the one writing his biography. Has something crawled out of the woodwork?'

Oliver's attention was firmly on Ralph Trudge-Smythe, but he noticed Juliette's jerk of surprise out of the corner of his eye.

'The exact opposite,' Oliver informed him. 'I've discovered Otis Coles is a very honourable man, and I believe he's one of the best things to happen to British politics since Winston Churchill.'

Ralph looked taken aback. 'Well, well, well, that is a grand statement to be making. It doesn't explain why he's taken a sudden interest in my affairs, though, does it?'

Oliver couldn't answer him.

But Juliette could. With a long look at Oliver, Juliette gave him a little nod, then turned to Ralph Trudge-Smythe. 'Actually, it does,' she said. 'My daughter is his niece.'

Oliver leapt in, worried Ralph would think Otis was simply taking care of his own. 'I'm sure he pointed out to you,' he said to Ralph, 'that accepting a lesser offer for the Tattler would be better than no offer at all. Isn't that the case?'

Ralph didn't say a word, but his financial adviser nodded. Ralph turned and glared at him. 'Keep out of it, Merton,' he hissed.

Oliver said, 'It's your decision, but I'm sure you're aware the Tattler isn't worth the paper it's printed on as things currently stand.'

'And whose fault is that?' Ralph's expression hardened, and he rounded on Juliette. 'You were the one put in charge, you were the one managing it. I don't expect my executives to run my businesses into the ground.'

Oliver laughed. 'You can hardly call Juliette an executive. She's a journalist. She was paid to write articles for the paper. The fact that she took on an awful lot more, is simply down to how much she loved the newspaper. If your father had been serious about carrying it on, he would have put in an experienced editor to head the Tattler, not a political correspondent. Therefore, if you want to point fingers, perhaps you should be pointing them in a different direction.'

Merton spoke quietly in Ralph's ear, cupping his hand around his mouth like a small child whispering in class.

Ralph didn't say anything for a few moments, then he shrugged. 'You win, you can have the Tattler, although I expect you to cover the costs of the legal and any other fees. Merton will discuss the specifics with you, and my legal department will be in touch.' And with that, he inclined his head to Juliette, then to Oliver, and left the room.

Oliver wanted to punch the air and shout "Yay!", but he resisted the urge. Juliette was still looking incredibly pale, but two spots of colour had appeared on either cheek and he could tell she was trying to suppress a smile.

'Shall we make an appointment for another day?' she asked Merton.

'I think that's a good idea,' Merton said. 'I've got your number, and I'll give you a ring once the contracts are drawn up.'

Oliver accompanied Juliette to the door, and out

onto the drive. His heart was hammering, and he was expecting her to start shouting at him at any minute. What a bloody fiasco. Ever since he'd met her, he'd had his head in the clouds, and he couldn't believe he hadn't realised that today was the day she was meeting Ralph Trudge-Smythe, or that he'd failed to spot her car on the drive. Although he could see why when they stepped outside; one of the vans had left, and her car had been parked behind it, where it would have been impossible for him to have seen it.

'I'm sorry, Juliette, I really am. I didn't mean to stick my nose in but—' he began.

'But you did, anyway,' she interrupted.

There was a very awkward silence, and Oliver cast about for something to say to fill it. The best he could come up with was, 'Congratulations on your acquisition of the Tattler.'

Juliette came to a halt. She wasn't looking at him, and he had the impression he wasn't going to like what she was about to say. Knowing that whatever she said, he probably deserved it, he steeled himself.

'Because of you,' she said, 'I now have to tell my daughter who her father is.'

'I'm sorry,' he began again, but she cut across him.

'That's a good thing, I think. I'll let you know after I've spoken to her.'

It took a second for her words to sink in. 'You

will?'

She turned slowly, so he could see her face in full. 'I will.'

'Are you saying that we're going to keep in touch?'

'I want to do more than keep in touch. I owe you an apology. When I found out you were writing Otis's biography, I assumed the worst.'

'You wouldn't have if I'd told you whose biography I was working on,' Oliver pointed out.

'But if you had, I'm not sure we would be where we are now.'

'And where is that, exactly?' His heart was pounding so hard, he was certain she could hear it. And he could do with sitting down because he didn't think his legs were going to hold him up for much longer.

'With me acquiring the Tattler. With me about to tell my daughter who her father is.'

His heart fell. That was what she'd meant. He could hardly expect anything else, could he?

She spoke again. 'And with me loving you.'

'You *love* me?' He didn't think his heart could take anymore. All this excitement was getting a bit much.

'You know I do. I already told you.'

He gulped, amazed at her bravery. If the shoe had been on the other foot, he probably wouldn't have wanted to speak to him ever again. 'I love you, too.'

'I hoped you'd say that.'

'What would have happened if I hadn't turned up today?'

'I would have come looking for you,' she told him. 'Hang on a sec, why *are* you here?'

'I was going to try to convince Ralph Trudge-Smythe to let me pay the difference for the Tattler. He wouldn't have needed any convincing for that, but he would have needed to be convinced not to tell you.' He decided not to mention his agreement with Otis who, it turned out, had made good on his promise of seeing what he could do – he'd more than made good, he'd actually done better than that, considering he'd managed to persuade Ralph to give Juliette the Tattler for nothing apart from the transfer costs. Oliver wasn't sure he wanted to know how Otis had managed it – he was simply grateful that he had.

Juliette said, 'Otis offered to do the same, but I refused.'

'I can fully understand why,' Oliver said. 'The Tattler is yours, and yours alone, and you don't want anyone else to be involved in it.'

'That's not true at all,' she said. 'I told Otis it wasn't a good idea for him to invest in it, because if someone found out then the whole story about me, his brother, and Brooke would come out.' She lifted her hand to her forehead. 'Oh God, I'd better tell

Brooke today, before Ralph Trudge-Smythe broadcasts it.' She lowered her hand, and gave him a shaky smile. 'I'd be quite happy for you to be involved in the running of the Tattler,' she told him, 'because without you, I wouldn't have believed I could carry it on.'

'I wouldn't have got involved,' he assured her.

'But what if I want you to be?'

'What are you saying?'

'I'm not sure. All I know is, that I want you in my life and considering the Tattler is a big part of that…'

Oliver couldn't take anymore; he didn't care about being involved in the Tattler, he didn't care about his next biography, the only thing he cared about was Juliette and how he felt about her.

With a groan, he closed the space between them and pulled her close.

His mouth hovering above hers, he said, 'If you want me to help, I will, but the Tattler is all yours. It's as much yours as I am. If you want me.'

'Oh, yes,' she said, her breath warm against his lips. 'I want you. I want you much more than I ever wanted the newspaper.'

'I take it I'm forgiven?'

'Only if you forgive me. I was silly not to trust you.'

'You'll always be able to trust me,' he told her.

'How about we put the past behind us and look to the future, because at the moment it's a blank page and it's up to us what we write on it. This is our story, and I'm determined this one will have a happy ending.'

'That's the most beautiful thing anyone has ever said to me,' Juliette said with a soft smile. 'I want to take you to bed, but there's something I need to do first.'

He knew what she was about to say. 'Brooke?'

She nodded.

Reluctantly he released her. There would be plenty of time; they had their whole lives ahead of them, and he couldn't wait to spend it with her.

CHAPTER 36

JULIETTE

'I was thinking you could do a couple of history pieces. Many of the buildings in Ticklemore go back an awful long way and people might be interested to read about them,' Benny said at the meeting of Team Tattler later that evening.

'Good idea, but that's one, maybe two, articles. What about going forward from that?' Sara said.

'How about if you select one item from a local shop to be featured in each edition?' Nell suggested. 'For instance, you could pick one of Silas's paintings, and interview him to ask him where he got the idea from. If it's one of his landscapes, you could show the painting itself alongside a photo of the scene – it would be free advertising for him as well as interesting for the readers. You could do the same for the other businesses in and around the village. It would be publicity for them, and you could ask them to subscribe to the newspaper in lieu of paying for an advert.' Nell's expression glowed with enthusiasm.

'You could write an article about one of the local farms,' Marge suggested. 'There are plenty of sheep farmers around. You could pick one that sells locally and write about how the lamb is produced, what it's fed on, that kind of thing. Or cheese? Cheese might be a good one. It's local interest, but readers might be learning something, and at least you'd have one guaranteed sale of the newspaper.' She chuckled.

Juliette laughed. 'Thanks. I'm aiming to have more than one reader, you know. I do like your idea though, and maybe I could do a veggie of the week. Benny, could you do something about the allotment, and perhaps the WI women could do a piece on, I don't know, jam-making? They're so heavily involved in the village and they do a whole load of good works. I need to focus on them more.'

Marge beamed and Benny also looked pleased. It was lovely to sit here and listen to all the ideas being thrown out there, Juliette thought. All of them were valid, and she was hastily scribbling notes. The first thing she had done when she'd entered the Tavern half an hour ago was to inform them Team Tattler was going to remain Team Tattler. The resulting cheer had made the glasses behind the bar rattle.

'You could visit the mother and toddler group in the church hall,' Father Todd suggested. 'Speak to some of the mums about the problems they face from pregnancy, through to when the children start school.'

'Good idea.' Juliette was prepared to consider anything and everything.

A slightly tinny voice emanated from her phone which was propped up against a pint of lager sitting on the table in front of an empty chair.

'I've done some canvassing, Mum, and the general consensus seems to be not so much local news, as national news,' Brooke said, her face tiny on the phone's small screen. 'Like the bigger picture things – climate change and child poverty, and so on. I know I mentioned it before, but the feeling among nearly everyone I've spoken to is that if we don't address the bigger things, the smaller ones aren't going to matter in the end.'

Juliette grinned at her daughter. She was the newest member of Team Tattler and it was only fair to include her, even if it had to be via WhatsApp. 'How can we make climate change relevant to the person on the street?' Juliette asked.

'Recycling is one way,' Brooke pointed out. 'So is reducing plastic, clothes swapping, not throwing anything out but putting it on Freecycle for someone else to use. I'm sure I could come up with lots more.'

Oliver said, 'How about if you write a column for the newspaper on that very thing? You could do other articles as well, but this could be a regular feature.' He glanced at Juliette for confirmation, and she smiled at him.

She'd only just made it back to Ticklemore in time for the meeting in the Tavern. She hadn't enjoyed phoning Brooke and telling her she needed to speak to her urgently, especially since she was just about to walk into her last lecture of the day. And she knew her daughter had worried all the way through it, because she'd told Juliette as much in Brooke's typical black and white fashion.

Her daughter had taken the news surprisingly well.

'I guessed he must have been important, or that he was married, or both,' Brooke had told her when Juliette had broken the news.

When Juliette had asked how she'd come to that conclusion, Brooke had said, 'I saw some of your bank statements. The same amount came from the same bank account every month. I guessed it might be from my father. I hoped the reason he was paying maintenance wasn't because he was forced to, but because he wanted to. And I hoped the reason he hadn't had anything to do with me because he hadn't been able to, not because he didn't care.'

Juliette cried at that. She'd been wrong not to tell Brooke about her father right from the start, and Otis had been wrong to have insisted she shouldn't. But hindsight is a wonderful thing, and they both thought they had been doing the best for everyone concerned. Juliette had reasoned that what Brooke had never known, she wouldn't miss. And it wasn't as though Finley could have been there for his daughter. Juliette knew he would have loved Brooke unconditionally if he hadn't been taken from them too soon.

Juliette had briefly mentioned Oliver to her, too, knowing she wouldn't be able to keep him a secret for much longer, but to her surprise Brooke hadn't batted an eyelid.

'Great, Mum!' she'd said. 'I was beginning to think I'd have to sign you up to a dating site. I wondered what had put a sparkle in your eye the last time I saw you, and now I know. You're going to have to tell me all about him.'

Juliette promised she would, but not right then as she had to get back, and there was someone else she needed to speak to before she went to the Tavern – her mother.

Audrey had taken it in her stride too, her only comment being, 'It's about time you told that poor girl, she deserves to know where she comes from. I'm just glad it wasn't some fly-by-night who didn't give a toss about you or Brooke. I'm sorry Finley passed on, though. It's a shame Brooke didn't know her father, but that's life for you. Always unpredictable. Which is why I'm so pleased you've found love at last.'

***

It was later that night, when Juliette and Oliver were curled up in bed together, Oliver being big spoon to Juliette's little spoon, that he murmured, 'All's well that ends well.'

Juliette twisted in his arms to face him. 'I love you, Oliver Pascoe,' she said.

'I love you, too, Juliette Seymour.'

'But there's something you need to know,' she added.

'Oh?' Even in the darkness she could see the faint alarm on his face and she chuckled.

'This isn't the ending, no matter how much Shakespeare you quote at me. This is the beginning, and I simply know it's going to be wonderful. As Hattie would say, I can feel it in my water!'

THE END

More from Liz Davies

Are you ready to revisit Ticklemore yet? If so, take a look at the Ticklemore Treasure Trove, available on Amazon, and read the next installment in this wonderful series.

Acknowledgements

Husband, of course, because he sees more of the top of my laptop than he does of my face most days (mind you, he might say that's a good thing!)

Catherine Mills, as always, for her unstinting enthusiasm for my stories and her willingness to gently put me right when I've drifted off course.

Mum for reading my stuff, Daughter for promising to (and for listening to me wittering about formatting when she has no idea what I'm rabbiting on about)

And my readers. Thank you for loving my books and making all the blood, sweat and tears – OK, coffee, sleepless nights and snivelling – worth it.

Liz x

ABOUT THE AUTHOR

Liz Davies writes feel-good, light-hearted stories with a hefty dose of romance, a smattering of humour, and a great deal of love.

She's married to her best friend, has one grown-up daughter, and when she isn't scribbling away in the notepad she carries with her everywhere (just in case inspiration strikes), you'll find her searching for that perfect pair of shoes. She loves to cook but isn't very good at it, and loves to eat - she's much better at that! Liz also enjoys walking (preferably on the flat), cycling (also on the flat), and lots of sitting around in the garden on warm, sunny days.

She currently lives with her family in Wales, but would ideally love to buy a camper van and travel the world in it.

Social Media Links:
Twitter https://twitter.com/lizdaviesauthor
Facebook: fb.me/LizDaviesAuthor1

Printed in Great Britain
by Amazon